I0616003

BLOOD ON THE TRACKS

BLOOD ON THE TRACKS

BLOOD ON THE TRACKS

THE CROCKETTS' WESTERN SAGA
BOOK 14

ROBERT VAUGHAN
ASH LINGAM

WOLFPACK
PUBLISHING
— EST 2013 —

Blood on the Tracks
Paperback Edition
Copyright © 2025 by Robert Vaughan and Ash Lingam

Wolfpack Publishing
1707 E. Diana Street
Tampa, FL 33610

wolfpackpublishing.com

All rights reserved. No part of this book may be reproduced in any
form or by any electronic or mechanical means, including
information storage and retrieval systems, without express written
permission from the publisher, except for the use of brief quotations
in reviews. Any use of this publication to train generative artificial
intelligence (AI) technologies is expressly prohibited.

This book is a work of fiction. References to historical events, real
people, or real places are used fictitiously. Any similarity to real
persons, living or dead, is purely coincidental and not intended by the
author.

All brand names and product names used in this book are
trademarks, registered trademarks, or trade names of their respective
holders. Wolfpack Publishing is not associated with any product or
vendor in this book.

Paperback ISBN 979-8-89567-790-2
Ebook ISBN 979-8-89567-789-6
LCCN 2025946667

BLOOD ON THE TRACKS

BLOOD ON THE TRACKS

CHAPTER ONE

"Hey, little brother," Will Crockett said as he pulled out a shiny pocket watch. The bezel opened with the click of the crown. He had a peek at the time and slipped it back into his vest, leaving the little leather tassel hanging.

"How about we go and get something to eat before the train arrives, and we get on board? It's 567 miles to El Paso, so it'll take us almost two days, if we don't run into trouble. The train runs day and night, but it's gotta stop for fuel and water. Even though it goes over forty miles an hour, its schedule depends on how many times it's gotta pull up to refill. It stops in San Antonio, too. That's where the train will fill up with both passengers and move the livestock into other wagons heading to the slaughterhouses back East. I reckon we'll mostly be the only passengers headin' to the farthest reaches of West Texas. Mostly cowboys will be hitchin' that ride."

"You know I'm always hungry. I fancy one of those juicy steaks from the Midnight Saloon, and a cold beer would be just the thing. Maybe an apple or peach pie to go with it. Someone said that second-class cars don't have a restaurant, only first-class cars do. I reckon we'll have to stop in the general store and buy something to travel with, too. We've got our canteens full. I'd hate to take such a long ride without somethin' to munch on."

Will smiled when his brother's stomach grumbled, as if listening to their conversation. He had lived with Gid his whole life and had never heard him turn down food. He entered the eating contest after eating contest, and he always won. Sometimes, he continued after all his opponents had dropped out, disturbing the saloon or bar that was hosting the event. He could eat a man out of his house and home.

"I don't look forward to being cooped up in a train all day and night. And we can't keep riding first class like we were kings or something. I get uncomfortable with all those fancy people. Ma and Pa didn't bring us up like that. I like things just as they are." Gid's shirt stretched tight across his broad back as his biceps, triceps, and forearms flexed. He wiggled his eyebrows with a handsome smile.

Santa Clara was only twenty-five miles southwest of San Antonio and had a circumference of 2.4 square miles. With two thousand five hundred residents, it was a busy little city. Of course, more than twenty thousand lived in the big city, dwarfing the small settlement that was only a short ride away. The Crocketts walked under the shadows of the bell tower. Wagon wheels churned up dust as buckboards rolled down the street, whips cracking over their heads with brown clouds in their wakes. A bustle of people hurried from business to business, delivering goods from warehouses on the edge of the town.

Fruit stores, haberdasheries, hardware stores, taverns, and hotels dotted the buildings. In the middle was the Rowdy Cowboy Saloon. Since it was a farming country, there was feed, fertilizer, and cultivation equipment on every corner of the small but prosperous town. Particles of dirt slowly floated in the rays of light as they headed for a meal, and hopefully, a cold drink.

"Did you know they had a battle here between the Americans and the Californios? That was back in 1847. I read about it in a magazine I bought at the fancy bookstore in San Antonio. The article said it was one of the last fights of the California Conquest."

"I don't know about any conquests, but I sure do like the climate. Still, there are too many people for my taste. I don't like it when you can reach out and touch somebody, no matter where you go. I long for the wide-open spaces."

"There are not that many people here. I read that there are twenty-five thousand residents in Santa Clara. That's nothing like San Francisco, where there are nearly three hundred thousand. I don't fancy visiting another big city again. At least not for a while. That's why we're headed for El Paso, ain't it? From there, it's not far to New Mexico and onward to Arizona, little brother."

Gid followed Will through the batwing doors as they whooshed closed behind them. Boot heels hammered the wood floor as the planks groaned under their weight. As soon as they walked in, they got the waiter's attention. They had tipped him handsomely in the past few days, and he treated them like they were special. The brothers wore denim trousers, chambray shirts, boots, and Stetson hats and looked like pretty much everybody else in town. Not at all like they felt back on the docks of the Barbary Coast in California.

"What'll it be today, fellas?" the gangly man asked through broken teeth. He wore thick, pop bottle glasses perched like a bird on the end of his nose. "We've got chicken dumplings, sirloin steak, and roasted chicken. Each comes with green beans, corn on the cob, and mashed potatoes. We've got apple pie for dessert. I know it's tasty because the wife made it herself."

"Yep, that'll do me."

"Whatta, you mean, Mr. Gid?"

"Why, everything you just said. I'll take one of each. They're all my favorite."

"I'll have chicken dumplings. Our ma used to make 'em for us. Let's see if yours are as good as hers." Will grinned as his stomach began to grumble too.

The last time they were looking forward to their mother's dumplings, they found her beside their bullet-ridden father with a gunshot wound to her chest. That was years ago, toward the end of the Civil War. Amanda Crockett had died in her sons' arms. With her last breath, she touched and kissed her sons' cheeks one last time. Dumplings remained the brothers' favorite meal. None had reached the mark when it came to their mother's cooking, but they were eager to try just the same. Someone out there had to know how to cook as well as their ma.

"I don't suppose you have more of those cold suds, do ya? Two icy beers will do us fine."

"Why, as a matter of fact, we do. Believe it or not, the

ice is shipped in by train. They say some of it comes in big blocks from as far away as Canada. Two frosty beers comin' up, gentlemen."

Every time the waiter called Gid a gentleman, he laughed. With as big as he was, he didn't believe he looked like one, but he appreciated the compliment just the same. When their drinks arrived frost coated the mugs, which were kept in an icebox, too. Once the food arrived at their table, no one spoke a word until Gid had consumed a portion of everything. To top it off, he had half of the apple pie.

He would have eaten it all, but the waiter said they had to share. Will took it all in with good humor. He had long since grown accustomed to his brother's appetite. He knew Gid ate two to three times as much as a normal man. Of course, his little brother wasn't little. He was several inches taller than him and was solid muscle.

When they finished, they paid the check and left an honest tip for their newfound friend. "I guess we'll see ya when we see ya, Joe. We're off on the train in a few minutes for West Texas. I'm afraid we don't know when we'll be back."

"Be careful. There are said to be desperate men in the Six-Gun Capital of the West. I reckon it wasn't get that reputation for growing flowers."

"If it's on the way to Arizona, I reckon we'll have to take our chances." Will smiled, tipping his Stetson.

They pushed their way back out through the swinging doors and pulled down two chairs hanging from pegs on the wall. They sat close to the building so they could kick back and lean against the wall and watch the people walk by. Both brothers enjoyed watching pretty girls, especially those who wore dresses that exposed their sensuous curves. Most fluttered fans before their faces as they made eyes at the brothers. Will and Gill tipped their hats and grinned in return.

When the Mission church bell rang, they knew it was time to head back to the train station. They already had their tickets as they threw their saddlebags over their shoulders. Since they were traveling by train, they sold their horses. They could buy new ones once they reached El Paso. From there, they would travel on horseback or stagecoach. Their plan was to return to Arizona to tend to some unfinished business.

———

Soon after, Will and Gid grabbed seats on a hard wooden bench under the depot's sunroof. Soon, they heard the blaring whistle of the arriving train. A sign hanging over their heads said, *Santa Clara Railway Station*. The massive engine roared as it bore down to its next stop. The big black beast came racing toward them, growing in size by the second as the teapot smokestack spewed thick black soot.

The moment the train set its brakes, incoming rounds started zinging past their ears. The Crocketts pulled their guns as they dove for cover behind three water barrels standing on the porch. Two bullets narrowly missed them, leaving streams of water spilling out and onto the floor. Had the staves not stopped the high-powered bullets, they both could have been killed.

Lead slugs slammed into the station's porch posts and building, shattering windows. Bullets went sailing through the air in all directions, indicating that the brothers weren't their targets, but now they asked themselves what was really going on and what was their target.

"Who're they shootin' at, Will?" Gid asked.

Another round of bullets peppered the train station behind them. Shards of glass and wooden splinters sailed through the air like bullets as the Crocketts covered their heads with their arms.

"I don't know, but I doubt it's us!" Gid replied. "At least, I don't think so."

He took a chance to have a peek at the chaos. As soon as he poked his head up and above the barrel's rim, another lead slug sang overhead, nicking the crown of his hat. He pulled his Stetson off and cursed.

"Damned fools! I figure they're shootin' at anything that moves," Gid growled, cursing again as he poked his little finger through the bullet hole.

"I reckon they're here to rob something. What it is, I'm not sure yet. There's a bank across the street, and another at the end. Here comes the train. Give 'em a minute to show their true colors. Then we can decide what to do. For now, hold your fire. It's best the shooters don't know we're here."

Puffs of black smoke stained the sky as the image of the massive black Baldwin locomotive came screeching down the tracks. The brakes locked, showering sparks from its sides as it skidded along the shiny steel rails. The town's citizens ducked for cover into shops and offices, some even diving through windows to escape. Gray smoke curled out of the outlaws' barrels, following flames and heavy-caliber rounds. Mothers grabbed their children, dragging them off their feet and to safety.

Horses' hooves hammered the ground as four men

rode out of an alley, sliding into a turn, gaining traction as they raced down the main drag toward the slowing train. Clouds of steam rose from the boiler of the screaming locomotive. The engineer poked his wind-burned face out the window, ducking just in time to dodge a bullet that ricocheted, singing into the air. Black paint chipped as slugs slammed into the steel. The fireman dove into the coalbin and to safety. The brakeman leaned, staring from the rear platform, holding onto the railing, wondering what in tarnation was going on.

The massive vermilion wheels contrasted with the black Baldwin engine that displayed gold, red, and blue linework. The locomotive tipped the scales at a whopping six hundred tons. Wooden cars strung behind the steam-breathing beast. Iron and steel moved forward with a mulish sure-footedness as the 54-inch wheels suddenly stopped turning, and the entire train shuddered in response. The jolt caused passengers' stomachs to lurch. Couplings clanked as the locomotive ground to a stop.

Four more outlaws came racing out of the alley across the street and joined their gang as they continued to shoot at anything that moved. In seconds, the streets were empty, save the assailants. The train's whistle gave three short blasts, followed by three long blasts, and then three more short blasts, the SOS signal of distress.

Clouds of dust followed eight outlaws down Main Street. They pulled to a sliding stop when they got to the panting engine. You could see by their horseflesh and guns they were serious about what they were doing and were prepared to shoot and kill anyone who stood in their way.

"Don't kill me, I've got a family!" the engineer cried out with his hands spread wide before him like they could stop a bullet.

When the round went through his palm and hit him in the chest, he staggered backward and toppled out the opposite opening, disappearing from sight. After falling his lifeless body rolled down the steep gravel grade that supported the railroad tracks.

Two riders pulled up at the front of the train, wheeling their horses around with guns in their fists. They were there to shoot any townspeople brave enough to interfere. The other six raced their horses for the string of passengers and livestock carriages. The one they were after was the mail wagon.

Ringo Moon wheeled his mount, siding up to the mail car. He tried to pull the thick wooden sliding door open, but it was locked. He made a fist, and hammered on the door and ordered whoever was inside to open up. A muffled voice refused, ignoring his threats.

"Bring me that stick of dynamite. Do you hear me in there? We're gonna blow ya to hell and back, so if you know what's good for ya, you'll open the door!"

"My orders are not to let anyone inside until the town law shows, mister," a frightened voice replied. "I don't wanna lose my job."

"You're gonna lose more than your job, fool. You're fixin' to lose your life. That marshal of yours ain't gonna show. Not with him tied and gagged in his own cell. Ya think, we didn't do our homework. This is a robbery, and we can do it the easy way or the hard way. It's your choice."

Ringo, typically impatient, tied the dynamite to the door latch. He puffed his cheroot to life and touched the tip to the fuse, then he and his gang set their spurs and rushed a safe distance away. The fuse sizzled and sparked to life, racing toward the bundle of explosives. The ground trembled when the door blew. Projectile-like splinters showered everyone within fifty feet. The mail coach guard came running out of the door, pitching himself to the ground as his clothing burned, smoked, and smoldered. The smell of singed hair and skin hung heavy in the air as tears cut a path down his browless face. He patted his cheeks to put his burning beard out.

Ringo whirled a loop overhead and lassoed the strongbox, tying it off on his saddle horn. When he pulled it off the train, it hit the ground with a loud thud. He shot the lock, blowing it apart and making the horses strain at their bits and rear. The gang leader slid out of his saddle and opened the box with the toe of his boot. He pulled out one of the small burlap sacks. He reached for a pocketknife and sliced a hole, spilling out gold eagles.

"We've got what we came lookin' for. Grab the loot, boys, and let's get out of here before somebody wakes up and starts shootin' back."

That was when bullets began spitting out of the Crockett's barrels. A horse went down, and another outlaw got winged in the shoulder. The bullet spun him around like a top. It was hard to take a good bead on the thieves as the never-ending puffs of steam from the Baldwin blurred their images. The light man poked his head around the corner of the end of the train from the caboose, then ran down the steps and raced back the way the train had come, veering off into a stretch of wooded land. He didn't want to end up like the engineer.

As one of the outlaws wheeled his horse and took aim at Gid, Will put a well-placed bullet into his horse's chest, spilling the rider. He hit the ground as if he was struck by a sledgehammer.

"Quick, grab the gold!" Ringo shouted as he returned fire. The horseless rider climbed onto the rump of Moon's horse and began firing his pistol. He emptied the cylinders like he was hammering out Morse code. Anyone in sight ducked for cover. In the blink of an eye, the outlaws stuffed the loot into saddlebags and burst from the scene of the crime as quickly as they arrived.

To Will and Gid, it seemed like it took forever, but it went down in a matter of minutes. One moment, the outlaws were there, and the next, they were racing away beside the railroad tracks and out of pistol range as the locomotive continued to huff and puff soot, smoke, and steam.

———

BY THE TIME the sheriff arrived, the gun smoke had cleared. The only thing left was the smell of cordite and blood from the dead horse. A breeze pushed dust across the ground as blowflies mysteriously arrived in the thousands. Will and Gid carefully walked toward the scene of the robbery with their pistols in their hands.

"Who are you two? You best holster them guns," the sheriff growled gruffly, swinging his pistol toward the brothers.

"Whoa now, Sheriff. We were shootin' back. I heard

the outlaws say they killed the town marshal," Will explained and lowered his pistol. He didn't put it in his holster, though. "And where were you when all this happened? I didn't see you arrive until the shootin' was over."

"Put down those guns," the town law threatened. "I'm Sheriff Pete Parson, and I'll say what's to be done or not."

Herman, the waiter, was standing among the gathering crowd. As soon as they saw the shooting was over, curiosity got the best of most people. Everybody in Santa Clara arrived to see what was up.

"Those men aren't outlaws. I can vouch for them myself, Sheriff Parson. Unlike you, it looks like they were the only ones defending us citizens from that lot of rambunctious killers," the waiter shouted. The gunshots still rang in his ears. "Take a look at the state of the buildings along this street. They plugged everything full of holes."

"Like I was saying," Will added. "We saw the whole thing. We were sittin' right there on the train station landing, waiting for it to arrive. They came from the alleys, hell-bent for leather, shootin' up a storm at anything that moved. Since we didn't know what they were after until they raced for the train, we held our fire. Then, when we saw what was happening, we started shootin' back. I shot that dead horse, along with a winged outlaw, but I reckon he got away. Gid here nicked another one, but I think he rode off with the outlaw gang. You may find them along the trail if you don't linger and get after 'em."

"Go after them?" Sheriff Parson asked. He looked at

the brothers like they were crazy. "I'm the town sheriff, not a Texas Ranger. That's *not* my job.

"With the marshal dead, you're the only law in town now," Gid replied. "So, it's time for you to step up."

Will watched as the voted-in sheriff squirmed at the thought.

"Are you the sheriff of Santa Clara or not? Because the marshal ain't gonna be much help from Boot Hill."

CHAPTER TWO

SPARKS ROSE FROM THE FLICKERING FIRE, DISAPPEARING AS the cinders reached the treetops. The flames flickered, casting dancing shadows on the men's faces as they sat in a circle. All seven listened as their boss laid out his plans. A choir of locusts started and stopped their chatter as they rubbed their legs against their wings. A string of smoke spiraled into the sky, disappearing into the night as the wood crackled and popped, puffing steam, as orange coals glowed in the men's eyes.

Ringo used a stick to make a square in the dust-covered ground. Beside it, he traced two lines heading west. Inside the square, he mapped out First Street and Santa Clara Streets, as well as the alleys adjoining the bank and those across from the railroad station. He scratched out the path they would use for their plan. Then he looked at each of his gang members to make sure they understood.

"We can hide with our horses in the shadows of the allies. The buildings will give us cover from the afternoon sun. There'll be a big herd waiting in the stockyards, so the town will be full of cowboys and strangers. That way, our presence should go unnoticed until we begin. Like always, we hit 'em hard and lightning fast. We've gotta strike before they know we're there to catch them helpless. Billy, you lead the other three men from the alley across the street. As soon as you see me break cover, you come right behind us, lickety-split. Everything should work out like clockwork, and we'll be out of there before they know what hit 'em."

"And what about the town sheriff?" Billy asked. "You want me to kill him, boss? I reckon he'll be our only threat besides the marshal."

"Nah, he'll have been appointed through elections. I wouldn't put much stock in the bravery of a politician."

"So, what about the marshal? In such a place, he won't be daisy. I know Santa Clara ain't as hard a town as many farther west, but odds are they'll have an experienced lawman to help the elected sheriff. With such a small town, I doubt there would be more than one deputy, if any."

"Yeah, we'll have to take care of the real town law before we rob the train. If we come in shootin' up a storm, most folks will run away and hide. Joey, you and Rob can take care of the real lawman. The train arrives tomorrow afternoon, and I expect him to be tended to by then. We don't wanna get messy. If we stick to the plan, everything will run like clockwork, and we'll get away with only a few shots. I'll take care of the engineer. They're usually feisty, just how I like 'em."

"And how are we supposed to do that?" Joey asked.

"Ride into Santa Clara tonight and keep an eye on the marshal. Find out where he eats breakfast, lunch, and dinner, and if he has a siesta or not. You know how folks are down here in Texas with all the Mexicans about. You two can take care of one little marshal, can't ya?"

"Why can't we ride in tomorrow morning, Ringo? I don't like roaming around out there in the dark. There might be hostile Indians about, and they would probably see us before we see them."

"Because that way, nobody important will see you boys ride into town. You two can't pass as cowhands. You don't have rope burns and calluses on your hands, and your boots ain't scuffed. Even your shirts and britches are new. You boys don't look like you just got off a cattle drive. You look like you're fixin' to go to a pleasure palace."

"Should we kill him, then, Ringo?" Joey asked.

"No. Then we'd have the state law after us. We just wanna stop him but not bury him. Then I reckon there'd be hell to pay. Knock him out and lock him in one of his cells. That will get him out of our way long enough to rob the train. I doubt the townsfolk will give us much grief. That way, the Texas Rangers won't come after us because if they do, we'll have real trouble on our hands. If we have a serious problem, I reckon that's where it's gonna be. Yep, they'll take revenge on killing a lawman, but they won't bother to come after us for a bank job. That'll be left to the local law enforcement. If it were the government's money, things would be different."

"Come on, Rob. It'll be dark before we know it. I know it's only a few hours' ride, but you heard the boss. The sooner we get to it, the better. That should put us in town between midnight and one in the morning. We might even catch the marshal on his last rounds so we can follow him home."

"You better make sure you're at his place waitin' for him before he gets there, or you'll have to bust in, and a Texan marshal won't go easily. Then you'll have to kill him for sure, and that won't serve our purpose. I don't care if you rough him up, but make sure he's breathing when you're done. Lock him in one of his cells, and when you leave, make sure you lock the front door. Once you lock it, get rid of the keys. If somebody does stop you, you don't want to have any evidence on you. Make sure you don't mess this up. I'm relying on you, Joey."

"The townsfolk will run and hide until they figure out we've taken their savings," Roby snickered. "By the time they realize what we've done, it'll be too late. Even if they did want to follow us, it'll take some brass to follow eight armed men into West Texas."

"What if we run into the sheriff, Ringo?" Joey asked, his eyes narrowing. "There are two lawmen in town, you know, even if one is a politician."

"Remember, I cased the place and know enough about him. He'll be asleep in that fancy hotel room of his. He's too highfalutin' to sleep in the cell bunk. See how our studying the town works in our favor? That way, we make sure we don't get any surprises. That's the same reason you need to arrive in town on time to check things out before making your move. Use your brains this time, boys. These days, you've gotta be smart to be successful in this game and stay alive."

"If you dance with the devil, the devil doesn't change. The devil changes you," Buck Butler whispered to Eric Turner. Gleefully drunk. He stifled another snicker. "Maybe we ought to think about havin' another boss. Ringo is always pickin' on us. Joey seems to do everything anyway. Maybe he would make a better boss, and he's nicer too."

When Buck realized Ringo was behind him, he drew himself straight as the blood drained from his face, and his body went tense. He quickly sobered up. As suddenly as rain, his guts turned to water. He knew that he talked too much when he was drunk, but he just couldn't help himself. Having all that gold had made him giddy, and he wasn't as careful as he should have been.

Ringo seemed to enjoy and even invite heated arguments and discourse. His face turned red as he shook with rage. His men backed away from his vehemence in his voice. His eyes narrowed as he hissed like a snake ready to strike.

Moon backhanded Buck, then grabbed a fistful of hair and pushed the end of his pistol barrel into the base of his skull. Butler felt it when the hammer clicked, resonating through his neck.

"You mouth off to me again, and it'll be the last thing you ever do." Moon's whisper hissed like a viper.

As Buck tried to speak, his eyes watered, his throat choked up, and he could barely talk. "I got cha, boss. I didn't mean nothin' by it. I'm drunk, is all. It won't happen again."

———

JUST AS ORDERED, Joey Burns and Rob Roy rode out of the secret outlaw hideout half an hour after they got their orders. It was only a three-hour ride to Santa

Clara. They carefully picked their way across the less-traveled trails with their rifles lying across their laps, ready for anything as they quietly slipped through the night. Of course, no lawmen were wandering around in the dark because it would be too dangerous, but that didn't mean that there weren't Comanche snooping around. Just the thought made goose bumps rise on Joey's arms, and hackles stood on end. He was more afraid of Indians than he was of his boss.

Neither of the men seemed to fear lawmen and ignored most gunmen, but Comanche and Apache warriors were something else. Anyone with any sense feared them both, especially at night. They had not only heard hair-raising accounts but had witnessed some, too, and neither one of them wanted to lose their hair. When they heard a twig break, for an instant, they froze, and everything went deathly quiet. They had to remind themselves to breathe. After ten minutes, all they heard was the wind blowing through the trees, so they continued with caution.

A man could never be careful enough when traveling across the Lone Star State countryside at night. When they looked up, they saw a sliver of the moon as a blanket of stars rolled from east to west, twinkling light years away. They made just enough illuminations to create hazy shadows. Joey bit his lip every time his horse stepped on dry twigs. To him, the noise felt like it could be heard a mile away.

Lucky for them, they made it to Santa Clara without being noticed and spent three hours worrying about nothing. When they rode into town, they used the allies to make sure they weren't seen. Finally, they saw the livery stables and corral, and they walked their horses out of the dark. To their surprise, despite the late hour, a lamp illuminated the front of the barn and part of the corral. A wedge of yellow light framed the ground through a partially open door.

"Whatcha doin' up and still workin' this time of night, old timer? Ain't it past your bedtime?" Joey asked as he leaned in his saddle and poked his head in the door.

"You're danged right that's where I should be, but you can see for yourself the corral is bustin' at the seams. I've gotta finish up shoeing this mare before I'm done for tonight. I'll get a fresh start tomorrow at first light." Curtains of gray hair hung around a full beard.

"Can you water, feed, and brush our horses down before you close up?" Rob asked, despite seeing that the man was exhausted.

"You can leave 'em in the corral, but you'll have to tend to 'em and brush 'em down yourselves. I'm dead on my feet, boys. My helper up and quit, and I haven't found anybody reliable since, and I'm the only livery in town, so you'll have to do with or do without."

As soon as Joey and Rob removed their saddles and harnesses and brushed their horses down, they led them to the watering trough and hung feedbags on their heads. Now it was time to get to work. Behind them, the lights went out, and the old farrier, Billy Bob Thorns, shut the barn door with a bang.

Just as they had planned, they had arrived in Santa Clara, and nobody had seen them. Now, all they had to do was act like they were there all along. Yet, their minds were on only one thing—something cool to wash down all the dust and hay. After they finished their refreshments, they would start the job. They believed it would be simple enough since it was two against one, and the marshal wasn't expecting trouble.

————

"COME ON, Rob. Let's get a whiskey and a cold beer to wash the dirt from our gullets. My mouth is so dry, my lips are stuck to my teeth."

They walked into the first bar they came across. The sign over the porch said, *The Rowdy Cowboy Saloon and Bunkhouse.* As soon as they stepped inside, they knew why. Most of the buckaroos were cheering for one of the two opponents. They saw a flurry of fists as a pair of rough-looking cowhands, with sunburned faces, pummeled each other with their fists. That was when Joey saw the glint of a blade from the lamplight and the dead, drunken eyes of the opponents.

A soiled dove screamed as the older cowhand buried his knife in the contender's belly, twisting it to cause maximum damage. The youngster looked down in shock at the handle: it was buried to the hilt. With one look, he knew he was going to die.

In a last-ditch effort for revenge, he doubled over and went for his boot gun. Two loud reports echoed in the room. Gun smoke hazed their vision, but there was no doubt. The apparent winner slapped his hand to his chest like it would stop the bleeding. Claret seeped through his fingers as he dropped to one knee and then keeled over. Both men bled out in seconds. The crowd stopped cheering, and everyone fell quiet. Nobody expected the dust-up to turn deadly.

It was as if the town law had a telegraph connection in his head, as he arrived just in time to see that the situation was hopeless. Nobody sent for him, but somehow, he knew something was about to happen. Like any good marshal, he had his finger on the pulse of Santa Clara, and nothing happened in town that he didn't know about.

"Joe," Marshal Bill Weston called out to the bartender. "Rush over and wake up Earl, the undertaker. We've gotta get all this mess cleaned up before I can call it a night. Something told me that it wasn't going to be a quiet evening. Come on, folks, break it up. That'll be the last fight tonight. Go on now. It's time to sleep it off. I'll take personal offense if anyone else is hurt or killed."

In minutes, a small man appeared dressed in a black frock and pants with a stained white shirt, pushing a wheelbarrow. A stovepipe hat sat on his head. Some of the shocked cowhands helped lift the bodies onto the cart. They were bewildered how things had gone so wrong, especially with two friends. The previous day, they had been riding the herd together. The pair had been best buddies and came from the same hometown, but too much whiskey changed everything. Tempers had flared, and the days on the trail had gotten to them, and the drink sparked a fire that no one could put out.

"Now we know where the marshal is," Joey whispered as they watched from the corner where they had taken a seat. "All we've gotta do is follow him home. Ringo said he sleeps in one of the jailhouse bunks. Stay sharp now. We'll catch him off guard when he walks into the marshal's office door."

"But what about my cold beer?" Rob complained.

"We can't take a chance on missing a perfect opportunity. You heard what the boss said. We're supposed to do this right. Once we're done, we need to go to the hideout, Ringo set up for us. If we do just like he says, we shouldn't mess this up."

Rob and Joey slipped out of the saloon's side door. With everyone's attention focused on the marshal and the killings, no one was the wiser. A few minutes later, they stepped into the alley's shadows next to the lawman's office, which housed the jail cells. Now, all they had to do was wait.

———

At such a late hour, the streets were abandoned, although the saloons were still heaving with cowhands fresh off the trail. They had brought in all the cattle waiting in pens to be shipped back East.

Joey and Rob heard the sound of boot heels walking down the sidewalk along the storefronts. The silhouette of a man slowly moved toward the marshal's office. They could see the outline of his guns. As Marshal Weston fiddled with his key, they took their chance. When they stepped onto the porch, the planks groaned under their feet.

As soon as the marshal heard it, he turned, pulling both guns. He reacted much faster than his assailants expected, but Joey was on top of him before he could fire. In the excitement of the moment, he hit him in the temple with his gun barrel, dropping him to the ground. He was so jacked up that he used all his strength.

"Why'd you have to hit him so hard?" Rob asked. He kneeled by the body, looking up at his friend.

"Because he was fixin' to shoot me, fool. What was I supposed to do? Did you see how fast he was? I'm lucky I'm not the one dead."

"Ringo said to knock him out and not kill him," Rob replied as he felt for a pulse. "Damn, he's as dead as a doornail. We've done messed up. If Ringo finds out, he's gonna be as angry as hell."

"You worry too much, Rob. Come on and help me drag him inside. By the time the town realizes he's dead, we'll have the gold and be long gone. Ringo never has to find out about this. In West Texas, nobody will be interested in a small-town marshal."

"Ya think? Don't you believe somebody will be snooping around here tomorrow when the marshal doesn't show in town? We'd better make sure nobody finds us."

"As long as Ringo doesn't find out, it won't matter. Come on, let's get to the house the boss said we could use as a hideout until it's time for the train. When it's getting close, we can wait in the alley like we were told. Killin' lawmen don't bother me none. He would have done the same if the tables were turned. Had I been a little slower, he'd have shot us both."

After dragging the marshal into the main office, Rob grabbed a mop and cleaned up the mess on the porch as best he could. Luckily, the marshal's wound hadn't bled too much. They rifled his body, taking everything of value.

"Come on, the keys are still in the door." Joey locked it and stuffed the key deep in his britches pocket. They had one last look around, but everything was dark. They dropped into the alley beside the jail and vanished into deep shadows on a dark night.

"Remember to get rid of that key as soon as we have the chance. That's what Ringo said to do. As it is, we don't wanna mess up any more than we've already done. Havin' to kill that marshal was just bad luck."

———

As SOON AS Joey knocked on the door, a small panel opened in the center as an eye squinted from the other side and asked suspiciously, "Who is it? What cha want?"

"We were told you were paid to hide us for the night and tomorrow. Open up so we can get off the street."

"Go away."

"Ringo sent us."

"All right then, come on in." Suddenly, the door swung open with a grueling squeak, and the outlaws disappeared inside. A triangle of yellow light spilled onto the small wooden porch. The ramshackle building was at the very end of town. Beyond that were a few covered wagons and several teepees. This was the slums of Santa Clara. Every town and city had one.

CHAPTER THREE

When Will saw that the sheriff was at a loss for what to do and say, he stepped up.

"The first thing we've gotta do is form a posse and quick. Every minute we let those robbers go, down goes our chances of catching them and getting the gold back. I assume that was what they were after, weren't they? A shipment of gold or silver."

Sheriff Parson nodded like he was in a dream, and he didn't quite understand what was going on. He had just been awoken from a deep sleep, and all this came as a huge surprise. Now, as the town law, he felt like he was the focal point of the whole community. He never imagined himself riding off to hunt down dangerous outlaws, but he found he was up against the wall, and he saw no apparent way out.

"How long have you been the Santa Clara sheriff?" Will raised his eyebrows as he waited, tapping his foot impatiently. "Maybe someone should go and find the marshal. Time is of the essence."

"I'll go fetch 'em," Billy Bob Thorns said. "Marshal Weston will know what to do. I'll be right back."

"Loan us some horses and we'll go with ya," Gid added, chomping at the bit.

The Crocketts hated it when men of reckless blood took what wasn't theirs and were ready to join the chase. Despite his brother's calm and quiet manner, he was quick to anger and always up for a scrap. Gid was always ready to fight, and prepared to die if needed.

The look on the sheriff's face was priceless. He truly hadn't planned to join the posse. The Crocketts didn't even know if the sheriff could raise one. Suddenly, he found himself in a position that he hadn't counted on, even though he wore the star. His idea of being a sheriff was eating meals with the mayor and planning how much to tax the new businesses. The violent part of the job hadn't been in his formula. It had suddenly fallen into his lap, and as his eyes looked around frantically for an excuse, he knew he had to be in charge, whether he wanted to or not.

"Where's the marshal?" Sheriff Parson asked. He couldn't help it when his voice cracked. "I could use some help right about now."

Billy Bob came running back. His face was as white as a sheet. "He's dead!"

"Who's dead?" Will asked.

"Marshal Weston, sir. He had a bad gash on the side of his head. I checked his pulse, but he was stone cold. He's mighty stiff, so I'd say it's been some hours since he was murdered. When I went to his office, I tried the door, but it was locked. Then I looked in the pain glass window and saw his boots. I kicked the door in and found the marshal lying there. I saw drag marks on the floor, so I reckon somebody bushwhacked him on the porch outside the door and pulled him in."

"Did you see any signs of who done it?" Will asked.

"With him being a marshal and all, it could be just about anybody. Maybe it was somebody he locked up."

"No, that's not why he's dead. The train robbers knew that if he were put out of commission, they would only have our sheriff to contend with. I bet they don't think that we would take chase."

Will turned and addressed the town's citizens who were crowding ever closer to the scene. Some gawked at the mess as others showed concern, but everybody wanted to know what was going to be done. These were the people who voted the sheriff into office. Many of them were also friends of Marshal Weston. Sheriff Parson felt all eyes on him, and he didn't like it one bit.

"How many of you folks had money on that train? Come on, let's see a show of hands."

"Half the town," Parson said in barely a whisper. "It was loaded with their savings from the San Antonio National Bank, headed for the savings and loans here in town."

Will counted until it was clear that more than half the town had their money in the San Antonio bank. Now that the Commercial and Savings Bank on First and Santa Cara Streets had installed a new security and posted two shotgun guards, the citizens who had always kept their hard-earned cash in San Antonio chose to deposit their life's earnings in the local bank for its easy access. That was why it was on the San Antonio to Santa Clara train.

Before, they considered it too much a risk with all

the Texan outlaws on the run. Now the population of Santa Clara had swelled, and the banks were upgrading their protection so the population would feel safe depositing their money locally.

Will figured the other half had their money in the McLaughin & Ryland Bank, since they were the only two in town. Lucky for some, only one of the banks was sending its money from San Antonio for more accessibility to their funds. Unfortunately, the gold double eagles didn't make it.

"Come on, this ain't gonna fix itself. I believe if we can get twenty men to chase these rascals, we can scare them into giving the money back. If not, then they'll have to pay the consequences. Any way you look at it, I figure they're goin' to jail."

"You sound awfully sure of yourself," Sheriff Parson dared say. The look in his eyes showed his doubt.

"That's because I've been doin' this for quite a spell. My little brother and me wore badges in the past, right here in Texas, among other states. It's been some time back, but we know something about keeping the law."

When the townsfolk realized their money was at risk, wives began to push their husbands forward to volunteer. Some of them had every penny they had ever earned among those gold coins. It could wipe out half the town. Sure, there was insurance, or so the banks and railroad company claimed, but they couldn't afford the expensive lawyers that the banks could, so the rich never had to pay the price that the poor did. It was getting their money back or the reformed bank would be closed by next week, and they would all lose their savings.

"Well, what are we waitin' for?" Billy Bob asked as

he stepped forward. The livery owner wore a heavy Colt Walker on his hip. From the look on his face, they could see that he wasn't scared.

Will pushed his gun belt lower on his hip as he tightened the buckle. He was ready to go to work. He leaned on the porch post with his Winchester rifle propped against the railing. Behind him, he heard footsteps step softly, and then Gid was standing at his side. His rifle was in the crook of his arm, and his pistols in his wide leather belt.

Just then, Billy Bob the blacksmith came riding up with a string of horses. "We can get extra saddles over at the livery stables." He had the extras that he rented out.

Before they left town to chase after the outlaws, they had heard the sheriff claim that America's future lay in the development of the West. That may be true, but if he didn't get his game together, he wouldn't live to see it. At the moment, he had yet to impress anyone, especially Will and Gid Crockett.

THEY RODE through the countryside with Gid and Will taking the lead. Few of the members of the posse had much knowledge of dealing with dangerous men, but with twenty-two members strong and a good plan, they believed they had a fighting chance. They recklessly rode through the afternoon, only slowing when night fell.

As the sun sat squat on the earth's rim, they saw a thin line of gray smoke as it climbed high into the sky. Will slid off his horse and pulled a handful of grass, letting it fall, indicating the direction of the wind. The blades drifted toward the smoke.

"We'll have to swing around so that we're upwind, or their horses will smell us and nicker or neigh, giving us away." Will lead them by the light of a quarter moon and billions of stars.

That was when the posse realized there was much more to wilderness knowledge than they ever imagined. The Crocketts seemed to know the earth's secrets. Things unknown to most White men. He also looked like he could take on a bear.

The land around them was full of rocky outcrops formed into mysterious shapes and shadows, creating dark places for a man to hide. It possessed a dark, desolate beauty, marked by pink bands and black rock.

"I'd say it's them all right, but that doesn't mean they're all there." Will closed his eyes and smelled the air for smoke. "If I was them, the first thing that I would do would be to split up to make several tracks to follow. Remember how fast these fellas came in for the robbery. That tells me they ain't beginners. They pulled off the robbery in under five minutes. We hardly had time to respond. That means they've done it before, and if we don't stop 'em, they'll do it again."

"They wouldn't dare mess with us. We're too many." Sheriff Person's voice didn't hold the confidence he wanted. He closed his eyes and tried to listen, just as the Crocketts did, but all he heard was the moaning wind.

"Hush up, or they'll hear you and know we're here." Will scolded Sheriff Parson with a sharp glare. "You men wait here. Give us ten minutes to get behind them. Then you all come in with your guns drawn. Don't come riding in like gangbusters either. Walk your horses in like you own the place. Spread out, too, so they can see our numbers. I want all their eyes on you, men. Meanwhile, we'll be comin' at 'em from the back."

Gid whispered, "Whoa now." He was usually the hothead, but he knew that the men they were tracking were dangerous as hell. "We've gotta think this through, brother. Our posse members here ain't as experienced as us."

"But they'll hear us like you said, Mr. Crocket. I believe it'll work," Sam Sneed, the bartender, said.

He sounded braver than the sheriff, but not by much. It was clear that the citizens of Santa Clara weren't used to chasing outlaws. Still, Will had to give them credit for having the grit to try.

"Watch yourselves, now. These outlaws won't panic. They're a bunch of killers and thieves, not freedom fighters." Will whispered as he looked into the men's eyes. "Take a bead as soon as you can and don't take your guns off 'em. Don't worry, they won't expect us to be behind 'em. Remember, ten minutes." Will pulled out his watch to check the time.

The Crocketts wheeled their horses and disappeared into the dark. The sound of hooves slowly vanished until all they heard was the wind blowing through the grass. When Will and Gid got close enough to see their faces, they saw four men sitting around a flickering fire. Six horses were tied to ground stakes as they grazed, whisking their tails and sliding their jaws at tufts of green grass. Just as Will had expected, the gang had split up.

The Crocketts' eyes flicked from one shadow to another, looking for signs of an ambush from a night guard, but it looked like the outlaws were confident enough that nobody in Santa Clara was up to tracking them down. Or maybe they were just reckless.

Right after they arrived at the back of the campsite, they heard someone complain in a gruff voice, and an ex-soldier stood to his feet. He wore the remnants of a Union officer's uniform but looked more like an outlaw and killer than a genuine soldier. The war had been over for a long time, but it was clear that he was among those fleeing their past and running for Texas.

It was so exciting, it was palpable. The glow on Gid's face said he wasn't worried and was ready for a fight. The Crocketts never left a job unfinished.

They stared across the vast, stretching plains and to the mountains on the other side. On a distant ridge, shadows stood long beside a pack of coyotes as they sang their nightly choir, but the brothers didn't make a sound. When the ten minutes were up, they were in position. The barrel-chested Gid snapped his head in the outlaw's direction as soon as he heard the voice. Just as the outlaw was about to look his way, the Crocketts made their move.

The outlaw was instantly rewarded with a series of lightning-swift punches from his massive fists, knocking Joey to the ground.

"If you know what's good for you, you'll stay down," Will said dryly. "So far, my brother's gone easy on ya."

Gid put a foot on his neck when he tried to sass back. A gurgling sound came from his throat as he struggled to breathe, and his eyes spread wide. They were on them before they had a chance to even pull a gun.

"The party's over, girls." Will smiled coldly.

When Joey pushed himself to his hands and knees while swearing at Gid, he gave him a swift kick in the gut to shut him up. "This must be one of those deaf train robbers. I told you to stay down. How about you boys? Any of you wanna sass me, too?"

The wind whispered through the leaves on the trees. Owls hooted in the darkness as the coyotes continued howling at the sliver of moon. On their way back to town with four prisoners, they rode under the great bowl of a sky in sober silence. All four outlaws knew what awaited them back in Santa Clara. They had all heard about the courts and the famous hanging judge.

Will carefully studied who he took as the gang leader of the four. His tired eyes stretched open, showing thin lines of veins, but somehow, he knew that this wasn't the real boss. It was probably his second man. When they got them back to town, they would make them talk, and if they didn't, Gid would have a round with them until they gave him the names they wanted.

Will slammed his pistol into his holster, slung his Winchester rifle over his shoulder, and turned on his heels. "It's time we get these fellas back to town."

They wheeled their horses toward Santa Clara and loped off into the dark. The thieves were surrounded by the posse with their leads in their fists.

The country climbed into a forest with cedar, elms, and huckleberries sprouting on the hillsides. This part of Texas was abundant with water, making it the perfect place to farm and ranch large herds of cattle and sheep.

When they returned to town, hundreds of people came to see what had happened. Many shouted at the outlaws, and some threw rocks. Sheriff Parson hooked his thumbs behind his suspenders like he was responsible for finding the gang members. Then he looked at Will and Gid, and his face turned red. All the other posse members stared at him, humbling him before courageous men. How dare he act like he did anything but ride along? During the outlaw's capture, he was as quiet as a mouse.

"Unfortunately, these boys don't have the money. The real boss took off with it using these four nitwits as bait, so they're guaranteed time to get away. Do you hear that, fools? Your boss sacrificed you to ensure his safety." Will spat in the dirt.

The sign hanging from a pole at the crossroads read, *Santa Clara Street*. It was only a block from the dead sheriff's office. Gid's shirt stretched tight around the shoulders of the heavy-boned man. He removed his cover, raked his fingers through his hair, and down his weathered face. His biceps and forearms bulged with every move.

"We'll never catch up with the other four. I reckon they got away clean. Maybe they rode for El Paso, where there is less law than even here. But if I were them, I'd ride off the trails and avoid towns. New Mexico ain't that far away. If they make it there, they'll go scot-free. No offense, Sheriff, but if you make it through the next six months or so, maybe you'll learn enough to stay alive." Will gave the greenhorn lawman a pat on the shoulder to show he held no hard feelings and wished him luck.

"Ah hah. You see now, don't you, Sheriff?" Gid smiled. "Being the town law ain't as easy as you thought. There's more to being a constable than collecting taxes and passing out fines."

The smug look froze on the sheriff's face. He

couldn't deny it and knew that Crockett was right. The sheriff stared at them like they were curious anatomical specimens from another world, but from then on, he held his tongue, knowing he was out of his league.

They sat on the porch with cigarettes and cheroots glowing in the dark. Everyone was too worked up to sleep, so they all waited for the sun to rise. Then they could send for the judge and get the show on the road. Their hands held tin cups of whiskey to take the edge off. No matter how many times they experienced such situations, they always left them tense, and the normal citizens were apprehensive. Some were nearly hysterical with excitement and joy, although this was mixed with the bitter taste of defeat since they had not recovered the gold.

"That's just one of the hundreds of things the sheriff doesn't know." Will grinned. "But give him time. Maybe he'll learn now that he's been humbled."

The sheriff was shocked when the Crocketts spoke as if he wasn't even there. He blinked his eyes like a bat in humiliation.

"Truth is a byproduct of a man's character. Honest men reveal their truths with every breath they take. But dishonest men distort the same." Will chuckled at the puzzled expression on the sheriff's face.

An orange streak showed on the distant eastern horizon. The sky was no longer completely dark. That was when the posse members on the porch began to see silhouettes moving in the growing light. The outline of shadows was the shape of men moving up and down the street, starting a new day just like they did their last. Despite the blow to the population, life continued.

As the sun began to climb into the sky, long shafts of

light passed through the trees like rain. Dogs barked at the end of town near a few scattered teepees and wagons. A rat ran across the street with a stray cat hot on its tail. Wagon wheels creaked as they hurried up and down the street.

CHAPTER FOUR

WHEN THEY HERDED THEIR PRISONERS TOWARD THE JAIL, they heard church bells when they rode into town. Hundreds of people were in his funeral procession as it slowly wound down the streets like a giant slug. At the head of the grieving people was a woman in black, walking beside a preacher. He wrapped his long arm around her as her shoulders shuddered while she cried.

"I figure the outlaw gang murdered him so they would have limited resistance when they robbed the train," Will said. "That makes two murders on their heads, plus the gold they stole from the mail car. It doesn't get any more serious than this."

"Did you boys hear that?" Gid yelled over his shoulder. "I reckon you fellas are perfect for the hanging judge, old Roy Bean. Yeah, you are all gonna swing for sure. There was no call to murder the marshal nor the engineer. If I had my way, I'd tear you apart, limb by limb, one at a time, right here and now. You're lucky my brother has more restraint and won't let me. But now you're gonna have a day or two to think about what you've done and where you're goin'. No matter where the judge is, I doubt it'll take him long to get to town once he hears what you riffraff have done. When he finds out you fellas killed the marshal, he'll be comin' fast and hard."

"It wasn't intentional," Rob huffed with pleading eyes. "Joey didn't mean to do it. We were only supposed to tie him up and lock him in his cell, close the front door, and throw away the key."

"Shut up, fool! Are you stupid, or what?" Joey spat. "Can't ya see the man's frightened to death. He don't know what he's talkin' about. We didn't rob no train. Did you find any gold coins on us? You've got the wrong men, mister. We're just cowhands lookin' for work."

"Then where's the blisters and calluses on your hands from loopin' a rope? Most buckaroos I know don't carry expensive guns either. You boys were armed to the teeth when we captured you. That was damned stupid, not leaving out a guard right after you robbed a train. I bet your boss would disapprove of that, wouldn't he?"

"So, which one of you really killed the marshal, or ya all in on it?" Gid asked. "I bet it was the mouthy one there. They called you Joey, didn't they? Whatcha got to say for yourself?"

"Like I said, we didn't kill anybody. And maybe we ain't cowboys. We're just a few men fallen on hard luck."

"Save your stories for the judge. What I wanna know is, where are the other four that helped rob the train? The fella I winged, I see right there. How's that shoulder feelin' about right now? I bet it hurts, don't it? You're lucky I just nicked ya. Usually, I don't miss, but I had to shoot ya through all that steam. So, don't tell me you weren't there. I saw you with my own eyes. You were quick, all right, but not quick enough. Had you been a little slower, you'd already be dead."

Eric Smith gave Will a look like he was angry as hell. He didn't like the way the lawmen talked to his boss. All it did was make Crockett laugh, though. The simpleton felt his neck redden and turned his eyes to the ground, embarrassed. He tried to be like the others, but he knew he didn't have what it took. Every time he tried to show his valor, he shamed himself. *I can't help it that I'm stupid,* he thought to himself.

"You won't be feelin' so damned spunky after the judge sentences you all to hang by the neck until you're dead. Whatcha say, little brother? They'll swing for sure, won't they?"

"There's no doubt about it."

"Well, there you go, gentlemen. The verdict has been announced. If I were you, I'd be makin' my peace with God."

That took some of the wind out of the outlaws, but Joey was too angry about being caught to think straight. After they filed in, both cell doors slammed shut with a bang. Large keys jingled in heavy-duty locks as the tumblers clicked and the mechanism drove home. Hundreds of people stood outside the jail, so even if they managed to break out, they were condemned to hang. The angry crowd was on the verge of becoming a mob.

"Have a good sleep, girls," Gid said as they walked out of the cell block and into the main office.

Two Winchesters hung on a rack over a small fire-place. Next to the cold fire was a wicker-seated chair and a small table, on which a pipe and a book sat along-side a pair of wire-rimmed glasses. It was close to a window that opened onto the alley, covered in steel bars.

"I reckon you're gonna have to telegraph for a new marshal, Billy Bob," Will said. "I even bet *you* would make a good lawman if you set your mind to it. You sure are brave enough. You've been the most helpful of the posse. Yes, sir, you're a fine man."

"Thank ya, Will, but I've already got a job. As the town grows, I'm takin' on help and all. We need somebody like Marshal Weston to take his place. In a settlement like Santa Clara, less won't do. It isn't one of the wildest towns in Texas, but we get our share of bad men in the state, and sometimes they're passing through. How about you and your brother? I bet you two could keep the law just fine in a town like ours. We'd be proud to have y'all. The sheriff here would see that you got paid well, too."

"I'm afraid that my brother and I are on our way to El Paso. We were just riding through. We wanna head back to Arizona to check on a few loose ends. We sure do appreciate the offer, though. The marshal's cell looks more comfortable than our bedrolls, that's for sure. You boys did a fine job holding the line like that. A man doesn't know what or who he is until his back is up against a wall."

Billy Bob Thorns was a tall, thin man, but powerful. He owned the local blacksmith's shop. Unlike most men of his profession, he was neatly dressed even though they were all covered from head to toe with trail dust. He was as tall as Will and nearly as strong as Gid. Will noticed that he was the only one who wasn't scared when they captured the outlaws without a shot.

He had heard some of the men's teeth chatter as

others cleared their throats and looked wildly all around. Most of them had been scared out of their wits. Still, they controlled their emotions and forged on with only a sneaking suspicion of what they might be getting themselves into.

A dozen men crowded the room, and they all talked at once as the rest of the posse occupied the porch. This was the worst thing that had ever happened in Santa Clara. If they didn't find the money, half the people in town were going to lose all their savings. In many cases, it represented their retirement. Then there was the loss of their marshal, which they also took personally. He had been in town long enough to become friends with the local population.

"Somebody is gonna have to send a wire to the judge," Billy Bob said. "Hopefully he'll be ridin' circuit and won't be too far away. Last I heard, he was down by Eagle's Pass, but that was a couple of weeks ago. Still, with today's trains, he can get here quickly enough. If we're patient, we'll have our day in court, and the law will punish these men for what they did."

"Ain'tcha afraid of a vigilante party, Sheriff?" Gid asked. "You might not have time for the judge to get here before the locals string 'em up. I take it you all liked Mashal Weston, didn't ya?"

"He was a hard man and sometimes even gruff, but he was always fair. He had his finger on the pulse of Santa Clara and at times felt bad things were coming even before they happened," Walter Math said. "I own Math's Haberdashery. If you boys need anything before you head to El Paso, just stop by and I'll be happy to offer you a special discount. I'll even throw in a couple of boxes of bullets to show our gratitude."

"Well, I'm afraid we've missed our train to West Texas."

"The El Paso direct runs again the day after tomorrow. You can stay in my hotel until then, free of charge. I'll even throw in three square meals a day. You two have done a great deal for our town, and we would like to express our sincere gratitude. You'll only be here for two days, so you might as well enjoy yourselves," Jed Hanlon said. "You both deserve it."

"You don't know what you've gotten yourself into when you offer Gid here free food. You might go broke before the train arrives to fetch us. We'll be happy to take the rooms, but we'll pay for our own meals."

"No, no, no. I insist."

"Don't say I didn't warn ya." Will's laugh was loud and friendly, and it reached his eyes.

That evening, they went to the Hanlon Hotel Restaurant for supper. It was finer than the Crockett brothers were accustomed to, except when they ate in restaurants with French menus back in San Francisco. Gid liked to eat, but he didn't like it when somebody threw a wrench in the works and slowed him down.

"I'd be careful how close you get your fingers to Gid's plate, ma'am." Will smiled at the waitress. "My brother might mistake it for food and bite one or two off."

———

THE ATTENDEES' voices crackled with expectations as murmurs rippled across the courtroom like an ocean wave. When the door behind the bench opened, everyone went silent. You could hear a pin hit the floor.

It was apparent that their interest had sparked, as they all sat up straighter and focused their eyes on the waiting outlaws and the looming figure of the hefty judge. At fifty-eight, he was nearly as round as he was tall. His white hair peeked from under a straw hat.

He didn't look like a judge, but then again, this far west, nobody worried so much about appearances. Still, he wore a white shirt, a shoestring tie, and a peasant's hat. The image set him apart, and his reputation followed him around like stink on a skunk.

Even before he had a chance to sit, everyone's eyes snapped toward the loud noise like branding irons.

BOOM-BOOM!

Some people almost turned to flee until they saw who was holding the gun. Her pale face contrasted with her black dress and veil. Then they all sat glued to their pews as their eyes shot toward the judge. His face turned dark purple as he hammered his gavel like he was chopping down a tree. The marshal's widow looked like a frightened animal cowering at the end of a boxed-in canyon with nowhere to escape. She was pale, white, and glistening with fear.

Will had already drawn and swung his pistols toward the blast, then swore as he lowered the hammers, blinking like a bird. Nobody could believe what they had just seen. It had taken everyone by surprise. At the door, they had large tables where the men checked their guns to avoid violence and blood-shed, but nobody thought to check the widow for weapons. Gun smoke squirreled out of the barrel as her white-knuckled fist held a pistol in her hands.

The excitement in the crowd was such that nobody really noticed Mrs. Weston was there until she shot two rounds before a guard wrenched the six-gun from her hands. A hint of a cruel smile touched the edges of her lips.

The women they had seen at the head of the funeral procession stood in the front pew. Gun smoke drifted through the closed space as two holes appeared in Joey's chest. He blinked rapidly as he tried to find his breath without success. He mouthed words, but no sound came out.

The smell of cordite hung heavily in the air. With his eyes open and empty, staring at the ceiling, it was clear Joey had given up the ghost.

Will and Gid drew away from the others to have a private word.

"What are they gonna do with that woman?" Gid asked. "I fear for her freedom. You can't really blame her for what she did. I'd have done the same, were it you, brother."

"As far as I can see, she had every right to shoot him, but I doubt the judge sees it that way. Not when it happened right here in his courtroom. Not Roy Bean. He ain't that kind of judge."

"But it don't seem right to me."

"The right and wrong of the law isn't for us to decide, little brother. Smarter men than us wrote them up to protect the people from the wicked. We can't fix every wrong in the world."

"It still don't seem right. The poor woman lost her husband at the hands of these men."

Sheriff Pete Parson looked desperately uncomfortable. The job of being the town law without the marshal's backup was proving to be more than he could handle. At least, now he was trying. Still, he was overwhelmed. It seemed that every time he absorbed the last thing that happened, something new, just as bad, popped up. The courtroom was now in total chaos.

Judge Roy Bean's face darkened as he spoke. In an instant, his eyes became flinty and dangerous. There were certain rules and laws a person didn't break, no matter who they were, even a grieving widow.

"The court register. Detain that woman at once and take her to my quarters. And make sure she doesn't have another gun. Somebody go and fetch Earl Gravely and tell him to bring his wheelbarrow. This one we'll have to judge in his absence."

To everyone's surprise, Judge Roy Bean continued like nothing had happened. It appeared that he didn't let anything interrupt his proceedings. An hour later, the jurors retired to the deliberation room to give the final verdict. All it took was one disagreeing vote to blow everything, but everybody knew that all twelve members would want to see the remaining outlaws hang.

Less than five minutes later, the same dozen people filed in and took their seats.

"What say yee, Foreperson?" the judge asked. "Give the clerk the paper."

When Bean opened the vote results, he had to force back a smile. If he had met any men who deserved to be punished to the fullest extent of the law, these three were them. To bushwhack and murder a United States Marshal outside his front door was unacceptable, and he knew he had to send a strong message. Not to mention robbing the train and killing the conductor.

"Will the accused please stand. It is by the order of this court that you all be hanged by the neck until dead tomorrow morning. I will prove witness, myself. Sheriff, you may take these men back to their jail cells, where I suggest they pray and repent for their sins. You three don't have much time left. Make the best with what you've got."

Without another word, the judge was up and out of his chair. For such a big man, he moved quickly and gracefully. He vanished behind the door as it clicked shut behind him.

———

"HAVE A SEAT, MA'AM," Judge Bean said to Mrs. Weston when they were alone in his quarters. "Why did you have to ruin my day? You know I can't let you off without some sort of punishment, don't you?"

"I'm ready to meet my maker, Judge Bean. I'm not afraid. I've made my peace with God. I knew before I shot him that I would pay. I'm just sorry that I didn't have the opportunity to kill all three of them. The second shot was unintentional because I got so nervous. I know what I did was a crime, and I am ready to serve justice."

Bean made a long, slow sigh. "First of all, I don't hang women, at least God-fearing women such as yourself. Second, you were avenging the blatant murder of one of our trusted marshals who risk their lives every day. Under the circumstances, I can't let you off Scott free. How would you do with six months in jail? There's a women's political prison in San Antonio. Maybe I can pull a few strings for you and let you spend your time there. You don't deserve to do hard prison. You've been put through enough. Still, like I said, I can't just let you off."

The widow sat with her head bowed in embarrassment. "Thank you, Judge, for being so lenient. That will suit me fine. I'll spend that time mourning Bill. You knew him. He was a fine man."

The marshal's wife looked like a frightened animal cowering in a corner with no escape. She was pale, white, and glistening with fear. Yet she was resigned and didn't regret what she had done. Her only regret was killing only one rather than them all.

CHAPTER FIVE

THE SUN WAS FOUR FINGERS FROM THE HORIZON AS IT continued to rise into the sky. There were so many people in town that it looked like a three-ring circus. Nobody knew how the word had spread so quickly around the county, but people came from far and wide —some in buckboard wagons, others on horseback, and even walking. Of course, the news of the train robbery was already old news, as was the capture of half of the culprits.

There was nothing like a hanging to get the blood up of those in the city and county. They had all made an effort to attend the demise of the gang members. Some of the farmers and ranchers had even lost money in the robbery. Others were there out of boredom and curiosity. Any event was considered a festival for those from the country outside of Santa Clara, and hangings drew the biggest crowds.

Salesmen mingled with the masses, selling their wares from trays hanging from their necks, as they claimed their soap or potion was a magic cure-all.

Scantily dressed ladies leaned coyly from balcony railings, showing their wares, hoping to attract a friendly stranger. One such saloon was across the street from all the excitement. In the corner, near some of the ladies of the night, Will and Gid sat as they solemnly watched. They fluttered around the Crocketts like birds seeking pollen.

"I never cared much for hangings," Will huffed. "They seem to bring the ugliness of humanity out in men. Look at how these people are gawking at the scaffolds with bloodshot eyes. Most of them don't even know who the outlaws are. All they want to do is watch someone die at the end of a rope while their eyes pop out of their heads. The more gruesome, the better."

"It doesn't bother me, especially with rattlers like these. You heard how they tried to deny what they did when we caught them. Why, we witnessed the robbery with our own eyes. After we found out they killed the marshal to make the train heist easier, they crossed the line of no return."

"Remember, they shot the train's engineer, too. That's two murders on their heads. The fact that these fellas are gonna pay for what they did doesn't bother me at all. It's how the people come to see them swing, making it like a circus for them to yell and gawk, and that disgusts me. Sometimes I feel it might be less of a fuss if they fight and die instead of being captured. It would save the government and townsfolk all this mess, along with time and money. Look over there. Why, some of 'em even brought their young kids, and they're eating sandwiches. It looks like they came to have a picnic."

When the sheriff followed Judge Roy Bean down the sidewalk with the prisoners trailing, all heads turned their way in unison. Every eye was on the outlaws. They stepped down into the street as small wakes of dust followed their feet to the gallows with their heads bowed. Some even silently moved their lips as they prayed for forgiveness. The condemned men looked up at the noose, stretching their necks. On the top stood Earl Gravely, the undertaker and executioner. In such a small town, one man had to do both jobs. The judge pointed a crooked accusing finger at the outlaws and nodded for the ceremony to proceed.

The train robbers and murderers climbed their way to their demise silently. Will closed his eyes and listened to the boot heels as they clopped up the thirteen steps to the top, where they were dispatched one by one. Each time the trapdoor slammed open, the crowd took a deep breath and then cheered as if it were some sort of sport. Will and Gid turned their heads away.

One by one, the hangman instructed that the bodies be laid out in cheap pine box coffins. They were destined to be displayed on the marshal's front porch for all those who broke the law to see. They intended to send a strong message to any future robbers who chose their town as their target.

"Ashes to ashes, dust to dust," Will whispered. "I never like seeing a man die, even fools. The lucky one was Joey. He went before they were even sentenced, so he still had the illusion of hope when he died. It was sudden, and he didn't have time to think about it. I'm afraid that his friends weren't so lucky."

"I wonder how it feels to be on the other side," Gid pondered.

"Whatcha mean, the other side? The other side of what?"

"You know, livin' the life of an outlaw and dying like an outlaw too. It must be a shock when you go from being a successful thief to standing on the gallows in the blink of an eye. I wonder what's going through those fellas' minds."

"You sure do say some strange things, little brother."

"Maybe it's that I ain't as smart as you and don't understand."

"You're plenty smart, Gid. It's the men like those over there in pine boxes that are stupid. We'll never be one of them. I don't think we could even get our heads around being like them. They're an entirely different species, little brother."

Even the half-breeds were huddled in groups, staring at the spectacle. Their eyes were like those of feral dogs, and their clothing was ragged and filthy. The Indians had drapes of ghostly black hair. They watched with greedy eyes as the White men welcomed the outlaws' demise.

"Am I too late?" Sheriff Parson asked, gobbling air from the run. "I don't know if I want to see all this or not. It seems barbaric to me. Isn't there a simpler way to do all this with some discretion?"

"No, you're not too late. There are two left, Sheriff. It wouldn't do for you to miss the whole show, would it?" Gid eyed the lawman with doubtful eyes. "You, along with us, are responsible for all this. How's that life of a lawman workin' out for ya now? It ain't as easy as you thought, is it?"

———

EVERY TIME the trapdoor banged opened, the women gasped in horror. One pretty, blonde-haired lady stood on the end of the porch as she teetered to and fro, threatening to faint.

Will rushed over and gently picked her up in his arms like a little child and carried her into the side street and into the shade. They watched as people continued to pour into the plaza, their faces full of curiosity. A scattering of nervous laughter rippled through the crowd.

Close to her cheek, Will asked, "What's your name, ma'am?" They blinked when their faces accidentally touched. She was warm, and her breath came short and quick and smelled sweet, like flowers.

"Linda." For an instant, they clung together like koala bears. "Thank you for saving me from an embarrassing moment. This is my first hanging, and I didn't know what to expect. Next time I'll know better and stay away."

Her hair was pulled into a bun, and her pale skin offset her sky-blue eyes. It made her face look smaller. Will felt uncomfortable with his stubble of beard and ruffled hair, but it was clear that Linda didn't mind. The pretty woman continued to stare at Will Crockett with pleading eyes, but he didn't know what to say, and it was unusual for him to be totally lost for words as his confidence wavered.

Everything was hazy as though her thoughts covered her eyes with a blindfold. She could barely pry them away from something that she felt she shouldn't see. She buried her face in Will's chest.

"Don't put me down yet, please. I'm still dizzy and my mouth is as dry as a corn bin after a drought." But Will saw the look in her eyes and saw something else in there. Perhaps desire mixed with a little mischief. The edge of her lips curled into a bashful smile as she snuggled closer.

As Gid watched, his muscles rippled up and down his arms and back. The veins in his neck looked like mooring lines, ridged and hard. He tried to ignore his brother, but he was too curious about this woman. He smiled as he watched Will come to her rescue just like one of those knights in shining armor of times past. She continued to shudder like a feather in a windstorm, but her eyes said something else.

Even though Linda tried to hold Will's confident gaze, she looked away after a few seconds and turned, as her neck reddened. She felt his heartbeat as she snuggled against his chest. She was a little bosomier than most of the women he'd known. She was a healthy-looking and vibrant individual.

Will's rugged, square-jawed face looked as though it was chiseled from granite. He wasn't only powerful, he was handsome, too. Something that Linda noticed despite the awful exhibition.

"I must admit, I'm rather smitten by you, ma'am." He said it with such solemnity that she didn't doubt a word, but when he said it, he surprised himself by his boldness. This woman wasn't a spoiled dove like most ladies in town. She was obviously a refined lady.

When Will replied, his voice was gravelly. From his tone, Linda knew she had moved him, but what comes next? She wasn't one of the saloon girls looking for a date. She was the daughter of the director of the second biggest bank in town. The one that hadn't been robbed of gold double eagles on the train.

Will moved his tongue over cracked lips, then his mouth broke into a smile which reached his eyes. His tongue was too dry as his heart roared in his chest and hammered between his ears. His palms were damp, and rivulets of sweat ran down his back. It had been a long time since a woman had such an effect on him. He, too, wondered what was to happen next.

When he saw Linda's smile, it softened his face. As soon as he turned away and looked back at the gallows, his smile faded, and reality hit him like the hot kiss at the end of a hard fist. He didn't want to tell her he was responsible for what was happening. Suddenly, the amusement in his eyes was gone, and his mouth tightened.

When he put Linda down, he said, "You had better run along now, Miss Linda. You don't want to see the rest of this. It's unsightly and not for young ladies such as yourself to see." Will twisted his mouth into a smile, but his eyes belied his true feelings. He saw the fear in her puzzled face.

––––––––

THE CROWD WAS SO DRENCHED in the excitement of the executions that as it washed through them, it created even more nervous tension along with their reason for life or death.

The sheriff scurried over to the Crocketts. He had run for the outhouse just as the executions began, as his guts turned to water. He exhaled a blast of cigarette smoke as he wiped the sweat from his brow. His eyes were full of fear as his jaw ground his teeth, but he couldn't take his eyes away. He realized, in part, he was responsible too.

"Maybe I'm not cut out to be an officer of the law. Maybe I'd be better working as a banker like I had originally planned." Sheriff Parson's voice sounded like it was full of pain and uncertainty. The last couple of days had been a whirlwind of confusing feelings, making him less certain of everything.

"Just the fact that you've admitted it and have had a look at yourself tells me you're a better man today than you were yesterday." Gid grinned as he patted the strange sheriff on the back. "You watch. You're gonna do just fine."

Will's skin tingled as a restless urge to move came over him. As Linda turned to go and scurried down the street, he nodded to Gid and headed back for the hotel. He wasn't up to seeing the last man swing. He frowned, making his cracked lips sting as his heart continued to hammer between his ears.

Will Crockett sat up the remainder of the night listening to his thoughts as they flashed through his mind at lightning speed. He not only thought about the hearing and the hanging, but he couldn't get his mind off the woman he had grabbed before she fainted.

Was it fate, or was it a simple accident in passing? Time would tell, but he already hoped he would see her again. Usually, the only kind of women he had the pleasure of meeting were percentage girls in the taverns and saloons. It was like a breath of fresh air for him to meet a wholesome woman. Then again, he wondered if he was as wholesome a man.

———

LINDA CHAPMAN WAS WAITING on the last bit of sidewalk on the road out of town. She raised her chin and stared boldly into Crockett's eyes with her fists perched on her hips. Will surprised both her *and* him, along with his brother, by taking her pretty face into his hands and lowering his mouth to hers. They kissed softly. Gid turned as red as a beet and didn't know what to say.

"I promise you I'll come and see you when we pass back through Sant Clara. First, we have some work to tend to in El Paso and eventually Arizona."

Linda didn't dare say a word because she knew her voice would betray her and reveal her true feelings, whatever they were. She had never been so confused in her life, and at the same time, she knew exactly what she wanted. She just didn't know how to obtain it.

"One day, I'll be back on the Southern Pacific Railroad and return to town. All you've gotta do is be patient."

As soon as Will said it, he realized that he had no idea what the future would bring or exactly when he would be back, if they made it back at all. It was dangerous work hunting down outlaws who knew that the only thing that awaited them was a noose and a six-foot fall. A man couldn't get any more desperate, so they would have to be on their toes.

Will mounted his horse and reached down and gave Linda's cheek a peck, but they both felt the electricity rush through them like roaring trains. Again, without another word, she turned on her heels and fled, instantly disappearing into the dense Santa Clara's crowded streets.

Will shrugged off his brother's questioning eyes and walked off, tight-lipped. Again, he was surprised by his actions. There was something about Linda Chapman that put him atilt. Both times he had seen her, his heart had melted, and he had forgotten what he was doing. Only women had the power to do such things to men like him.

CHAPTER SIX

"WE SHOULD'VE TAKEN THE TRAIN, YOU KNOW. THAT WAS our plan anyway," Gid grumbled. "Now we've gotta ride six hundred miles to get to where we're goin'. At first, you said we were gonna go by train and here we are on horseback."

"Yeah, but then we wouldn't have any chance of locating the outlaws. Plus, we aren't gonna go the whole distance on horseback. If we don't find their tracks in a few days, we'll stop at the next way station along the railroad tracks and hitch a ride for us and the horses. We might get lucky like we did with the first four. We can't try to track them if we go by train, at least not at first. I'd like to get those folks' hard-earned money back. It sticks in my craw that we let them get away."

They rode with the sun in their faces. The creek gurgled beside them. Vultures made lazy circles high above, looking for their next meal. Occasionally, they would see a bald eagle fold its wings and drop into a dive, vanishing under the tree line, then climbing again with its prey in its talons.

"Lookee there, fresh horse droppings on the trail," Will said as he slid out of his saddle and kneeled to study the six sets of tracks.

"How are we gonna know it's them?"

"I studied their tracks back in Santa Clara, close to the railway station, and one of their boot heels was broken and easy to see. Two of those horses don't have riders. That means that those are their spares just in case one of the others comes up lame. These fellas are professionals. I don't doubt the gang leader is with them."

"Yeah, that was smart. I figured they might have some spares stashed nearby. These boys aren't beginners," Gid replied. "They've done their homework."

"I figure the outlaws didn't believe we'd be reckless enough to follow them after they robbed the train," Will said. "They were counting on the new sheriff balking and giving up the chase before it got started. I wonder if he had any money in the same bank as the others. I still don't see why the other four made camp without a guard, though I can see why they might split up."

"They must have felt that without the money, nobody could prove they were involved. They didn't count on you recognizing the one you shot. Still, I figure it was laziness that got them caught. We got lucky with that one. The rest of the gang seems smarter and more on top of things."

"Scouting is thirsty work, Gid. Sometimes you end up hot, hungry, freezing, and tired all at the same time. Then again, what can I tell you that you haven't already experienced? I reckon I've rattled on long enough and maybe more than I should have."

"Why, when you ride alone, I reckon you'd talk to

yourself if you had to." Gid smiled. "And most folks think you're quiet. Nobody knows you like I do. Do you really believe we'll be able to tell which tracks belong to Ringo Moon and the rest of his gang as we move forward? There seems to be steady traffic on the road to El Paso, not to mention all the cattle."

"Yeah, you're right, little brother. I guess they got away long ago. It's a sham about all that town's folk's money. You know that there's some things we just can't fix."

"To be honest, I figure even Billy Bob, not alone the sheriff, was scared stiff most of the time when we were closing in on Joey and his boys."

"I've never much thought about us ignoring the risk. With our lifestyle, it's unhealthy."

"Why would a man worry when he can plan?"

Will slapped his knee and laughed. "Good for you, Gid. Spoken like an honest man. Be honorable above all else. They had grit, I'll give them that. In the end, even the sheriff. The truth is, if you don't have a wagon-load of grit, you'll never make it in this country. Not with men of reckless blood, rain, lightning storms, and flash floods, not to mention the wild animals and Indians. If you're unprepared, you won't last."

Gid nodded as he thought about how slick the outlaws were and how unprepared the town was, especially the sheriff.

"That's why most of the folks in Santa Clara hardly ever leave town, just like those in the posse. None of them holds a light to you, little brother."

Will could see the light in Gid's eyes grow brighter with the compliment. He even jutted out his chin and puffed up his chest in response. He appeared almost manic with satisfaction.

"I sure do hope we get lucky and run into Ringo and his outlaw gang. It would be mighty nice to get those poor folks their money back."

"I thought we were heading for Arizona?"

"When have we left something like this unattended, Will? If we run into 'em, we'll have to try to nab 'em and escort them to jail. Still, I doubt they'd be so dumb as to run for El Paso. It's too obvious."

"The other four members of his gang sure weren't very smart. Why do you expect these to be different?"

AFTER RIDING FOR THREE DAYS, they realized they were looking for a needle in a haystack. There were so many tracks that, after a while, they all became indistinguishable. There were also dozens of smaller paths and trails that ran off the main road. They could have taken any of them and been anywhere by then. They didn't even know if the four remaining gang members had split up or not. Maybe they had divided up the loot and each one headed for home, wherever that might be. Soon, they could even be out of the state or even the country without a trace of the money. The Mexican border wasn't that far away.

Gid's paint suddenly reared up, kicking his front hooves. That was when they heard the snake's rattle. As quickly as lightning, Will pulled his pistol, and a single shot rang out. The rattler's head disintegrated right before it struck.

"I hope that outlaw gang isn't close, or they'll have heard that gunshot."

"What was I supposed to do? Let the rattler bite you, little brother? You were a second from gettin' poisoned."

They stopped to refresh the horses at a small watering hole they passed along the trail. Bunches of healthy grass surrounded its bank. The horses bobbed their heads as beads of water rolled off their hairy chins. Their mouths and tongues slurped the cool liquid.

When they got to the next watering and coal station, they waited there to board the train and give up the chase. It was still almost six hundred miles to El Paso, and what was left of the outlaw gang was long gone and could be anywhere by now.

When the train for El Paso came into view, an old black dust-covered dog barked dispiritedly and lazily crawled under the station master's porch. Gid watched the cars pass by one by one until they pulled up to a grinding halt. The sound of the couplings clanging filled the air as the engine began to idle.

———

HE PUT the cup to his lips and had another sip. "This coffee is thick enough to float a rock," Gid grumbled as he set it down and pushed the cup aside, grabbing the jug and taking a belt of corn liquor, making his mouth pucker as he shook his head.

"I know it's been a long, boring ride, but we don't want to drink too much. This is the most dangerous city in Texas, and until we can see how the situation is, we'd better be on our best game."

"Have you got a feeling, Will? Lately, I think that you worry too much."

"Many men wiser than us say worrying is for fools and horses. It's the opposite of faith, so how can somebody be a godly man if they worry all day?" Will laughed.

"Worryin' is like you believe in a problem that might never come." Gid turned and looked at his brother. "Come on, let's see what's goin' on in town."

———

ERIC SMITH WAS surprised when a low-hanging limb unseated him. He sat on the ground, puzzled as he pushed through the pain. He blinked his eyes as his head slowly stopped spinning. The other three outlaws all laughed. They were just a few miles from El Paso. They had traveled a week and a half, day and night, catching naps when they could. As the moon filled, they rode deeper into the evenings, pushing their horses to their limits, even with the spares. They knew they had to put as many miles between them and Santa Clara as they could.

Ringo didn't leave Joey and his other men behind, hoping they would get caught. The truth was, he hadn't expected a posse to follow, knowing the type of sheriff Santa Clara had. He was more of a politician than a lawman and wasn't someone that Moon feared. Still, it wasn't a bad idea to have them split up just in case they did manage to form some sort of posse.

If something *did* happen, they would go down, not Moon and his men, and they had the money, which was the most critical factor. Now they were rich, so they would wait and see if Joey and the boys showed up over the course of the following days as planned. If not, even better. The money would be split into four ways rather than seven. They never gave Eric his cut because he was dense and didn't even know he deserved it.

When they had the chance, they stopped and counted their loot, finding that it was much more money than they had ever expected. This was all well and good, but it also meant that there was a greater possibility for the law to take action. But Ringo knew when they made it to El Paso, they were home safe and sound. From there, it was a short ride over both the New Mexican and Mexican borders. Additionally, the town was teeming with outlaws and gunslingers who were hiding from the law. Sure, they had a sheriff, but there was only so much a lawman and a couple of deputies could do with a place as big as El Paso County with a population of three thousand eight-hundred-forty-five.

"Well, since my friend here has chosen the spot, I reckon we can bury the gold right here by that oak tree that knocked you on the head, Eric." Ringo snickered. "Remember to leave enough out for the party in El Paso. I never did like Santa Clara. There are too many farmers, ranchers, and decent folk for my taste. Nowhere is like the Six-Gun Capital of the West. I'll take El Paso over any place in Texas, and I'm ready for a party. Too much work and no play makes for an unhappy outlaw gang. Grab that shovel and get to work, Eric. We don't wanna hang around here all day."

———

A FEW HOURS LATER, Ringo, Eric, Wayne, and Jessy rode their worn-out horses into the town of El Paso. They headed straight for the livery stables to sell their exhausted horses and buy six more. It was essential that they had healthy, fresh animals in case things suddenly went awry. Of course, they weren't expecting trouble, but a smart outlaw always had a fresh horse somewhere close by just in case. If you broke the law, you were always on the run.

"Come on, let's go get something to eat and drink. We can rest later. I'm so hungry I could eat a bear." Ringo's belly grumbled right on cue.

"I don't think I could sleep without a few drinks anyway," Eric said as he rubbed the lump the size of an egg on his head. "I need some whiskey to kill the pain."

"Next time you'll look where you're ridin', won't ya? You've gotta stop sleepin' in the saddle and expecting us to keep an eye on ya. You've got to learn to watch where you're goin' or one of these days it's gonna cost you your life, Fool. Or are you too stupid to get that through that thick skull of yours?"

"That was a tough ride, boss. I know it was the right thing to do, but that doesn't make it easier. I know I'm not the best outlaw, but I'm a hard worker. I do wish you'd stop callin' me names, though."

"Well, was it worth it or not? We struck it rich, boys. Come on, let's head for the Wigwam Saloon and see what's goin' on with the ladies. Maybe I'll sleep in one of those rented rooms tonight. It's time to splurge."

When Ringo and what was left of his gang pushed their way through the batwing doors, most people in the crowded room looked their way. The tension was palpable, and everyone was armed to the teeth. This was the environment in which Ringo felt most comfortable. He was in a room with people like him. Smoke hovered a foot from the ceiling in the stifling heat. The windows were open, but they could hardly feel the breeze. The smell of patchouli oil filled the room, masking the unpleasant odor of unwashed bodies.

When they brought their beers, they were so cold the mugs frosted, and beads of condensation ran down the sides. It was the perfect cure for the parched men.

CHAPTER SEVEN

HALFWAY DOWN SAN FRANCISCO STREET, THEY TURNED down Mesa Street and toward the rumbling noise pouring out of the saloon's doors and windows. It was the largest tavern and hotel in town and was always the center of attraction for both the honest and the dishonest.

When the Crockett brothers walked in, a few people looked their way, but since they didn't look like your typical gunslingers, they returned their gaze to what they were doing. In general, they were hardly noticed, and that was the way they liked it.

A massive bar ran the entire length of the side of the room, and behind it was a continuous mirror with glass shelves filled with various types of alcohol and glasses of every size and shape. Clouds of cigarette and cheroot smoke hung thick in the air. Kerosene lamps were perched all along the walls, keeping the room in a fair but hazy light. The yellow glare glinted off the shiny, polished spittoons scattered across the building's sawdust-covered floors.

It was hard to make out what anyone said. With so many drunken voices, the sound was a constant din. Bartenders and waitresses with long, knee-length aprons scurried to and from the bar and kitchen. Inside, it was stiflingly hot, with temperatures over a hundred degrees, making the frosty cold beers even more desirable. The servers relentlessly tried to keep their customers' glasses full.

They hadn't even finished their first beer before they saw the men who robbed the train with the money destined for the Commercial and Savings Bank in Santa Clara. The four of them were sitting at a table not far from the brothers. Gid swiveled his gaze toward Will with raised eyebrows. They both instantly recognized them. At first sight, it gave them a jolt, making them stop in their tracks.

Will and Gid raised their icy mugs in salute, but the outlaws didn't recognize them. They returned the gesture with frowns and angry faces.

"Whatcha lookin' at, fools?"

"Not much," Gid replied, grinning. They still didn't know who they were talking to, but it was clear that they were getting angry just the same. Ringo and his gang members scowled and spat at everyone in the room.

As soon as the waitress saw Ringo with that look in his eyes, she dropped her tray of beers and screamed and ran for the kitchen as her heart flooded with fear. She hurdled for safety as fast as her legs could carry her. She didn't know who he was, but the Crocketts knew he was a rabble-rousing troublemaker as well as a thief and killer. His hands hung beside his guns.

"Be careful now, or I'll sic my brother on ya." Will grinned. A startled look appeared in Ringo's eyes when he saw that the two strangers weren't afraid. "I'll warn ya now, he's a terror."

Suddenly, the outlaw gang leader realized who he was talking to. They were the men who took shots at them as they fled the scene of the crime back in Santa Clara. All the color drained from Ringo's face as his eyes swelled. He suddenly realized he was caught and there was nothing he could do but stand up and fight, otherwise, he was going to jail. If the men who were shooting at them when they robbed the train, were in El Paso, Ringo figured they could only be there for one reason.

"An honest man this far west is as rare as hen's teeth," Will whispered to his brother. "I reckon it'll be any second now."

Will gritted his teeth, his eyes on his opponent's revolver. The outlaw took another step backward as his fingers caressed his pistol grip.

The gang leader suddenly felt as though he had ice water in his veins and a fire in his brain. "A man can always speak his mind as long as he has his guns and a fast horse," Ringo said, as he looked down his nose at the Crocketts.

A grin crept onto Gid's face, then he smiled wolfishly and balled his hands into fists.

The outlaw forced a smile, showing his tobacco-stained teeth. After squinting for a moment, he spat a long stream of brown juice onto the floor, missing the spittoon entirely. He stood there with shining eyes.

When Will didn't draw, Ringo hesitated, knocked off balance. The younger Crockett followed fast with lightning-quick smashing lefts and rights, snapping his head from side to side. He kept the blows raining down, driving Ringo into the ground. When he was done,

Ringo's features were swollen and rearranged. He was a bloody mess. Will stood watching, ready to pull on the other three if they dared step in.

The spectators broke out of their paralysis, turning and fleeing the scene, while others lingered, laughing, and some even clapped. For the locals, Ringo and his men had been a nuisance since they set foot in the saloon. Gid's knuckles were dark with blood.

Of course, Will understood the euphoria of war, when you tried to kill your enemy, and he tried to kill you. Both he and his brother had fought for the South during the entire conflict. But when the opportunity arose, they would rather capture their man than kill him in cold blood.

As soon as Gid was done with the gang leader, Sheriff James White burst in with his pistols in his hands, his thumbs drawing back the hammers.

"Nobody move! What's goin' on here? Is that you, Will Crockett? Why, it's been a while, ain't it?"

"That it has, Jim. It's good to see you, even if it's not in the best of situations. These four fellas are responsible for robbin' the Santa Clara to El Paso train of the Commercial and Savings Bank's gold and killing both the engineer and Marshal Bill Weston."

Sheriff James White lit a cheroot, inhaling deeply as he observed the situation and tried to determine the right course of action.

"We could give them a trial here. No matter where it's at, the results will be the same. All a lawyer has to do is put the local citizens of Santa Clara in their shoes. Still, it rubs me wrong if they don't have a chance to see their own justice played out. I believe we owe them that. Mind you now, it'll be a risky job if I've gotta go it alone with four dangerous outlaws. I'm sure the bank will cover the costs if I hire you boys. I know you ain't lookin' for a job, but it would help out an old friend. Whatcha say, Will...Gid? We can take the train."

White looked at Will with pleading eyes while he exchanged looks with his brother. Gid nodded without hesitation. Then again, he was the hothead of the two.

James kicked off another round of questions, but Will didn't mind. It had been a long time since they had seen each other. No matter the circumstances, it was fine to meet up with old friends.

"I can't take my deputies. Somebody's gotta stay here and keep things under control in town. Whatcha say, Boys? I know you wanna see that these thugs get their justice. It would be risky business to go it alone, even if we are on the train. There will also be innocent people in the passenger cars. If I'm on my own, they will probably try something, and chances are innocent people will get hurt."

"If you put it like that, I reckon we don't have a choice, do we. My brother is hell-bent on seein' these four get justice just like the others did anyway. Back in Santa Clara, three were hanged a week ago, and one was shot and killed."

"I heard about that. Is it true that the marshal's widow shot a fella by the name of Joey Burns? I heard she did it right in the middle of a hearing with Judge Roy Bean presiding. That must have been something to see."

"Come on, let's get these jailbirds locked up safe and sound. We should probably leave on the first train heading east. El Paso has a reputation for vigilante gangs taking the law into their own hands, and it gets ugly. I don't wanna get my deputies or me shot for trash like this."

"All right, then. We were headed for Arizona, but I reckon it can wait. We started all this, so we might as well finish it, too. I hate to leave such things half done."

"Come on, then," Will growled. "Let's lock these fools up and buy some tickets on the next train eastbound."

CHAPTER EIGHT

IT WAS ALMOST IMPOSSIBLE TO DETERMINE HOW THE FIRE started. Of course, there was no electricity, so there were no fire alarms yet. It happened so quickly that many people on the other side of town read about it the following day in the Times, which was published at four a.m. In the end, it left six large businesses in ruins, as everything attached burned to the ground in the blazing inferno.

The only ones available to fight the blaze were the stovepipe workers and a small team of firefighters who joined forces to challenge the fire. If it weren't for them, the entire business section of El Paso would have been reduced to charred ashes.

The Senate Saloon, Disman Co.'s clothing store, Kerns & Co.'s jewelry store, Kaplan's extensive bazaar, and Dun's restaurant were no more than glowing orange cinders. The Williamson drugstore was also lost to the dangerous fire that threatened the very existence of El Paso, Texas. Where it started was anyone's guess, but most signs pointed to the piles of tinder behind all the buildings. They consisted of empty boxes, broken barrels, staves, straw, sawdust, and pretty much anything of no use.

Suddenly, Sheriff White was called to help with new fire inspections across all the businesses in town. They had been lucky this time, but they had to make sure it didn't happen again. After the fire, the fire marshal was vested with sufficient power to compel the local shops and saloons to follow the new code to the letter. The first order of the day was the elimination of the fire traps behind every business in the city.

Anyone who valued the scorched buildings and those that went unscathed was due to the city's chief engineer, Chas L. Pierce. It was he who orchestrated the fire control, or the entire town might have burned to the ground, and that would have been the end of El Paso.

Mr. Pierce's statement was as follows: "I retired at midnight and was awakened at two thirty a.m. by a pistol shot followed by cries of fire and help. Upon reaching the scene, I found volunteers carrying Kern's goods out of the store. I pushed my way through the quickly growing crowd and to the rear of the building, where I discovered that the fire had started in Williamson's store. The firefighters had already deployed their number one hose, but they had difficulty getting it to work as the flames grew. They got the number two hose working before number one finally was back in commission.

"When the fire reached the shell roofs, the fierce heat melted the windows in the business across the street and blistered and peeled the paint all along the block. This temporarily drove the firefighters out of El Paso Street, but only for a moment. The call went out to all the town seeking assistance as dozens more joined in and battled the blazing fire.

"As it roared, the wind changed several times, making the task all the more difficult. The engineer sent a team with a hose up to the second story and finally began to control the flames. From there, they sprayed a stream of water directly at the hottest part of the fire.

"When it was all said and done, the damage was extensive and believed to be more than $35,000. If that amount really covered the damage, it was never proven. However, the estimate appeared in the newspaper the following day. The adjacent buildings escaped with no more than broken windows from the heat, and all the nearby storefronts needed a new paint job as the old paint had melted in the soaring heat. Everything nearby was badly scorched.

"Afterward, El Paso suffered as its water stocks were depleted to such a level that they became scarce and restricted for some time. Some of the items carried out of the stores were stolen by the many thieves that populated the six-gun capital."

Pierce continued, "I saw a small boy with a score of watches and silver and gold chains around his neck as he disappeared into the smoke-filled alleys and escaped. Sheriff White had his hands full, so Will and Gid Crockett pitched in. They had already agreed to help escort the train robbery prisoners back to Santa Clara, so they were on the payroll and did their best to help contain the fire."

Everyone who fought the blaze was covered in mud and glory by eleven o'clock that morning, including the Crocketts. Water puddles dotted the ground as some of the buildings still glowed orange, reflecting on their surfaces.

"We're gonna have to get a steam fire engine and an alarm bell to safeguard the future," Sheriff White said to the fire department chief.

"Those ladies from the upper rooms sure are frightened," Gid said, as he nodded toward the soiled doves. They saw a woman work her mouth into a scream, but all that came out was a moan. They all had their eyes spread wide and were scared stiff.

An entire family of Mexican children was tucked away in bed at Sheriff White's house during the progress of the fire. They were so afraid that they didn't quite understand what was going on.

One man, who was hit by a blast of water from the firehose, was knocked off the second story of a building as the spray carried him off his feet. He fell onto the veranda and then onto the ground, but miraculously survived unscathed. A few of the businesses had insurance, but the majority had to take the financial loss.

In the end, arson was suspected, as half an hour before the fire broke out, several men were seen in the yard behind the buildings. Will immediately thought it might have been set by someone in cahoots with Ringo Moon and his men. How better to disguise an escape than with such a distraction?

"Gid, run back and check on the prisoners. If one of their connections set this fire, they might try to use this chaos to their advantage and make a break for freedom. I'll stay here with the sheriff until it's time to retrieve the young Mexican children, once we've ensured that everything is safe. Those kids' fathers did a fine job helping us put out the fire. You have yourself one hell of a community, Jim."

Will nodded, picturing the charred ruins. They had been awakened by the smell of smoke. As soon as the older Crockett brother blinked his eyes open, he cupped his hands to his mouth and screamed, "Fire!" In the quiet, it sounded like gunfire. As chaos prevailed, they were all unmindful of time.

Somebody hung a sign over the charred entrance of Dunn's Restaurant. It read: *disfigured but still in the ring.*

Will watched with the palm of his hand shading his eyes from the bright, glowing cinders and glaring sun. His hair and eyebrows were singed, and the smell of burning hair was strong in the air.

As the end of the day came and went, they moved into a fast-falling gloom. The dimness clung close to the ground. The sheriff chewed on the end of a dead cheroot. He watched a struggling-to-breathe store clerk who had a short-haired skull, which was thin and hatless. The sun glared off his brow. Everyone's faces were smudged black with smoke and soot.

———

WHEN GID REACHED THE JAILHOUSE, he felt something was atilt. He didn't see the glowing lamp at the end of the cell block, which was visible from the outside window. He quickly checked the lock to see if it had been forced, but there were no signs of entry. He stood up to the door and peeked through a pane of glass. Everything was black. He thought he saw the reflection of glass on the floor from the bright lights on the street in front of the local jail.

They must have thrown a tin cup at the lamp and busted it, he thought.

He held his breath and listened. That was when he heard the whispering voices, making him believe that Ringo and his men were up to something. Gid had to find out what it was before sounding the alarm because he was all alone. Of course, this didn't put him off the slightest. He relished a good fight even if he was outnumbered. He knew his ferocity and feared no man.

That confidence was partly why he had made it through the war and all the violent years that followed. He pressed himself stiff-backed against the stone wall. Gid jumped when he felt the heat. His heart jerked in spasms, and his chest heaved for breath.

He tiptoed across the porch, dropped into the dirt-covered alley, and moved down the building with his back to the warm stone wall. When he reached the corner, he was surprised to see a man with a team of two mules. He had a rope tied to the bars and was urging the animals of burden forward, hoping to break them out of the wall. The building was made of stone and steel. Gid smiled as they held and didn't budge. Whoever he was, it was a hopeless mission. He chuckled to himself.

"Don't move a muscle, mister," Gid growled. The metallic sound of a cocking hammer was loud and clear. "I've got a bead on ya and I won't hesitate to shoot. Just ask your friends there behind the bars."

The stranger didn't budge as he dropped the reins, his face still hidden in the brim's shadow of his hat. When he looked up, Gid took a deep breath as shock showed on his face, and he shook his head.

"Why, you're no more than a boy. Who sent you here to break those fools out? You best mind who you get yourself involved with, or you might end up behind bars just like them, or maybe even dead." Gid hooked his thumb over his shoulder. "Go on, scat. Get on out of here before I change my mind. I doubt you're much more than ten years old, and here you're about to ruin your life forever. Feel lucky, I was the one who caught ya. Had it been the sheriff, you might have ended up shot or at least in prison for your efforts."

The kid hesitated for an instant, like he was going to say something. His green eyes and red hair stood out against a sunburned face. One moment, he was standing there beside the pair of scraggly mules, and the next, he had vanished. He ran so fast that a wake of dust followed his tattered shoes.

Gid used the extra key the sheriff had given them when they signed up. He carefully slipped it into the lock, turning it slowly so as not to make any noise. He wanted to hear what Ringo and his men were saying. Still, they probably had heard him when he threatened what turned out to be a boy. The last thing he wanted to do was shoot a young lad.

The door squeaked on rusty hinges. Still, silence came from the back cells. When he stepped inside, they saw the glass lamp cover broken on the floor, as he had thought. When he reached the cells, he looked at the back window and saw the rope.

"Well, well, aren't we the busy ones. When the boss is away, the boys will play, won't they?"

"If these bars weren't holding me back, I'd show you what I'm made of," Ringo grumbled.

"You couldn't whoop me in your wildest dreams, fool. You were just about to get a young boy mixed up with you scallywags. Had that happened, then you would have had the chance to get at me because I would have locked myself in that cell with you and torn you apart."

The angry faces that stared back at him out of the dim light made him laugh until he got a stitch. Gid pulled out a Lucifer, flicking it to life with his thumbnail, and lit the wick. He grabbed the broom and swept up the broken glass.

"For your effort, you gentlemen can go without your meals today. Maybe you'll settle down if you don't have any energy."

"You can't do that. That's not civilized," Ringo spat.

"Who said that anybody here was civilized?" Gid replied as he fingered his knife in his belt. "Maybe I ought to teach you another lesson. The first beating I gave you didn't seem to do much good."

When the key turned in the jail cell lock, it made a loud noise. Suddenly, Ringo wasn't so brave anymore. The sound of hard fists slamming into his face was loud in the quiet room as Eric pushed himself into the corner, hoping that he wasn't next.

CHAPTER NINE

When the shriek of the whistle blasted from the top of the black Baldwin locomotive, Sheriff James White, Will, and Gid herded their horses aboard the livestock car and climbed up the metal steps to the second-class passenger carriage. They pushed the four outlaws with guns at their backs. They knew not to trust them after all they had done. Especially since Gid had caught them trying to break out of jail.

Now they knew that the gang had friends, or maybe it was just other outlaws looking to make some money. They were sure Ringo would be willing to pay a pretty price for someone to come and break him out, especially since he was headed to hang along with his friends. When there were no more options, outlaws became desperate. What they didn't know was how their criminal buddies planned to help free the gang. They didn't even know how many there were or if they really existed, but the safest assumption was that they were a clear and present danger.

Once aboard, they cleared the car of its occupants.

They shackled the men's hands and feet to the metal railing and seat supports along the inside of the passenger carriage. That way, their hands and feet were bound so tightly they could hardly move. If they had to shoot, they wouldn't hit anyone but the gang members.

The sheriff had thought ahead and brought a burlap sack full of food. Sausage, bread, cheese, dried fruit, and jerky would be enough to keep them going since there was no restaurant or bar in the second-class car. It would take thirty days to get to their destination if they didn't encounter trouble, but trouble was Ringo's middle name.

Gid ignored the prisoners' stares and dug in like he hadn't eaten in a week. "Remember what I said about feeding you. You four don't deserve a meal after the way you've been actin'."

"Why, all we had so far is bread and water," Ringo huffed.

"I'm thirsty," Wayne said. "You haven't given us any water for hours."

"How's that life of an outlaw workin' out for ya? And why should I treat you boys kindly?" Gid asked. "You men have been a disappointment from the start. Why did you shoot the poor engineer on the train? He didn't even have a gun in his hand. Senseless killing is something that I won't tolerate."

"Ringo said it was to make a point," Eric replied.

"Shut up, fool. Every time you open your mouth, you make things worse. I should have left you back where you were knocked off your horse by that low-hanging limb. Or even better, shoot ya and put you out of your stupid misery. I don't know why I gave you a job doin' our dirty work. You're not even good at simple tasks."

"Is that where you buried the money, Eric?" Will asked with kind eyes. "I know you're not like the others. You're just a little slow, is all, and were led astray by these wickey men. Nobody can help how we're born, but we can all choose how we live."

"Don't you say another word, you bastard," Ringo spat. "Remember whose side you're on, moron. If you open your mouth again, I'm gonna cut you from ear to ear."

"Why are you always calling me names? I never talk to any of you boys like that. Every day you go and pick on me, and I've never threatened you once. What did I do to make you all so mean to me? I'm tired of being a whipping boy."

"Don't expect them to be honest or kind to you, Eric. We understand how a man like you could get mixed up with people like this. Gid, unlock his bracelets and let him sit with us over here. Maybe you're feeling a little hungry. Go ahead and help yourself to whatever you want. How about a glass of warm beer to cool you down?"

Eric looked at his partners in crime, and what he saw just made him angrier. They continued to give him dirty looks. The men who arrested them treated him better than his supposed friends. He suddenly remembered how they laughed at him when the limb knocked him off his horse. He thought they would split a gut, and nobody offered to help him up. He let the feeling stick in his craw.

"Yeah, I'm thirsty and hungry, too." Eric shot a dirty look at Ringo Moon. "You're right, I'm not like them.

The only reason I joined is that nobody else would give me work since I'm a little slow, and Jessy is my second cousin. He was the one who recruited me to be their whipping boy."

He got up, moved across the aisle, and took a seat across from Will and the sheriff and beside the massive Gid. At first, he hesitated, but then Will's little brother smiled. When it reached his eyes, it set the poor man at ease. They all could see he was hired to be the fool of the outlaw gang and was supposed to tend to all their needs and do all the chores. They apparently all picked on him, too.

Gid had been hard on them with their meals since he caught them trying to escape, and now they were suspected of being involved in the town fire, too.

The sheriff reached into his sack and pulled out a long, juicy piece of dried meat. He cut off a large chunk of cheese and sliced a dozen pieces of spicy sausage as thick as his arm, then cut thin slices of Mexican cured ham and placed them all on the wooden bench beside Eric. He even had a pint flask full of warm beer.

Ringo, Wayne, and Jessy's mouths watered at the sight of the delicious food. They were all hungry, and their mouths were as dry as the desert, and their tongues stuck to the roofs of their mouths. They couldn't take their eyes off the meal their traitor gang member was devouring without even glancing their way.

"Here you go, buddy," the sheriff said as he brought him several fresh peaches for dessert. "Enjoy your meal."

"So, tell me now, where was that tree you bumped your noggin' on?" Will asked as he raised an eyebrow, then he looked at the other three prisoners out of the corner of his eye.

"It's not far from the railroad tracks, close to town. I'd say an hour's ride out of El Paso by train. Maybe an hour and ten minutes. I don't know much about trains. I've only ridden on a few."

"About an hour and a bit by train, is it? Whatcha say, Sheriff?"

"That sounds about right. How far from there did you hide the gold?"

The question came up so casually, and suddenly Eric answered before he thought. "Why, it's right beside the tree on the other side of the limb that whacked me. I dug the hole myself. The others don't like to use picks and shovels. They make me do all the work."

"Could you point it out when we get there? I know you don't want to go against your buddies, but believe me, they'd throw you under the wagon as soon as they thought you were no good to them anymore. As it is, it sounds like they use you for the hard labor while they lie about. It seems that they don't treat you much better than a slave."

"Yeah, that and collect and cut the firewood, brush down the horses, and everything they don't like doing, which is pretty much nothing but drinking night and day. I like beer, but whiskey gives me gas."

"Well, what if the sheriff and me talked to the judge in your favor and got you a light sentence for cooperating with us?"

"Coo-what?"

"For helping us, son. Help us recover the hard-earned savings of all those people in Santa Clara. Maybe a good word will keep you from a lynching party, too." The sheriff gave him a wink and a smile, and Eric caved. It was almost like he had been waiting for someone to offer him the chance.

He wasn't as bad as the others. He was just too dumb to know better than getting mixed up with outlaws like the other three, who were actual killers.

"Whatcha say, buddy?" Gid asked as he nudged him with his elbow. "How about helpin' us out?"

Eric glanced at Ringo, Wayne, and Jessy, and all he saw was hate. Sure, he knew he was simple. People had been telling him that all his life. Now, he felt he had the opportunity to turn over a new leaf and rid himself of the men who constantly badgered him. At this point, he would prefer to be in jail than continue to tolerate their abusive nature. He looked back at Will and blinked.

"All right, then. I'll tell you when to stop. However, it would be better if we could watch from where the conductor is, so I don't miss the spot as we roll by. Maybe we can ask him to slow the train down a bit. I don't think I'd miss it then. I don't want to let you down, Mr. Crockett."

"I think the sheriff can arrange that. Whatcha say, James?"

Sheriff White sat for a moment, chewing on what Will said, then he slapped the table and laughed. Across the aisle sat the four outlaws staring at the sack of food.

"You no-good, stupid bastard. I'll kill you if it's the last thing that I ever do," Ringo snarled as he pulled on his chains, struggling to get his hands on Eric, the gang's fool.

"Why don't you two take Eric forward to the engineer while I explain things to Ringo again. It sounds like he didn't understand what I told him the first time. I hate it when I have to repeat myself."

The three got up and headed to the double doors between the cars as the train swayed on the tracks. When they opened the door, the noise came rushing in. As soon as it closed, Gid hit Ringo with a haymaker that nearly broke his jaw. It cracked like he was opening a coconut as it swiveled loosely from his face. He tried to talk, but his jaw jiggled around as his tongue flapped in the air. Moon grabbed it with his hands and pushed it back into place as tears of pain streamed down his face.

"Here, take my banana and tie your jaw in place," Gid said, emotionless. "You broke pretty easily. I thought you were gonna be tougher than that. Most men your size don't go down until I hit them two or three times. I guess you're one of those sissified outlaws. I noticed those soft hands of yours. Maybe they won't be so pretty if I stomped on 'em some."

———

AS THEY SLOWLY MADE THEIR way forward, they passed through all four passenger cars. The last one was first-class, and the occupants gave them dirty looks. When they arrived at the coal car, they had to walk up the ramp on the sides, clinging to the railing. The look of surprise filled the conductor's face when he looked back and saw the sheriff's badge.

"How're ya doin', Henry? I didn't know you were running today's train."

"Yeah, you heard about Robert. He was killed in the train robbery a couple of weeks back. They shot him in the heart for no reason at all. Why, he was a gentle giant, he was, and never hurt a fly. I'm taking his place until the Southern Pacific Railroad sends us another engineer. Then I'll be back in town at my desk in El Paso. I don't like to travel across the country anymore like I used to. I reckon that now I've gotten accustomed to my missus. What are you doing up here anyway? Don't you know you could fall off and break your necks or worse?"

"My everyday life is more dangerous than that. It's a lot easier than gettin' shot at. Can you do us a favor and stop the train for a minute when this fella says to? Maybe even slow down a little first? This here is Eric Smith. He's gonna help us recover the stolen money from the same robbery you're talkin' about."

"Any way I can help, I'm willin'. You know that, James. Nice to meet ya, Mr. Smith. My name's Henry Bates. You just give me the word and hold on. When I set the brakes, this baby is like a bucking bronco, but she'll stop on a dime."

On the way out of El Paso, they crossed a herd of longhorns, which were distant descendants of cattle abandoned by the Spanish nearly 180 years earlier. The string of animals seemed to go on forever. Around the lazily walking cattle rode men, some of whom were still in their teens and others old, worn, and gray. The animals walked with their heads down as the cowboys twirled ropes over their horns and whistled.

The fifty-four-inch wheels sang as they raced down the shiny tracks with a clickity clack. Eric was ecstatic as he held on with his white-knuckled fists for dear life. A smile creased his face from ear to ear. He had always dreamed of being something important, like an engi-neer, where he could do his job alone. He eyed the fireman, but he smiled between shovels of coal, setting Eric at ease.

"There it is, Mr. Crocket," Sheriff White said.

"See that big tree with lots of leaves over there? Are we too late to stop, Mr. Robert?" Eric asked.

"Not for me. Hold on to your hats, boys."

When the engineer moved several levers, clouds of steam rose on the sides of the black locomotive, and the brakes suddenly locked as sparks clouded the tracks beside them. From the cars in the back, they heard the shouts from disgruntled passengers, but Henry only laughed. He was having the time of his life during his few days out of retirement, and he knew that nobody was going to fire him. This could be his last days at the controls, and he wanted them to last.

After what seemed like minutes but was only seconds, the massive iron engine stopped as still as a stone as it panted slower and slower until it ran at an idle. Black puffs of smoke and soot continued to spout out of the teapot's smokestack.

"Jump to it, boys. We'll have the passengers up here before we know it if we don't get a move-on. They weren't expecting an unscheduled stop."

"Don't worry about the passengers, Robert. They won't mess with a sheriff on official business. The railroad company certainly won't complain, since it was their train that was robbed. If they ask, just tell 'em the sheriff was takin' care of business and they'll stick their noses somewhere else."

THEY FOUND a narrow draw dense with oaks and cedars strung out up and down the hills. Trees bent over the draw, creating a tangled arch.

When they arrived at the spot where he thought the tree was, it appeared Eric was confused. "They all look the same to me now. Lookee over there. I think it's that one."

They all rushed to where he pointed, but then Eric realized it wasn't the same tree. He looked up as he rubbed the place on his head where he had the bump. He looked at another, but it wasn't that one either.

Will studied the ground and saw no signs until they moved farther away from the tracks and the trail. When he saw prints from several horses, he called Eric over. That was when he saw the print of the broken boot heel. Then he knew this was the place.

"It ain't rained since you boys were here, so I reckon these old tracks could be yours." Will dropped to one knee and felt the outline of the hoofprints. Then he saw what looked like a butt print. When he looked up, there was a tree limb above him. "Is that where you fell after hitting that thick branch up there?"

A large limb hung about eight feet over their heads. It seemed to be the right height if he was riding a big horse.

Eric scratched his head as he looked to where Will indicated and bobbed his head up and down. "That's it for sure. I fell right there. Look on the other side of the tree trunk and under that brush, and you should see where I dug the hole."

"Are you sure?" Sheriff White asked.

"There's one way to find out," Gid said as he grabbed

the shovel the fireman used to shovel coal into the belly of the panting train.

Using it to scrape away the surface rubbish, he soon saw that beneath the now-dried-out branches and leaves, the earth had been turned. In less than five minutes, he uncovered the burlap sacks that had *US Mail* written on the sides in black letters.

He let breath pass his lips in a long sigh. "Well, I'll be damned. There it is." Gid reached over and pulled out the sacks full of gold. "Is all the gold here?"

"Nope, Ringo kept some out for the party in town, but I'd say that most of it's there. There're thousands of dollars in that sack. At least that's what Ringo said. It was supposed to be split seven ways, and I'd get my paycheck like always. But when they didn't hear anything about Joey and the others, Ringo seemed happy enough to ride off without going to look for them and keep it all for the three of them. Mind you, I would have gotten paid too, so I understand I ain't an innocent man."

"How much were they gonna give you?"

"I reckon the same two hundred I get every six months."

"Did you know that there was over ten thousand dollars in those mail pouches?" Will asked. "And they pay you four hundred dollars a year?"

"No, Mr. Crockett. They give me two hundred dollars every six months. That's more than I spend anyway. Mostly it's money for bullets to hunt for them to eat when we're on the trail. That and nice duds. Ringo said I can't ride with them if I look like white trash."

The sun was almost overhead, crowding the sky

with its bright white light. Eric pushed his hat back from his forehead, easing the hot grip of the headband.

Sheriff White's graying mustache hid his mouth, but you could see the iron-willed anger in the tight line of his jaw.

"So, this is the gold you boys stole?" Sheriff White asked.

Eric waited until the heat of embarrassment drained from his face. "Uh-huh," Eric replied. "Yes, sir, I reckon it is."

Will Crockett was in his forties, and his eyes were beginning to well up with anger, but the fire in them belonged to a younger man. They were white, caged in ridged, red lines. He furrowed his brow, making wrinkles of concern appear on his forehead.

Eric's fear drained away like the ground after a flash storm when Will smiled and said, "Without you, Eric, we'd never have recovered the stolen loot. That puts you on our side, partner. I think we might even be able to get you off since most of the gold coins are still here."

THEY SQUINTED through the afternoon glare and the end of the train as they reboarded. Eric's face glistened with oily preparation. It was obvious he was nervous as he looked at the sheriff and back at Will. He paused to catch his breath. He wiped his face with a grimy hand. He was sweating bullets for what he had done, but if the truth be told, he felt better inside, and his conscience had lightened considerably.

A thick stream of black curled skyward in a thick, bold line as the massive engine spewed soot. The soft blue of a cloudless sky was the only redeeming factor in the ragged, wild-looking valley until the train left a string of smoke, blemishing the land.

To the Comanche and Apache Indians, the land was already scarred by the shiny tracks that crisscrossed the countryside—that, and a telegraph post that strung wire across the country to facilitate communication.

As the fireman frantically shoveled coal into the iron beast, the boiler value rose constantly. Some people had disembarked without permission. They did so mostly to complain, and the vast majority came from the first-class carriage.

The sheriff studied the scene stoically beneath impassive eyes. The cooperating outlaw stared wide-eyed and swallowed hard.

"Don't worry, Eric. Sure, you might do some jail time, but it won't be as much as Ringo, Wayne, and Jessy, and you sure as hell won't hang." The sheriff tried to smile, but it only made White look more menacing.

After thanking the engineer, they climbed aboard the passenger car where Ringo and his boys were not only shackled, but the sheriff had tied their feet and hands together behind their backs so there was no chance of escape. Nobody was allowed into their passenger car.

CHAPTER TEN

"YOU DON'T HAVE TO SIT WITH THOSE FOOLS ANYMORE, Eric. You're workin' for the law now. You can stay on this side of the car with us and not have to hang around with your old, smelly friends." Sheriff White smiled. "They're in a lot of trouble. You had best stay away from them. I'm afraid they're headed for the gallows. The circuit judge isn't a forgiving man."

The other three prisoners lay on the floor trussed up like hogs. They had rags stuffed in their mouths with bandanas tied around their heads so they couldn't spit them out. Gid was an expert knot maker and knew how to ensure those who struggled would be even more uncomfortable. The more they fought their bindings, the tighter they got. He used freshly cut, wet pigging string that shrank when it dried. Had they cooperated, things would have been different, but if they wanted to do it the hard way, that was fine with the Crocketts.

"See? We shut 'em up and all. They won't be pickin' on you again as long as I'm here. At least they won't if they know what's good for 'em." Gid gave the gang members an evil look. With one glance, they saw he meant to keep his promise.

Even while the Crocketts were talking, Ringo continued to struggle with his bindings. He tried to yell muffled insults, but they were unintelligible with a sock in his mouth. Still, the daggers he shot the lawmen with his eyes were full of defiance and hate, especially their old gang member, Eric, though he had always secretly hated him. He only let him ride with them because he was a family member of one of the gang members. If looks could kill, he'd be dead.

In 1883, the Galveston, Harrisburg & San Antonio Railway (GH&SA), part of the Southern Pacific, completed its line from San Antonio to El Paso. This marked the completion of Southern Pacific's Sunset Route across Texas, connecting San Antonio with points west, with the hope that the future of the border city in West Texas would become the railroad hub for the entire southern route.

The tracks ran on narrow-gauge tracks along the Rio Grande, which flowed two to three hundred feet below. After this stretch, they turned toward the mountains farther from the river. The segment along the border costs the railroad $100,000 a mile to build. The train passed through two large tunnels, and it crossed the Pecos on a low-level bridge near the river's junction.

"Now that we have dangerous prisoners on board, I reckon maybe I should deputize you and Gid, Will. In case we've gotta shoot one of these thieves and murderers, it'll eliminate lots of red tape and make it all legal. If it comes to it, the other passengers will listen to you both better if they see tin stars on your chests. Have you worked as a lawman before? I always carry a couple of tin stars in my saddlebags for just such occasions. "

"Yep, we've worked as lawmen more than once, so we know the drill. Do you think these fellas are gonna give us any more trouble, Eric? Are you all that's left of Ringo's outlaw gang? I'm sure everyone in El Paso knows what happened. The population is only a few thousand."

"Yes, sir." Eric jumped at the chance to give his two cents. He seemed eager to bury his bullies. "Ringo has lots of friends, and they're all outlaws like them. Some are famous, too. A few of 'em are even meaner than him. There's Black Bart, Dakota Dick, and Bella Star. Why, he even knows what's left of the old Younger and James gang? Some of 'em stuck together after Jessy was killed in 1875. Ringo Moon's been around for some time. Everybody likes a successful outlaw—at least in West Texas. I always thought there wasn't a marshal or sheriff in the state who could take him. It turns out it wasn't so hard after all. At least not with you men."

The prairie lay around them like a big plate wavering in the heat. They roared by a massive field of sunflowers, six feet tall, as their yellow faces dished toward the sun.

RINGO'S FRIEND turned his head and pinched his nose with thumb and finger, blowing twin strings of snot onto the dirt. He wiped his hand on his thin cotton shirt. If the truth were known, they weren't really friends, although they did rob a couple of banks together. Most outlaws had few friends and generally distrusted everyone. Only brothers like the Youngers and James had the luxury of being loyal and honest with each other.

He cocked his head when he heard the first signs of churning wheels on steel tracks—then came the blast of a locomotive's whistle. Behind the sound, the wind moaned like a nightmare's beast as the unbearable humidity weighed heavy. The horizon was just turning red, and he knew that in seconds, everything would be lit up. Now was the time to act. He chuckled to himself, imagining seeing Ringo's face when he saved him. He was gonna owe him big.

Days of riding where no white souls venture save one troublemaker—yours truly.

The thought made Dakota Dick smile and even laugh. He wondered if the train would stop in time, or if he would get to watch the locomotive spill into the hole in the bridge and two hundred feet down. He and his horse sat perched on the topmost rim of a hill like misflown birds. He stared through his spyglass, looking for black puffs of smoke in the sky. He was just a few steps away from where the bridge met the dirt, right where he had planned to place the explosives. He knew he had plenty of time to execute his plan. He was going to do the unexpected and derail the train.

"It'll be any time now. The day the law outsmarts me will be the day monkeys fly out of my ass," Dick snickered to himself. "Who would have thought to blow up the bridge? It'll stop the railway for weeks. Ringo's gonna owe me for this, and I'm gonna name my price. Maybe he'll let me lead the gang with him. I'm already more famous than him, anyway. Maybe I'll even take it over in the end. He ain't so tough. I might have more opportunities here than I thought."

Dick's knee touched his long gun in its sheath. He drew it in his mind, taking aim. If he ran into trouble, he was ready. He pulled his horse to a stop just short of the tracks. At first, he saw a tiny black dot in the distance. Then it drew closer and grew into a massive engine, blowing smoke and soot, staining the sky. Soon, he could hear it roaring toward him. Suddenly, he heard the brakes lock as the big steel wheels screamed, making a shower of sparks.

Dakota was shocked when he saw someone on top of the train. It was something he hadn't expected or hadn't prepared for. He was sure that nobody had seen him leave town. He had taken care to ensure he wasn't followed. He used his binoculars to have a closer look. At first, all he saw was a black, blurry image until he focused on the massive locomotive. He saw a man on the roof of the first carriage holding a long gun, much like his, and it was pointed at him. Dick ducked, then he heard the bullet crack.

Whoa, now. I barely dodged it! Move, man, move!

He reeled from the narrow escape, but then the realization hit him like a ton of bricks, and his heart sank. The shock of the bullet numbed the pain. He hadn't dodged the bullet after all. It was a solid and deadly hit. Whoever it was knew how to use a rifle. Dick had thought he was too far away.

On impact, he grunted a tooth-clenching curse. Dick suddenly realized he wasn't on his horse anymore. He was lying spread-eagled on the ground, looking up at the sky. He wondered how the vultures got up there so quickly. His world turned slowly on its axis, making the clouds seem to race in circles across the heavens. He heaved with all his might, trying to gobble air, but he couldn't. He felt his heart struggle and skipped a beat as his eyes throbbed. They felt too big for his head. A dizziness came over him, and right then, he knew he was going to die.

———————

"WE'LL SOON BE at the bridge. Maybe we might wanna keep an eye on things. This is where we're most vulnerable," Sheriff White said.

Will slapped at the flies with his hat as he stared toward the horizon out the window. Hooking his thumb over his shoulder, he asked, "Well, whaddaya say, Sheriff? Do I take him, or do you wanna make the shot?"

"Be my guest. From what I hear, you may well outshoot me with a long gun anyway. That's still a hell of a distance. I'm not sure if I could hit anything from that far away or not. Then again, we don't really know if anyone is there. Maybe you think that Ringo and his friends are smarter than they are. Most outlaws don't give a damned about each other."

"Well, regardless, let's not just stand here like mannequins. If someone is waiting at the start of the bridge, we'd better be ready. I think I might just be able to make that shot if they are, so let's get moving. Gid can watch over Eric and this bunch. I think we can trust him now. The rest of the prisoners won't be giving us any trouble hog-tied, anyway."

Will climbed the swaying ladder outside and then staggered along the top of the train with his rifle strapped across his back. As the first sign of red showed on the skyline, he knew that in a few minutes their surroundings would be bathed in light. In moments, the dawn-broached sky turned a hellish red.

Will framed the idea to himself as he stared blindly at the blur of country from on top of the first-class passenger car. It was a Baldwin engine, and the heaviest locomotive ever produced in Pennsylvania.

Will felt the Texan lawman beside him. "Sheriff, get yourself on up front and tell the engineer to stop the train right where the bridge starts. Tell him somebody is gonna blow it all to hell. That should get his attention. I know train people, and they like to be on time."

"You want me to lie to him?"

"I want you to make sure he does what you ask. If it means scarin' him, then so be it. With a bunch like this, we can't be too careful. Remember, these boys are headed to hang and don't have anything to lose."

Will pulled his binoculars from their case and traced the distance. When he focused on what he was looking for, he saw lank, greasy hair fall around large butterfly ears under a hat with a big floppy brim. In one of his hands, the outlaw held his reins, and in the other, several sticks of dynamite bound together. Will instantly saw what he planned to do. He had a one-in-a-million shot from this distance, but he knew he'd done it before, and he was gonna do his best to do it again. If he let him blow the bridge, things were going to get complicated for everybody.

Black shadows of the horse and rider were painted on the ground. The bridge stretched over the river before him as it stood up to the tacks. A person could lie there and hide, never to be discovered by anything but the sun. But this outlaw wasn't even hiding. He was sitting on his horse on the top of a hill near the bridge.

"We've got a confident one here. I reckon he's made his last mistake."

———

SWIRLS OF GLOWING red sparks spewed from the smokestack, drifting to the stars. Smoke as dark as night streamed along the top of the passenger and cattle cars. The yellow lens of a lantern threw a beam of light ahead of the train. From the fire bin, the orange light filled the conductor's room as the boiler temperature rose to one hundred sixty PSI, leaving a good head of steam.

The fireman held a tin cup under a barrel and cleared his throat with the tepid water. Behind the engine and tender box came the baggage cars, and after them the first-class passenger car. Trailing further behind came the second-class passenger and livestock cars. Three men in the mail car were busy sorting out letters and packages to be delivered at the next stop. This train stopped at every station on the route.

The flagman sat all alone in the caboose, bathed in soft light, as he read a thick book while occasionally checking the train's movement from the cupola, looking for dragging equipment and hot boxes. A yellow kerosene lantern hung from the gimbals on the car's walls. The brakeman checked his watch. It said it was past midnight.

"What the hell?" Henry asked.

"It looks like somebody's on the bridge and he's got a burning rag in his hand. Is that dynamite in the other?"

In a panic, the engineer pulled the brake lever as the driver's wheels and all those in the following cars activated the air brake system, and the entire train began to slide down the tracks, spraying the night with sparks from the iron grinding on the shiny steel. Smoke gushed and spewed steam from the drive cylinders.

Thrusting piston rods spilled hot cinders from the firebox, leaving a glowing path between the tracks. The train screamed as all the wheels suddenly locked. The boiler water bubbled, and the bearings popped and snapped.

———

WILL SPOTTED the shooter and brought his Sharps rifle to bear. A long tube scope sat over the thirty-four-inch barrel. The fifteen-pound gun felt weighty in his hands. Suddenly, the nerves in Will's body went dead, and he froze like he had been injected with ice. He took the last deep breath, and when he exhaled, he gently squeezed the trigger. He felt the recoil against his shoulder. He sucked in a bolstering breath of air. He instantly saw it was a good shot.

———

A BANG RANG out from a heavy-caliber rifle as he watched through the telescope. The outlaw's horse bared its teeth and swung its head from side to side with its ears flattened against its skull. Spooked by the loud nose, little birds chattered with the wind as vultures rose from the ground with bony wings: whoop, whoop, whooping like children's puppets on a string. Field mice, rats, and squirrels fled for the underbrush.

The shot sounded dead, flat, and empty. Smoke

rolled out of the long barrel. Will looked beside him and saw that Gid had taken a position near him on the top of the first-class passenger car just after the coal wagon.

"Who's watching Eric?"

"Sheriff White's with him. The engineer wasn't a problem. He's already seen enough. That was one hell of a shot, brother."

They scrambled down the ladder, dropping to the ground, and ran to the downed man. Where he fell turned dark with blood. Gid pushed the dying man over with the toe of his boot. His sightless face turned up with dirt stuck to his cheeks. A bullet hole punctured his sternum. The mortally wounded man wheezed through red-stained teeth. His chest sank with a pneumatic sigh, and he died.

Three vultures, with yellow beaks, hobbled out, waiting for their turn to pick at the remains. Gid clapped his hands loudly, scaring them away, but they waited, perched on the crossmembers of the bridge. They wouldn't have to wait long for their next meal.

"Attaway!" Gid yelled as he slapped his knee. "Sometimes, the lion's gotta show the jackals who he is." He spat a stream of brown juice across the dead man's head. "I wonder who he was."

"I would have preferred to have a word with him before he died," Will said with tired eyes. "Now he's not gonna be talkin' to anybody. I wonder how many more friends Ringo has out there watching us. Where you find one, there's usually more. Maybe he has a stash of money put away, and this fella was looking for a big payday. Why else would he try to help trash like him? A man like this would only take such a chance for money."

When they returned to the train, it immediately began to puff and chug, slowly picking up steam as it lurched forward. They safely crossed the bridge as they kept an eye out the window. Now they knew they had to be careful because Ringo's friends could telegraph ahead and have somebody else waiting for them somewhere down the tracks. They still had over four hundred miles to go.

From the passenger car window, they watched a column of Indians wind down the trail a mile below them. They could see how they lazily marched on in dreary unison, never missing a beat. They didn't even glance up at the smoke-spouting steel beast but continued on their weary way. Nobody could have imagined where they were going. As long as they didn't bother them, they didn't care. The sun continued to spray orange rays of light.

Will looked relieved as he let out a breath. He felt like he'd been holding it for hours. His look was lit with elation—and vindication. He knew he had done an excellent job and that few men could make that shot. Gid curled an amused smile.

Before hooking his wire-rimmed spectacles around his ears, James cleaned them with the tail of his shirt. Will smiled. The sheriff looked meek and humble with four eyes. It betrayed the true nature of a dangerous man.

Eric was afraid to open his mouth because his voice would crack and give him away. He was so scared that he was having a hard time hiding it. Still, all three lawkeepers noticed it despite his efforts. It made him avert his eyes as he looked at the toes of his boots.

"Here, put a dash of this in your coffee, Eric," Gid said as he uncorked the whiskey jug and poured him a dose. "It'll help settle your nerves. You look a little distraught."

When Eric took a sip, he spilled the liquor nervously and then wiped his chin with the heel of his hand. "Thank ya kindly. I don't really drink often. Ringo said givin' me whiskey was a waste of money because my mind's already drunk."

"That just goes to show ya what kind of friend he was. With amigos like that, you don't need enemies." Gid clapped him on the back.

The sheriff tried the whiskey but made a sour face. "Maybe I'm spoiled, but this corn liquor tastes like horse piss. It would choke a mule. How about we mosey down to the first-class passenger car? They have a fully stocked bar and restaurant for the rich folk."

"One of us has got to stay here and watch the prisoners now that we know we're gonna have men trying to break them out before we reach Santa Clara."

"You two go ahead without me, Will. I don't mind the corn liquor so much, and there's plenty of food left in the burlap sack. I fancy some more of that Mexican sausage anyway. While I'm at it, I'll keep an eye on Mr. Ringo here. He's close to getting the whippin' of a lifetime."

"Don't you worry, we'll bring back a bottle of labeled whiskey. Four hundred miles is still more than a day's ride. We'll be right back, won't we, Will?"

As THEY PASSED through the second-class passenger cars, they saw thin-lipped, sun-darkened men in range cloths and worn leather chaps of all ages. Some were from the south of the border and others from north of the Rio Grande. They all carried the distinct smell of cattle.

The elder Crockett followed the sheriff's broad back inside. The first-class passenger car bar seemed dark after the bright sunlight. The shades were half-closed, and ceiling fans whirled above them, cooling the environment.

When they entered the compartment, the passengers were completely indifferent. Most wore fine clothing and looked down their noses at the three men with badges but didn't say a word. That was when Will noticed two men with dark skin and expensive guns in rigs hanging low on their hips. These men weren't cowboys, and they didn't fit in with the first-class passengers.

Sheriff White rested his elbows on the fancy passenger car bar and ordered, "A fresh bottle of whiskey and two glasses."

"Do you have your first-class tickets? If not, I'm afraid, you'll have to return to second class."

When James showed his badge, the bartender frowned but served him anyway. He didn't look like a man to cross, and the shiny tin star made it official.

Out the windows, they saw several teepees standing in the distance, surrounded by numerous Indian ponies. Their black silhouetted figures wandered around their camp.

Will pulled his binoculars from his saddlebag and put the glasses to his eyes, edging it along the distance.

"Whatcha see down there?" James asked.

"The same thing as you, but only bigger."

"These were the vast areas that were populated by savage Aboriginal tribes. This used to be their land, and some of them still think it is. Mind you now, I believe they have every right, but you go and try to tell that to a politician."

"You don't think they would try to stop a train, do you?"

"You just never know what's going on in a Comanche's mind," the sheriff grinned, as he swallowed his second drink in one go. "I gave up trying to second-guess them years ago."

Sheriff White's eyes shone like dark chips of polished obsidian. As he stared at his new friend, he carefully assessed him. So far, he and his brother had surprised him at every turn.

Will was the older of the two brothers and stood five feet ten inches tall with sandy, graying hair and the blue eyes of a man with more experience than his age. He was wiry and tough: his great strengths were his wits, quickness, and cunning.

His brother, Gid, was six feet three, with broad shoulders and light brown hair. It was apparent they were brothers because they had the same easily recognizable eyes and measured life with the same scrutiny. This was where the similarities stopped. The younger brother was powerful, and his strength often drove his first solution to a problem, and he was also quick to anger. Only his darker skin and size set them apart, but both were ruggedly handsome.

CHAPTER ELEVEN

GID WAS DOZING OFF AND ON IN THE SECOND-CLASS passenger car. He kept one eye open to check on Ringo, Wayne, and Jessy. Eric was curled up on the seat, sound asleep despite the train rocking back and forth. Or maybe it was *because* of it, like a baby rocking in a mother's arms. The constant clickety-clack was hypnotic, drawing him into a deep and peaceful slumber. He smiled as he dreamed of home many years ago. He grasped his girlfriend's hand as they skipped down the road, fingers linked together. He looked over and saw a happy smile on her face.

She said something to him, and he tried to answer, but no words came out. He saw her mouth move again, but he heard no sound. Suddenly, they were being chased by a massive band of Comanche warriors, and they weren't back in Hazard, Kentucky anymore. They were on the Texan plains, but how did Sara get there? He watched them run from above like a third eye. From above, like an observer, Eric saw himself looking back with wide, frightened eyes.

In his sleep, he heard people talking somewhere in the background. It began to draw him away from his dream. He wanted to get away from the hostile warriors but was reluctant to let go of Sara's hand. His eyes shifted nervously under his eyelids as his legs and feet moved as he ran. His breath came quick and short.

He suddenly felt someone shaking his shoulder. "Wake up, Eric. You sound like a wounded pup. Open your eyes there, buddy. You're having a nightmare." Gid looked at him with deep concern. The converted outlaw still wasn't sure where he was.

Eric wasn't so worried about the outlaw friends of Ringo, but he was nervous about the Indians. As the train continued across the state eastbound, he saw abandoned cookfires and carcasses from animals Comanche hunted and ate in bloody steaks. He had never had a run-in with the Native Americans and didn't fancy having his first encounter.

As long as I stay on the train, I'll be all right, Eric thought.

He repeated to himself over and over. He shoved his hand into his britches pocket and felt his lucky rabbit's foot. It instantly gave him some comfort. It had gotten him this far, and he was still alive and had all his limbs.

Aboriginal people hunted the Great Western Plains for thousands of years. The original inhabitants witnessed the recession of the glaciers when the land began to warm. They accelerated the demise of the saber-toothed tiger, the great mastodons, and the hippo. They hunted the same land when it was densely forested, and now it is a sea of grass.

Through all these changes, these people continued to live as nomadic hunters on the vast stretches of land, despite the army successfully forcing them from their homes that had been in place for thousands of years. At least, not until then. The Indian wars raged on from 1775 to 1883, but it looked like their days were numbered. They had lost the Hundred-Year War. The only resistance that remained was limited to young men seeking praise or old men seeking death.

Nineteenth-century Indians were colorful, mystical, and warlike. The antiquity of their rituals and the intricate organization of their many tribes were unknown to most. They were a hunting society built around the horse, even though the four-legged animals didn't exist until the Spanish introduced them three hundred years earlier.

———

A LONG, oblong mahogany table stretched across the first-class dining car. It was so highly polished that the room reflected off the table like a mirror. At the end of the bar stood a squat, fat man who made the drinks. He wore a thigh-length apron, along with a matching shirt and pants that were as white as snow, without a single stain. His black shoes were as shiny as the table.

Two men stood at the other end across the bar top with their faces in the shadows of their hats' brims. They were dressed in expensive dark clothes and carried heavy armor. Braces of pistols hung from both their hips, and knife handles protruded from the tops of their fancy, stitched boots. It was clear that these weren't cattlemen, although they were mingling with the rich. Both Will and the sheriff knew they could only be there for one reason, and that was to break Ringo Moon out and flee.

"Maybe we should have taken the law into our own hands and strung up the lot. It's proving to be a bother taking them back alive."

"But that's our job, ain't it, Sheriff?" Will asked. "Otherwise, we would be the ones breakin' the law, and I don't abide by that. We have to set an example to honest folk."

"I'm just saying it's a hassle draggin' them halfway across the state only to watch them hang a few days after. And here we have to risk our lives over it all."

"Nobody made you become a sheriff, no more than you put a gun to our heads when you offered us a job as your deputies. We all know the downside of the bein' a lawman, and we're all grown up here. Either you're gonna wear the badge and uphold the law, or you might as well take that badge off your chest. Rather than being the cure, you'll become the problem."

A well-dressed man with wiry red hair with a goatee and mustache stood over six feet tall when he leaned against the bar. He wore formal dress, a stiff collar, and a frock coat even though they were in the middle of nowhere and the temperatures soared. He sat staring out the window as he smoked a large, expensive cigar as big around as a tree branch.

The band wrapping said Havana, Cuba, and the smell of the rising smoke was exotic and almost sweet. His gold cufflinks twinkled in the sunlight from the window. But Will noticed the two men in black weren't interested in his gold. They were there for something different, and he thought he knew what it was.

As fresh drinks were delivered to the sheriff and his

new deputy, a Mexican suddenly lowered his head, dropped his shoulder, and took a step to his left as he brought up a knife. James White heard it through half-closed eyes. The first swipe sliced through the lawman's shirtsleeve, barely missing his skin. It happened so fast that James didn't even see it happen—but he felt it when it passed within millimeters of his body. It was the last thing he expected in the first-class train lounge. But not Will Crockett. He had smelled that something was up. It was as if he possessed some special instinct, akin to a third sense.

Pedro flicked another, quick, short arch, just missing the sheriff's sucked in stomach. That was when the assailant saw the look in Will's eyes, and he heard the click of his Colts' hammers, but it was too late. It was either fight or die. Will pulled the triggers, shooting him in the chest, slamming him against the carriage wall. The bandito gasped as his legs turned to rubber, and he slid down to the floor. Flores stopped dead in his tracks as he held his hands over his heart. It had stopped pumping.

Suddenly, the plush carriage exploded in violence. Bullets whined by, thudding into the walls and breaking glass, sailing out the windows, ricocheting into the distance.

The second Mexican said something in a low-voiced string of unintelligible, heavily accented Spanish. It was obvious he was so angry that he had lost all reason, thus all fear. He pulled his guns, but Will already had both of his Colts in his hands. The last thing the Mexican outlaw remembered was the double metal clicks. They sounded crisp despite the humid air. Crockett pulled the triggers, and his face disappeared.

As soon as the gunfire stopped, the bartender continued to ramble like nothing had happened. Maybe such disturbances were more common than they thought.

As soon as the smoke cleared, both men wearing badges had a stiff drink of labeled whiskey to calm their nerves.

———

"WE'LL PASS through Del Rio and Sotol City next, among other small towns that provide fuel for the locomotive. There we'll take on coal and water. Maybe even some food, for the first-class passengers. The second-class passengers have gotta feed themselves. From there, it's 154 miles to San Antonio and another thirty miles to Santa Clara."

"Then we should consider ourselves lucky, shouldn't we?" Will showed a wicked smile, raising an eyebrow. "Just think if it hadn't been for all this, you'd have missed endless conversations with me. I've been told that I'm an interesting man. I have so many stories and tales that I believe one day I'll become a writer and pen a volume of journals on my life's experiences."

Will Crocket grinned, but there was a serious look in his eyes. Perhaps someday he *would* become an author when he retired from endlessly roaming the country, much like the Comanches that the politicians were trying to push off their land. Then again, he would have to stay in the same place for months on end, and he didn't know if he was capable.

"Help me drag these two outside in between the cars, beside the couplings, before they start to smell,"

Will said, grabbing a limp arm. "The passengers are shocked enough as it is. There's a space there in the corner, one on each side. Out there, the smell will blow away with the wind. You just never know. Odds are, these fellas are wanted men. It'll be handy to have their faces when we check the wanted posters. I've got a stack ten inches high. I bet the one we left back at the bridge had a bounty on his head, too. Some of them fetch a handsome reward. I don't hunt men for money, but everyone can use some extra cash once in a while."

"Sorry, folks. I hope nobody got hurt," Will said to the passengers in a loud, confident voice. "I'm Deputy Sheriff Crockett. I'm afraid that you just never know where an outlaw will pop up in West Texas. You might wanna patch that window, Steward, before the glass breaks more and somebody gets cut. As it is, we don't seem to have anybody hit by a stray bullet. The only ones to suffer were the two fellas that started the fight."

"How 'bout we walk the length of the train from one end to the other, checking the passengers in every car to make sure we don't have any more of Ringo's buddies on board. Hell, this train might be full of outlaws and bounty hunters looking for a reward. When we're done, I wanna go back and question, Ringo. It's high time we had a word."

"All right, Will. I'll be right behind ya," the sheriff said as he pulled his gun.

"Maybe you ought to put your pistol away, James. We don't want to provoke a gunfight if we *do* run into an outlaw or two. So far, nobody innocent's gotten shot and we wanna keep it that way."

Will punched the empty shell casing out of his pistols, replacing them with new bullets. He nodded, and he and the sheriff put their guns away. They holstered their pistols but never let their hands stray too far from the revolvers' grips.

Sheriff White's mustache curled down around each side of his mouth, contrasting with his clean-shaven cheeks.

"I bet this'll piss those fellas you have hog-tied off." The bartender snickered. "It's an honor to meet ya, sir." He proffered his hand.

When they grasped, the stranger shook them up and down like a water pump, and he grinned like a possum. He was strangely unperturbed by the situation.

"This here is my friend, Sheriff White from El Paso."

"Oh, everybody in these parts knows who Sheriff James White is. To be honest, sir, some like ya and some don't. I reckon I like ya fine, though."

"I'm afraid that bein' a sheriff is that kind of job. Either they hate ya or they love ya."

Will looked at his pocket watch. He pushed the winder, and the cover popped open to reveal a white face with Roman numerals. He looked at Eric, his face long and thin with large self-conscious eyes. He squinted in the dim light as the sun fell off the end of the world and night followed.

They eyed the darkness from inside the carriage, which was racing across the Texas countryside in the pitch-black of night. A large silhouette raced down the shiny tracks.

———

GID SAT inside the second-class carriage, waiting with his heavy Colt Walker in his hand. His other pistol was in his holster. In his massive paws, they looked like pea shooters. When he cocked the hammer, the click seemed loud, making the outlaw's eyes spread wide with paranoia.

"Listen up, boys. If you make a move, I'm gonna pull this trigger until my pistol's empty. Now, I'm gonna remove the gags and tie your hands in front of ya, but if you act up, you'll pay dearly. We've made it this far, but we aren't home free yet. Until the fat woman signs, I'll shoot ya if you so much as twitch. I'll warn ya now. I've got a nervous trigger finger, and sometimes it does what it wants."

"What's that?" Eric asked. He was growing increasingly paranoid, especially as darkness approached. "Look outside. I see the silhouettes of two horses and riders." His eyes blinked, and he shook his head, then cupped his hands, staring out the window, looking into the dark.

"I don't see anybody," Will replied, smiling. His eyes were like two calm pools of water. "You worry too much. Whatever happens, I'll take care of ya, buddy. You're doing your part, and I promise we'll do our part as best as we can, too."

No matter what he did, Eric's mind always went back to the Comanche. He couldn't seem to get them out of his mind ever since they saw the dreary party. He wondered if it was a war party. He knew they were superb horsemen, as they rode fast but with apparent easy grace, trailed by clouds of dust. He knew it wasn't logical to be so apprehensive while on the train, but still, he had a bad feeling about this ride and the hostiles, and he couldn't seem to shake it.

In addition to the train, six stages a week kept Soto

City transport busy, even for those with limited funds, and were suitable for the more rugged journey. First thing that morning, they saw a coach behind charging horses as they stared out the train's window, but it was going in the opposite direction. Still, there was something romantic about a song of yesteryear.

Eric could see Gid relax the hard line of his jaw, his face rugged and leathery until he looked at Smith, which brought a smile to his mug. He seemed to like Gid best of the bunch, despite his grizzly nature and the fact that he seemed so large.

Back in the day, the sheriff's family insisted that he go west. He felt almost impatient to see Indians and cowboys back then. Initially, James intended to make it rich in the goldfields like thousands before him and after. However, he wasn't to have such luck, and when he fell on hard times, he took a job as deputy sheriff for fifty dollars a month and free room and board. Eventually, he became the Santa Clara sheriff.

CHAPTER TWELVE

DEL RIO WAS A SMALL SETTLEMENT SOUTH OF THE RIO Grande. Only twenty miles away, across the river, was Soto City, Texas, which was just big enough to have a telegraph office. Three men waited outside in the shade of the porch, but the blistering midday heat wore them down and made them nod off on and off. They were waiting for the train, but for all the wrong reasons. Heavy-caliber pistols hung from leather holsters on their waists as long guns leaned against the building.

The town was recently established after the arrival of the railroad station, as its planners hoped to attract business from the other side of the Rio Grande. The towns began to grow and blossom with the arrival of the train, which crisscrossed the state on shiny steel tracks. This was something that the local Comanche and Apache saw as eyesores and insults, but in most cases, their sheer size and power scared the local hostiles off. The resistance dwindled as the White population in the Wild West soured. It appeared that now, nothing could stop the invasion of Easterners.

Much of the country was run by Indian agency agents whose positions were often handed out to men who hated the local natives. Many profited by selling the rations intended for the reservation Indians of their government's beef and grain to local homesteads or even back to the army, which had provided the meat in the first place. Such was the corruption of West Texas and most of the state as they continued to pressure the Indians, both roaming free and those already starving on reservations.

The Indian wars raged for the last hundred years. With the invention of the repeater rifles and the onslaught of hundreds of thousands of Americans heading west, the time of the Native Americans was quickly passing by as their population dramatically diminished. Still, some resistance remained, and those left were now fighting for a cause, and they willingly sacrificed their lives in battle rather than dropping to their knees and succumbing to the White men's desires.

From inside the car as sunset came, they saw antelope bounding across the hillside in the hundreds. They ran as though something was chasing them, but as they watched, nothing appeared. Then the Crocketts caught a glimpse of a mountain lion. It was eight feet in length and seemed to weigh nearly a hundred and fifty pounds. It was one of the kings of the forest and feared by all. Only the grizzly bear refused to flee from them, but it often cost them their lives.

The Soto City railroad station had been built with hostile Indians in mind, considering it was some 200 miles to San Antonio, leaving it in the middle of nowhere. The closest town was Eagle Pass, sixty miles to the south.

THERE WAS AN OBLONG, thick-walled log building with several open stable sheds and a corral at the end, and a sign that said: *Blacksmith* hung on the front of the barn. This was the stagecoach way station whose future was in question with the newfangled trains.

There were a few dozen houses surrounded by as many teepees, sitting squat under a large wooden water tower. The train idled as they filled the boiler. Another large-diameter chute allowed the coal to be loaded by gravity into the coal bin, making the process take no more than two hours from start to finish. Four men climbed out of the coal tower, black with soot from head to toe.

One side held a local stage depot with spare teams of horses. Circling the stagecoach station, fifty yards out, was another five-foot-tall and four-inch-thick wooden wall to protect the coaches and animals from hostile attacks in the past by both Indians and Mexican outlaws. They could make the station guard out in the doorway on their way to eat. The railroad had built the barn, corral, and buildings to last, and the army and Texas Rangers had promised to defend it to the last man if it were deemed necessary.

Weak, frightened words whispered between Eric's lips. "I reckon I'm in over my head. I thank you, men, kindly, for helping me stay alive. But be forewarned that getting Ringo Moon to jail will be a bigger feat than you men think is possible. He is said to have enough money buried across West Texas to get his friends and acquaintances alike interested in freeing him before he hangs."

There was little honor among thieves, but when

gold and silver coins were in the equation, demeanors changed, and so did personal codes. By the time the train left El Paso, half the outlaws in town had heard the stories and were deciding whether they would take part or not. Some of those didn't have the means or even a horse and saddle, and others couldn't convince the rest of their gangs. But with a town partially populated by outlaws hiding out in broad daylight, there were always desperate men ready and willing to disregard the danger and take the bait.

"Let's lock these three in the mail car so we can go and have a meal. The engineer, Henry Bats, said that we have about an hour and a half. That gives us time to check the train, as he said he would pull out in two hours sharp."

Will removed his watch from his pocket and flicked the cover open to have a peek. "That'll be at three o'clock. If we eat in the same place as train employees from the Southern Pacific Railroad, we know we won't be late. Eric, you can come with us. It's time to get some fresh air."

"What about guarding the mail car?" Gid asked. "Do you want me to stay behind?"

"And miss a meal? Then I wouldn't be able to live with you for the rest of the day. We can give the train company guard a generous tip to keep a close watch. If they're locked inside and they guard the door so nobody lets them out, we should be all right. We can have him shoot off a round if he suspects something, just to be safe. But a man has to eat, and today I'm just as hungry as Gid."

"Our next stop will be San Antonio, and from there it all depends on the connections. We may be better off riding our horses, but that always leaves us with the chance that one of these fools will try to run off, and we'll have to chase him. We can't have that because it'll expose us too much. It'll be safer by train, even if we do have to change lines in the San Antonio rail yards, but we can cross that bridge when we come to it. Right now, we've gotta make sure we get through this stop without a mishap."

————

WHEN THEY WALKED into the center of Soto City, they saw that it had much to be desired. Of course, the town popped up overnight with the arrival of the train. This was the perfect location for a refueling station, and due to the plentiful water source on the lake, they began building a town around the railroad landing. It wasn't much yet, but history proved that it would soon become a bustling city with locomotives coming and going from all directions.

"Over there's a good place to eat," Sheriff White said. "The price is reasonable, and the portions are large. Mind you, there're only two saloons to choose from, plus a Mexican cantina that serves good tacos, but their beer is warm, and they have tequila instead of whiskey."

As soon as they stepped into the tavern, the owner looked at Will like he knew who he was, smiling like an old friend. Of course, this brought unwanted attention as his muscles tensed. Still, he knew that he and Gid had been in several dime novels from back east and the local newspapers. When you did the kind of work they did, your reputation grew and eventually followed you around.

No sooner did the saloon employee see Will Crockett and his brother Gid, than he spoke up, "I read about you two fellas in a few of them dime novels. I think one was called *The Texas Shootout*," the squat bartender said. "Your name's Will Crockett, ain't it, and you must be his brother Gid? Come on in and refresh yourselves. For two such famous men, drinks are on the house. Are you kin to Davy Crockett, like they say? You know, the one who fell in the Alamo, God rest his soul."

When Will walked in, he stopped, framed in the doorway, a silhouette in the morning midday light highlighting his outline, including the guns on his hips.

Inside the saloon, Will lounged against the wall with his face close to the windowpane. His Sharps rifle rested on the windowsill as he studied everyone in the street while Gid looked for a table. They knew better than to let their guard down now that they were most of the way to their destination. History told them this was when they were their most vulnerable.

"He's a distant relative," Will replied, "but I've never met the man before he died on March sixth, 1836. I have met his nieces and nephews, though. As soon as we were introduced, I was reminded of the stories I'd heard about her uncle and my distant cousin."

"I've never seen a man wolf down so much food. You must have a hollow leg, Gid," Sheriff White said as soon as their meals were served.

Will's little brother raised his eyes, wiggling his eyebrows, and grinned. Without missing a beat, Gid devoured yet another serving of food. He had eaten with such gusto from an early age. He had also watched as his muscles grew hard and thick. For two brothers, so alike in some ways, in others, they were as different as day and night.

The town would soon be renamed after the railroad dispatcher, John. B. Comstock. It would quickly become a hub for the wool and lamb industry across the United States. It also served as a post for the local Texas Rangers. There was a full patrol housed in their barracks on the outskirts of town. The commanding officer was well known, and although strict, his men knew he was honest and brave as they followed him into hellish situations. Their job in West Texas was a difficult one, but none of them wavered. Only the bravest of men became Rangers.

"Just because you have a crazy notion, doesn't mean that everybody wants to go with you and get shot to hell," Sheriff White said. "So, be on your best behavior, Gid. I agree, it would be safer if we rode the train all the way to Santa Clara. If for nothing more, it'll give us cover if things go south. There are too many places to lay in wait for an ambush if we travel by road. Every Tom, Dick, and Harry will be on our trail by now. At least riding the train will thin out the outlaws and gunslingers and make it harder to reach the prisoners."

Eric passed his tongue over his dry, cracked lips. He was so anxious that he hardly touched his food. He felt like rats were eating at the lining of his stomach and was just about to upchuck despite not eating for a full day. He quickly excused himself and ran outside to dry heave off the edge of the rickety porch. For him, it seemed forever when it was probably only a few seconds of embarrassment. He knew he would have to eat something because he was starting to feel dizzy.

Finally, he pushed his way back into the bar and retook his seat. This time his face was pale.

"You worry too much, Eric. That's why your stomach is upset all the time. Wherever you die,"—Gid grinned —"it's still the same distance to hell, so stop your fretting, son. Pessimism never saved anyone. If you live each minute like it was your last, you'll never miss a moment of enjoyment through life, but if you worry all day and night, you'll make your life a prison where there's no escape."

Eric suddenly turned. He felt the blood drain from his face until he saw the younger Crockett wink. He wasn't trying to scare him but tried to make light of a serious situation. What started as a simple outlaw transport seemed to be turning into a running battle, and they had no idea of how many men were on the other side or even who they might be. Time would tell if they got all the prisoners to Santa Clara intact. If not, they would have to bring them in over the backs of their horses, dead.

A wooden sign hung over a small space. It said: *Shave—50 Cents.* A barber in the corner busied himself with the posh first-class passenger with red hair while cutting his long locks and shaving his freckled face. Finally, he dipped his fingers into the grease bucket and then twisted the tips of his mustache into sharp points. He spun the barber's chair around so his new customer could have a look at his handiwork in the mirror.

The barber chair was right beside the window to provide sufficient light. As soon as the first-class passengers finished eating, they formed a line to wait for the excellent value shave. In San Antonio, it would cost twice or thrice the price. They weren't the kind of men who enjoyed going unshaven, and even less the type to shave themselves. Besides that, most wealthy individuals were stingy and couldn't pass up such a bargain.

Halfway through their meal, they began to hear a commotion outside the open windows. At first, it was more like a murmur, but soon it became an angry crowd. They couldn't make out what they said, but it was clear by the nooses in the leader's hand that they intended to hang somebody, if not more than one man.

A cluster of axe handle-bearing men roared down the main street of town, kicking up dust, making all those they passed shudder with revulsion. They were heading for the three men wearing badges, and then once they had the keys, they planned to visit the mail wagon and make four wrongs right. Of course, they didn't know that Eric had helped the law in exchange for a reduced sentence. To them, he was just another outlaw who needed to be hanged.

Sheriff White and the Crocketts moved outside, but Eric stayed seated by the table. He didn't want to be lynched now that he had helped and obeyed the local law, leaving him on the other side of the angry mob. Of course, there was no way for them to know this, so he knew his best course of action was to try to go unseen and not heard.

"How about I give you all to the count of three before I start shootin'?" Will growled. "There's no way you're gonna coax the prisoner from our custody. Do you know what the penalty is for assaulting a law enforcement officer? It's to hang by the neck until dead. All right then, one, two, three..." As Will counted, his eyes narrowed to slits.

Despite the crowd's gruff mannerisms and tough

talk, when they faced real gunmen who were willing to fight back, they lost their thunder and backed down. They suddenly realized that all three men with badges already had their pistols in their fists, and from what they saw in their eyes, they were ready to use them.

Suddenly, Gid shot off two rounds into the porch ceiling to get the angry men's attention. Plaster sprayed them from above. He stood on the edge of the landing and talked in an angry voice. "The next one is for anyone who crosses this line." He made an imaginary line across the wood-plank floor with the toe of his boot.

A red-tinged calm settled over them all when his gun fell silent. Will Crockett hadn't had that feeling since his last battle in the war. It felt as if ice flowed through his veins. A cold chill ran up his spine as his anger spiked. "Don't make me repeat myself, gentlemen. My patience has run out. The first man who moves on me dies, and that's not a threat. It's a promise."

"Hell, no!" the vigilante gang leader said with a voice full of iron. It was clear he wouldn't be moved. "We ain't goin' nowhere until we see these thieves hang. They robbed us not three months back and got away with all our money. How do you expect us to feel? I, for one, ain't in a forgiving mood."

Will, Gid, and the marshal exchanged looks. They could see that they were fifty to three, and all that was keeping things calm was their bravado, but such courage only went so far when the odds were so against their favor.

"Either stand down or suffer the consequences," Sheriff White growled, hoping his voice sounded authoritative. "I'll tell you boys what. I'll give you a personal invitation to watch them hang in Santa Clara, and I assure you, hang, they will. You'll have ringside seats to their demise, and you can make a claim with the local law in case they find any of your loot, so you might even get some of your money back. That's a lot better than the nasty task of tar and feathering someone and putting them to death, aside from murder being a crime, and you'd all end up with your faces on wanted posters. I'm afraid that I'd be obliged to take you in, too. I'm a stickler for the law."

Will raised his open palms, trying to calm the angry crowd, especially his brother. He watched as his face got redder. "Take it easy, folks. You too, Gid, or you're going to blow a gasket. We don't want a fight with the town locals. We're here for one thing only. Y'all can mouth off all you want. No matter what you do or say, you'll walk away empty-handed. That much I can promise. All you're gonna find is more problems than you bargained for. So, whatcha wanna do?"

Inwardly, Will chuckled to himself. He was used to his brother's quick jump to anger with the slightest nudge, and when he had good reason, he was even harder to stop. Lucky for the townsfolk, his older brother was the only man he really listened to. If he hadn't been there, things would have already spun out of control.

He loved his little brother, but sometimes he did fly off the handle and attacked, asking questions later. But while they were wearing deputy sheriffs' stars, they couldn't go down that road, if for no other reason than their mutual respect for Sheriff James White.

His brother could see that Gid was suddenly filled with conflicting feelings, ready to unleash a cataclysmic storm. He physically had to grit his teeth until they hurt, and with bunched fists, as he dug his fingernails into his palms until they bled.

Finally, when the crowd didn't disperse, Will Crockett dropped his hands to his hips, as he brushed his coat aside, showing the Colt-45 revolvers in his holsters as he eyed the men leading the crowd.

Will pointed a finger and said, "You, you, and you will be the first men to die. I might not be able to kill you all, but you three big mouths will never know what happened because you'll be dead. My brother will get three more, and the sheriff, his share too. That will leave nine of you dead before you can even clear leather, and I bet the number would be closer to fifteen or twenty. Once we kill you, half will run away, anyway. We're used to this because it's our job. How many of you can say the same?"

Will stared at his new friend, Sheriff James White, with keen interest, wondering what they would have done if the crowd of vigilantes refused to give up the fight. Lucky for them, that day they wouldn't be tested. Who knew what the results would have been? Undoubtedly, a bunch of men would die for nothing but a few hotheads and loudmouths.

CHAPTER THIRTEEN

COMSTOCK, FORMERLY KNOWN AS SOTOL CITY, IS located near Ozona in Val Verde County. This journey on horseback, wagon, or on foot was a grueling experience until the train arrived, running twenty-four hours a day, making the time west only a few days' ride.

F Company of the Frontier Battalion was stationed in the new railroad hub and soon-to-be-thriving city. Captain Gus Harvey was known for his leadership and bravery in the war against hostile Indians and Mexican forces, be they of a military nature or international bandits. At fifty years old, he was still as strong and determined as he was at twenty. He had come a long way from his birthplace in Cincinnati, Ohio. Now he spent his time on the Texas Plains attempting to control the violent Comanche and the incursions of Mexicans from over the border to rustle horses and cattle, only to sell them back again north of the river.

Six companies of Texas Rangers, each comprising seventy-five men, were organized in 1874 to create the state's own force to protect the Texas Frontier. John B.

Jones was commissioned major of the force. In its first seventeen months, they reported twenty-one engagements with hostile Indians. The Rangers made arrests, escorted prisoners, guarded jails, and attended courts. Hundreds of lawless men were arrested and thousands fled, but there were always a few outlaw gangs that refused to give it up, like that of Ringo Moon, remnants of the James Gang, and Black Bart.

In 1877, the Texas Rangers cleared the outlaws out of Kimble County, ending the Horrell-Higgins Feud, terminating the Salt War of San Elizario, and capturing Sam Bass. When the frontier was considered relatively safe, a skeleton crew of Rangers was attached to Comstock to ensure the railroad ran on time and hopefully warded off any threats.

During the following years, Harvey led a campaign against the Comanche, and they slowly succeeded in weakening their willpower. They also handled the thieves who attempted to rob the railroad company blind. If it weren't already tied down and attached, they would try to steal it. Now, they found some of their trains under attack by organized bandits. They had finally graduated to follow the shiny tacks to their pots of gold.

With the Texas Rangers, the town almost had as many lawmen as citizens. But the railroads had big plans for Comstock. It was to become a central hub for shipping across the western United States.

When the locomotive rolled into town, they didn't find a wall of wooden storefronts like they had in other prosperous cities. There were a few saloons, bathhouses, and boarding houses. They also had a general store, a hardware store, and a haberdashery, all combined into one. They provided most of what the residents needed to survive. Mixed in with the Easterners seeking to strike it rich or start sheep, cattle and horse ranches, was a small group of European immigrants.

They spoke strange languages, ate odd-smelling food, and mingled little with the other White men. Most of them lived in covered wagons at the end of town and minded their own business. The few men that populated Comstock were as hard as they come and challenged most who visited, and the Crocketts were no exception.

Will, Gid, James, and their cooperative prisoner, Eric, walked down the street with their heads down against the glare and their hats pulled low to shade their eyes. The bright sunlight glinted off their shiny stars. Wind whipped down the street, propelling tumbleweeds in the opposite direction.

A cowboy yelled out, "Yippee-ki-yay!" making the three turn as their hands moved for their guns. When they saw how drunk the buckaroo was, they relaxed their tense muscles and smiled. He didn't even have a pistol in his hand. Suddenly, his horse started to buck unexpectedly, racing down the street, unsaddling the rider halfway to the end. Everyone who saw it burst out laughing.

When they walked past the blacksmith's shop, Will and Gid could smell the smoke from the forge and hear the loud clanging of the smithy's hammer as he worked on a piece of red-hot, gleaming metal. Beside the blacksmith's stood the restaurant. It didn't look like much, but it was bustling with clientele, which usually told the story of whether it was good or not.

"Why're y'all so jumpy? Let's go and have some fun." Gid smiled, having already forgotten their dangerous mission. He never got scared and usually took things with a grain of salt, especially when he was food to be found.

"Neither one of us has much experience in just having fun. How will we know it when we're having it?" Will asked, looking at his brother, amused.

"Don't you worry. I'll let you know when it happens. I'm starving. Let's get something to eat. I could eat a whole cow. Lookee over there, it's a saloon too. That'll do it."

"When aren't you starvin', little brother?"

Few customers were to be found in the Comstock Tavern. There weren't that many pedestrians on the single, long street either. Most of it was occupied by the bank, post office, mineral office, and Ranger post, along with a few more government buildings. They were preparing the town for a significant population boom, but would the railroad be enough to sustain it?

As soon as they walked into the bar, they saw several girls wearing scant dresses exposing their sexual charms, as they stood eyeing the handsome brothers, but neither noticed. Despite the scenery, Will and the sheriff never stopped their eyes from moving from face to face, looking for ones they'd seen on wanted posters, while Gid followed his nose. But the moment the ladies saw the Crocketts, they stared because they were both so handsome. They also looked like they might have some money.

Gid finally noticed the percentage of girls as they went from table to table like bees going from flower to flower, flirting with customers as they arrived, making them smile. Despite its size, Comstock already had a couple of tents of women sharing beds as they worked in shifts. Other than them, there were a few other ladies in town. Thus was the way of the creation of settlements in the Wild West.

For a small town, it seemed to hold its own, but the larger centers of vice and crime were back in the cities like San Antonio, Dallas, Fort Worth, and Austin. Comstock's heart was just beginning to beat, but its day would come soon enough.

Across from the lawmen were what appeared to be soldiers from times past, much like the Crocketts. They wore remnants of Union uniforms and were all heavily armed. One's face was scarred, and another was missing an arm, and none of them appeared friendly. Nobody in the saloon did anything but frown upon their apparently unwanted interruption. Or maybe it was precisely what they were waiting for.

"Look at the way that son of bitch eats. Why, he's like a wild dog. And look at the face on that sheriff. It looks like he has a corncob up his ass. We have our own lawmen in Comstock, and we don't need others stickin' their noses into our business." He hacked a wad from his throat and spat onto the sawdust-covered floor. The message was clear.

"I recognize that sheriff. He's the town law from El Paso, and I must say, there ain't no love lost between him and me." His words were clipped and patronizing. He had a misshapen nose and a sleepy eye. "You might wanna be nicer and less of a horse's ass next time we cross paths, lawman."

Empty bottles covered their tables along with half-filled glasses. Cheroot smoke squirreled upward, hovering a foot from the ceiling. All the men at the table were gruff and impolite.

Sheriff White's eyes shot daggers at the insult as he eyed Gid to see what he would do.

"You loudmouthed bastard," Gid replied, growling. "I'm not gonna let you talk to my friend like that. Keep it up, and I'm gonna teach you a lesson."

When the waitress brought a tray of donuts for dessert, Gid's eyes widened as he grabbed two in each hand, instantly forgetting the insults. When food was on the table, he had a one-track mind. He continued to ignore the banter between his brother, the sheriff, and the strangers across the room as he wolfed down the sweets.

A frontiersman's buckskin shirt, stained by sweat, clung to his massive chest. His hair and beard looked like they had never seen a pair of scissors. He sat silently in the corner, sipping on a glass of store-bought whiskey. The rest of the bottle sat idle on the table. It was clear that he was in no hurry but watched everything happen without missing a detail.

He seemed to be the epitome of awareness. It was obvious that he lived somewhere in the wilderness, and he wasn't in his usual habitat. Maybe he was just hanging around town waiting for something to happen to kill the boredom.

Deputy Crockett studied his broad, pockmarked, rugged face. They exchanged looks, both knowing they had seen him somewhere before. Most of the usual faces they saw were on wanted posters, but others were famous from newspapers like themselves. Then again, as they had their hands full with their prisoners, they would be served best if they left well enough alone. They still had to get their outlaws to Santa Clara and the courts.

Will removed his hat and passed his shirt sleeve across his forehead, then slipped it back on, pulling the brim low over his eyes. They lay still in the shadows cast by the lamplight. Still, he didn't budge his gaze from the mountain man. Then it hit him. It was the sixty-five-year-old frontiersman he had seen in the newspapers.

Jim Baker was one of the last of the mountain men still alive. He wasn't as famous as some from prior decades, but he was an expert trapper, hunter, and scout. His longevity made him the last man standing from the fur trade and buffalo hunts from years past.

When Will tipped his hat, Baker nodded but didn't say a word. He seemed pleased enough with watching and not engaging in conversation. Crockett understood because sometimes he felt the same way.

When the train's whistle began to blow long blasts and it wasn't yet time to leave, they knew that something was wrong. It went quiet for a moment, then the long blasts resumed. It wasn't Morris' code, so it was probably the fireman. Somebody must be in a panic. The first to jump to his feet was the engineer sitting in the corner, nursing a glass of whiskey. It was his train, and his charge.

"I reckon I best go see Henry and see what's goin' on," Sheriff White sighed. "There never seems to be a dull moment."

"I'll come with ya. Gid, you watch Eric here. Make

sure he doesn't get beaten up or shot. We don't want anything to happen to our witness."

Gid nodded, barely lifting his eyes from his nearly empty plate. When he was eating, there was little he paid attention to. But despite his apparent focus on his meal, he listened to every word said. He immediately noticed the change in their tone of voice. He also knew that alone he would be more of a target if somebody were to start something. However, this didn't deter him from hesitating or missing a bite of food.

If they wanted something from him, he would deal with them when the time came. Nobody seemed to notice Eric. That was probably more by design than by chance. He sat huddled in the corner, barely visible behind Crockett's burly body, and was as quiet as a church mouse.

WHEN THEY HAD FIRST ARRIVED at the Comstock Saloon, the crowd gave them dirty looks. They ignored the patrons and took the nearest empty table, one of several.

"Is there anything else ya want?" the waitress asked as she walked up with a scrap of paper in her hand. She wetted the tip of the yellow pencil with her tongue and looked at the men quizzically.

"What else ya got?" Gid replied.

For the sheriff, the Crocketts stank of duty and honor. The sheriff gave them both a dubious look, but up until now, they had shown he wasn't wrong. Maybe they *were* the men he read about in the dime novels.

From the farthest corners, the mountain man

chuckled humorously, shaking his curtain of long gray hair and beard as he sat and watched. He nursed a tepid beer and a shot of whiskey. After living in the wilderness for years, everything became entertaining. He laughed and snickered the whole time.

Gid counted out two dollars and fifty cents, as it clattered on the bar top. "We'll be back for another drink once we find out what that racket is. It sounds like it's coming from the train."

Bottles and glasses strung out the bar's length. The bartender wiped his hands back and forth on his apron as dirty looks were shot Gid's way. Still, he didn't seem to notice, or maybe he just didn't care.

"Are you the kind of fella that walks under a flock of birds and doesn't expect to get shit on your face?" Gid finally looked up as he smiled and bunched his hands into fists.

"And what's a tub of lard like you gonna do about it?" the stranger replied.

Gid suddenly waded into the stranger, clubbing his face with his hammer-like paws. He backed him into a corner and hit him with a roundhouse haymaker. His eyes rolled back into his head, and he slumped to the ground. When he nudged him with his toe, he moaned.

Crockett's next opponent's smile was cocky and cruel as another local tried to come at him from behind. He saw him out of the corner of his eye. Now it was two against one.

Gid stepped back a half-step, then drove his left fist into his gut. A gasp came from the fighter's open mouth. Finally came the uppercut against his jaw, sending him back with arms flailing. When his fingers touched his cheekbone, it made him wince.

"You broke my face!"

"You should consider who you're mouthin' off to before you pick another fight." Gid wiped the blood from his knuckles with his napkin.

AT FIRST, the sound came gradually. It was faint as it emerged from the distance. It sounded like lots of yelling, then they heard and felt the ground tremble under their feet. When they looked into the sun, they saw the faint outline of a cloud of dust. Below the dust was a sizable Comanche war party as they yelped and wailed, giving warnings to all those in their path. Several more blasts came from the Baldwin's steam whistle as the fireman frantically pulled the cord.

In seconds, everybody who had gotten off the train was making a beeline, running as fast as they could to get back on board and to relative safety. The rich man with red hair and the fancy suit pushed two women aside to clamber up the ladder before them, leaving them lying in the dust. He didn't even look back.

The hostile Indians continued to whoop and shout while wasting ammunition far out of range. Nobody in town was frightened enough to return fire. At two cents a bullet, it was a foolish waste of money. For the Indians, it was probably just to make a point of how brave they were. It was as though they hadn't decided whether to attack or not.

When Will saw what the red-haired man had done, he became furious, taking long strides to the ladder, climbing two rungs at a time. He reached out just before the wealthy passenger disappeared into the first-class carriage. Crockett grabbed his ear right before he disappeared, nearly jerking the arrogant snob off his feet as he screamed like a girl.

"I saw what you did to those two women back there! Who do you think you are?" Will roared in his face as spittle covered the freckled cheeks, and his eyes grew wide in horror.

"Get your hands off me! How dare you?" the supposed gentleman yelled as he held on to the railing to keep from falling off and into the dirt. But Will wasn't going to let him get away. He used his reddening ear to pull him back down the carriage steps and back to the street.

"Now, apologize for your actions!" Will ordered, red-faced, ignoring the occasional gunshot from the Comanche across the ridge. He knew enough about hostile Indians that he didn't think they were in danger yet.

When he didn't respond, the open-handed slap came like the sound of a whip cracking, and the rich man clamped his mouth shut as his face drained white. Blood dribbled down his mouth and chin. He bunched his lips, ready to mouth off again, but thought better of it and clamped his teeth, leaving a gash of a hard line.

"Now you're gettin' the idea, mister. When I'm around, you'll get treated as you treat others." Will raised his hand like he was going to strike him again, but he was just faking. Still, the wealthy business owner flinched and covered his face like the coward he was and whimpered like a small child.

"Your main defect is that you're only interested in your money and that you're too stupid to know that's not what makes a man. If you were only as smart as you think you are. Just because you're rich don't mean that you're a genius or can go around treating people like dirt. Especially women. You remember now. I'll be watching."

Gunfire continued to explode like popcorn in a frying pan, but they were still out of range, and most of the rounds were fired into the air. The big black engine hissed clouds of steam, and the tee-pot smokestack began to spew black smoke while the fireman struggled to build up steam. The engineer was back at the controls and was preparing to depart as quickly as possible.

Will and James watched and waited calmly to see what the Indians did.

"I don't think these boys are really lookin' for a fight. If they were, they'd have charged us by now." Will took off his hat and held it up to shade his face as he stared into the distance. "They look pretty skinny to me. Maybe they just want something to eat."

They continued to watch for a few more minutes, but the war party still didn't budge, and none of them knew what they would do next.

"Help me cut one of those longhorns back in the cattle car out for these fellas, James," Will said. "Maybe we can get them to go away without a fight. They could be all over us by the time the locomotive builds enough speed to outrun a horse at a sprint. If they haven't wasted too many bullets, that is. Most Indians don't have but a few. If you don't want trouble with hostiles, treat them as you would want them to treat you."

The Indians stared at them like hungry wolves but maintained their distance, skulking behind the scattered brush. Most of the tribes feared soldiers and men with badges, yet a few still resisted. These were poor, dirty, and ragged, and acted like the defeated men they were, and all for what? To steal their land and erase their history? These weren't the feared Comanche or Apache. These men are no more than youngsters. That was why they fired into the sky. They weren't looking for war. All they wanted was something to eat.

"Only a White man would cut two inches from the top of a blanket and sew it on the bottom, thinking he's made it longer." Will chuckled. "Instead of fighting, why don't we try to make friends."

In minutes, Will leaped out of the cattle car riding his horse chasing a longhorn steer out the door. He waved a white cloth over his head then calmly walked toward the war party. The closer he got, the younger they saw they were. Some couldn't be more than thirteen. They were just boys.

Grinning, Will slapped the steer's rump. He bunched his fingers and put them to his mouth, indicating food. The young Comanche warriors rode out and herded the steer and turned and rode to the top of the ridge. When they reached the summit, one stopped and waved. He had a smile on his face that stretched from ear to ear.

"That went a lot better than I expected." Will chuckled to himself, as he wheeled his horse, nudged its flanks, and headed back to the train. *Sometimes kindness is the best path, especially when you're outnumbered.*

———

LATE THAT NIGHT, after it was all over, Eric sat exhausted from the tension while he watched the dark pass by through the carriage window. For a moment, the young outlaw's mind drifted to his family and what once was. Although he missed them, he knew that fretting over them did him no good. He would probably never find out if they survived or not.

Unfortunately, everyone was going to find out what course he had taken in life. It would be plastered all over the newspapers beside Ringo Moon's name. He dreaded the thought. He hoped they didn't make them pose for photographs, but he doubted it. Ringo was famous but not like Jesse James or John Wesley Hardin.

Suddenly, he gasped. What would have happened if he had made the wrong decision? Now he began to doubt going against Ringo Moon and making friends with lawmen he really didn't know. Maybe the devil you knew was better than the one you didn't.

What if Ringo does succeed in escaping? Then I'll be looking over my shoulder for the rest of my days if I don't rot in prison first. Or maybe he'll just kill me outright for being a traitor.

For the first time, Eric questioned his rash decision. He had let the lawmen talk him into turning on his gang so quickly that he didn't understand how it had happened. Now he wasn't so sure what he should do. They were only a day from Santa Clara, and then it would be too late to consider a new course of action.

If Ringo *did* get away, Eric believed that the deal with the sheriff wouldn't hold much water while standing in the defendant's booth all on his own. Of course, then the judge would throw the book at him, as there was no one else to punish. Somebody was going to swing for the train robbery and the murders, and Eric suddenly realized it could be him.

CHAPTER FOURTEEN

As soon as the Indians disappeared and the gunfire stopped, two men rode up with beige hats and badges, and a wake of dust followed. It was apparent they were Texas Rangers. Will was just arriving back from giving the Comanche a longhorn steer for food so the young Indian boys wouldn't starve. Five tin stars flashed in the sunlight as the men eyed each other before speaking. Everybody was heavily armed.

"What's going on here, gentlemen? Sheriff? We were just riding back into town to catch the train to San Antonio when we heard the gunfire. I'm Captain Gus Harvy, and this is my right-hand man, Ranger Jimmy Jackson. I run the Texas Ranger post here in Comstock. Mark my words: one day this his gonna be an important part of Texas and we're here to make sure it doesn't fall apart before it happens."

"Pleased to meet cha. This is the El Paso Sheriff James White, my brother Gid, and I'm Will Crockett. Those fellas over there are the Ringo Moon gang. This one here,"—he pointed to Eric—"has decided to turn over a new leaf and is gonna help us send his old outlaw friends to the gallows if that's what old Judge Roy Bean decides to do. Or what's left of 'em. Four are already dead. As soon as we get these fellas back to Santa Clara, we're gonna see that they swing for train robbery and murder."

"What was going on with those young Comanche? They weren't shootin' at you men, were they? It's not like them to be aggressive. They're just young boys living in the wrong times. I try to keep an eye on them, so they stay out of trouble. I'd hate to have to send 'em to Fort Sill, or the Anadarko reservations. They haven't even gotten to enjoy their teens like most young boys their age."

"Whatcha think's gonna become of 'em?" Will asked, concerned. "I'd hate to see harm come to those boys. They were just hungry, that's all, and didn't know how to ask for help. Mind ya now, if most men in Texas see Indians shooting guns, they normally fire back. But I don't take to killin' needlessly. I'd rather take a man before the judge and let the law do its work than shoot him dead. Not unless they try to take my life. Then I'll protect myself like we all do."

"It sounds like we're similar thinkin' men. I have much worse bandits to look out for than a few wannabe warriors. We have some hard Texan and Mexican outlaw gangs around here. They like to hang out in out-of-the-way places like Comstock or Eagle Pass, just south of here. You'll find all sorts hangin' around, tryin' to hide out in plain sight. The thing is, we don't have enough Rangers to cover a state the size of Texas, but we do the best we can."

"So, you'll be ridin' with us on the train, will ya? Gid

asked. "It'll be good to have a couple of extra guns. So far, we've been hit at every turn. It appears that Mr. Ringo there, has money stashed all over West Texas, and it was all stolen from banks, trains, and stagecoaches. That means that every Tom, Dick, and Harry is gunnin' for us, lookin' to bust Ringo and his boys out and get a nice reward. But we're here to make sure that ain't gonna happen."

"We've also got to return the stolen gold eagles. There're sacks of 'em. It represents the Santa Clara citizens' savings. They had it deposited in a big, safe bank in San Antonio. After the local savings and loan built a new vault and added shotgun guards, they ordered their money to be shipped by train back to Santa Clara where it was handy, but it was stolen before it got there," Will said. "We intend to give it back, and the local sheriff, Parson, will lock 'em up in his jail until the circuit judge shows. Like Gid said, we could use some extra help."

"We're leaving our horses here, or we won't catch the train in time. It looks like you're just about to pull out. I have one of my Rangers comin' in a while to fetch 'em home. Do you fellas mind if we ride on your coach? Maybe we can pick each other's brains for information. We're all on the same side, ain't we?"

"By all means," Will replied, smiling. "We have the whole car to ourselves except for our prisoners."

"What about the gang? I've heard that Ringo is a mouthy one. I don't tolerate sass well. If he mouths off to me, he'll be eatin' the end of my pistol barrel. I can't count the number of prisoners I've left with no front teeth. Mind ya now, I'm a peaceful man but I must admit, when my dander's up I get a mite reckless."

"There's no problem there. We welcome recklessness if it's aimed at criminals. Last time they wouldn't shut up, we stuck socks in their mouths and hog-tied 'em. So, if they act up, they know what's comin', unless you get to 'em first." Will chuckled.

―――――

"PSHAW," Sheriff White said, then spat a brown stream of juice into a spittoon beside the wooden bench seat, making it ring. "I ain't ever even heard of nothin' like that. It's hard to believe that even Gid can beat four men at once. Most folks in Comstock ain't whatcha call daisies."

The scenery flashed by two large windows on either side of the wagon. Wooden benches wrapped around the carriage, and another split the middle of the train. All the seats were empty, save nine. Four of the passengers wore shackles on their hands and feet and frowned with hate-filled eyes. Ringo ground his teeth to keep from mouthing off, knowing what he would get in return. The Texas Rangers didn't try to hide their distaste for the outlaws.

There was something strange in Moon's eyes. It was as though he was sure he would get away before they reached their destination. It was reflected in his manner despite the fact he was chained to the railing that runs around the outside seats. Still, his arrogance couldn't be mistaken. He didn't act like a man who was headed for the wrong end of a noose.

It was hard to tell with Wayne and Jessy, his gang members, because they followed Ringo's suit no matter what he did. They were like little puppies, and their only interest was making their master happy. His attitude also gave them a boost of confidence despite being watched by what was now five lawmen. The mountain man, Jim Baker, had also decided to join them. It turned out he was quite the storyteller.

"Well, I'll swear to it," Jim Baker said. "Yeah, I knew who you fellas were as soon as you walked into the saloon. I saw your pictures in the newspapers and dime novels. Just because I'm a mountain man don't mean that I don't know how to read and write. Gid there took on four men and whooped 'em all. You should have seen the state of 'em. They could hardly walk, let alone talk. I think one's got a busted jaw. It hung from his face like it was on a spring."

"That sounds like my little brother, all right."

Eric blinked in wonder. And here he thought that Gid was the friendly one. Now he seemed much meaner than his brother. He doubted he could get up after such a beating. He discreetly stole a look at his massive paws as a cold shiver ran up his spine.

"He's lucky he doesn't have a busted head." Will snickered. "I've seen Gid take on four men and cut through them like hot butter. It wouldn't be the first one he gave a fella a concussion."

"These days, Comstock has the garden variety of outlaws." Sheriff White chuckled. "I wouldn't worry too much about them. Now, the boys we have captured, that's a different story. They're as dangerous a bunch as I've seen for neigh-on twenty years. They don't use fists. They'll be usin' guns iffin they escape."

A hint of a smile tugged at the edges of Gid's mouth as he nodded his head in recognition. He didn't like people doting on him for doing what he thought was right or teaching lessons to rude men. After the fight, he had let the woman paw, hug, and kiss him on the cheek. It seemed that every lady in the saloon wanted to be his friend.

Maybe being noticed wasn't so bad after all. Gid smiled at the thought.

While they were distracted, the sheriff took a fresh look at the brothers, sizing them up after all that had happened in the last couple of days. I was true that you couldn't judge a book by its cover, but then again, some things and people never change. The Crocketts appeared to be two such men. They certainly lived up to their reputation. If he had to take the prisoners back *alone*, he would have never made it.

"I love a good story if you know how to tell one." Will laughed. "I know who you are, too, Mr. Baker. You're the last of the mountain men and fur trappers."

"That's what they tell me. So, do you wanna hear what your brother did or not? I have a hankerin' to tell a good tale."

"I apologize for interrupting, Mr. Baker." Will smiled. The man sitting before them probably had more knowledge about the wilderness than all of them combined.

"Call me Jim. All my friends do. Now, where was I? Oh, yeah. Why, the women went wild when they saw Gid in action and immediately began kissing his cheeks, and he turned as red as a beet. Mind ya now, I wouldn't have done any different if they doted on me like that. I could only wish. One was so bold as to squeeze his biceps after she kissed his cheek. She saw that scar on his arm and outlined it with her finger."

"'That's just one of many, ma'am,' your brother replied, all humble like." It was suddenly apparent that

Jim was not only a mountain man, but he was a hell of a storyteller, too.

"At the girl's request, your brother pulled up his cotton shirt, showing several purple, spider-like scars. Muscles rippled across his arms and chest. The ladies touched the ancient wounds and cooed and awed." He had to stop and laugh when he saw Gid's face turn red. "Ain't I doin' a good job of tellin' what happened?"

Light slanted through the open window as dust danced in the sun's rays, falling into yellow squares on the floor. The train began to build steam in the boiler as a stream of black smoke rolled out of the smokestack. It was just about to get underway.

"When Gid is eatin', he doesn't take interruptions lightly. Especially when they can't seem to keep their mouths shut. Then again, you've been mighty quiet of late, Mr. Smith. What's the matter? Cat got your tongue?"

Eric frowned. "Weren't you afraid, Gid?"

"Until it started, I didn't know what was going on. Lots of brilliant ideas are risky. Plus, I'm hard to kill. Especially by four nitwits."

"Most of the cemeteries I've seen are full of men who claimed they were difficult to bury." Jim Baker laughed like he didn't have a care in the world. "Then again, I reckon most mountain men are a bit like you, Amigo."

Eric gave a little shudder when he thought about getting hit by Gid. Then his mind was drawn back to swinging at the end of a rope. Maybe his only real family was Ringo and the gang. Again, it occurred to him he might have made a mistake. Gid Crockett sounded damned mean when Mr. Baker was telling the story of how he whopped all four men alone. From the look on his face, it appeared he had enjoyed it.

He glanced at the El Paso law. Sheriff White had treated him well enough for now, but he saw how they dealt with criminals, and at the end of the day, that's what he was, like it or not. Even if they did as promised, and he got a lighter sentence, he knew how a man such as himself would fare behind bars. Maybe making new choices was the wrong thing to do. Eric was too confused to make up his mind. He was having difficulty weighing his options.

"And you think that I'm supposed to believe that?" Ranger Harvey asked as he spread his hands, but he was laughing. Still, it wasn't clear that he believed that Gid could beat four men at once or not. Especially the hard men that populated Comstock, regardless of what the sheriff said.

ERIC SMITH RECOVERED ENOUGH to hide his genuine emotions. He hid them with a mask of good-natured innocence. Still, a worm began to eat at his brain as he considered what would happen if the sheriff and the Crocketts didn't keep their word.

Suddenly, he felt both Will and James staring at him. It was like they all knew his secret as soon as his face was twisted with shock and disappointment. He felt they were all suddenly aware that Eric was having second thoughts. Every time he closed his eyes, he saw himself swinging from the end of a rope. Eric's guts turned to water, and he went as rigid as a block of ice.

He waited until the heat of the moment drained from his face.

Nobody can hear what you're thinking, fool. Careful now, or you're going to give yourself away.

Smoke came from the corner of the car in which the prisoners were. When the lawmen saw that it was only a smoldering attempt made up of their light jackets, they realized it was meant to distract their attention. Ringo looked at the lawmen defiantly, but the others looked as guilty as hell. That instant, they knew that somebody else would be waiting for them somewhere, and they wouldn't be far away.

"How did you fools manage to start a fire all trussed up like that?" Will Crockett asked, but then he looked away. He could feel that something wasn't right, even though he had yet to know what it was.

Sheriff White slid down the ladder and stood square in the middle of the street beside the tracks. He planted his feet wide as he blinked. It is evident that he was beyond angry and had descended to that dark place where men who upheld the law often went. The friendliness in his voice disappeared as it turned coldly polite.

A knot tightened Will's mouth. Still, the smile remained, but now it didn't reach his eyes and lost its meaning. He looked at Ringo like he was a dead tree: completely free of emotion. For him, this part of the job was automatic. He knew there was no time to think, or feelings would intervene, and he would lose his edge. He followed the sheriff out the door. They must have started the fire for something, and they planned to find out what it was.

As soon as two silhouettes stepped into the sunlight, a bullet roared out of the sheriff's barrel and closed the distance between his gun and his target as it shattered bone and ripped into his opponent's heart. When another man appeared, Will rolled across the ground as his pistols came up, one behind the other, squeezing both triggers at once. The recoil made the barrels jerk. When the bullets hit the bandit, his head snapped back, and his body followed. His heels dug in the dirt and toppled him over, spread-eagled on the ground.

When the train's fireman arrived, he was breathless and wheezing, his eyes full of excitement. "I've got the fire out, so we can go now. The engineer said he wants to get out of here and fast." He had hardly noticed the gunfight. Ever since the lawmen got on the train with their prisoners, they had encountered trouble at every stop and turn. The fireman climbed the ladder to the engine room and began stoking the boiler as the engineer started throwing levers. Black smoke poured from the teapot smokestack as the engine panted faster.

When the engineer released the brake lever, the massive wheels slipped before gaining traction. The couplings jerked one by one the entire length of the train. Finally, the locomotive lurched into motion as it gradually began to pick up speed.

CHAPTER FIFTEEN

LATE THAT NIGHT, RINGO SAT IN THE SHADOWS OF THE kerosene lamp. His eyes were ridged with red lines, and had large, puffy bags. He had hardly slept since they were captured. He kept an eye out, knowing that sooner or later the lawmen would slip up and he would have his chance, but if he was asleep, he might miss that special moment when opportunity opened its door and he would finally get away.

He didn't care if his gang members made it or not. When things got bad, they all knew it was every man for themselves. Still, there was one thing that Ringo felt he had to take care of before he left. He intended to shove a knife into Eric's heart as he watched life go out in his eyes. If he had to, he would take Smith with him, if he couldn't kill him then and there. If he got what he wanted in the end, it didn't matter how it worked out. Still, betrayal could never be forgiven. One way or another, he would see that Eric Smith died, and the sooner the better.

Moon knew he would have to take extra risks, but if

he let Eric get away with threatening to turn him and his gang in, he would never be able to trust anyone again. He would have to set an example and ensure that everyone left understood the message. That, in turn, would be relayed to places like El Paso, informing everyone that Ringo Moon wasn't to be betrayed.

Ringo carefully felt his belt. Unbeknownst to the lawmen, his belt buckle doubled as a knife, but he had to wait for the right moment to reveal his secret. Still, he felt confident that the time would come, and probably sooner rather than later. They were still two hundred miles from San Antonio and thirty miles more to Santa Clara. Moon didn't believe there was any way the lawmen were going to get that far before he and his men escaped, and if he was lucky, he would see the lawmen dead in the process.

Of course, he knew that killing sheriffs and deputies would make him more of a wanted man, but he also wanted to make a statement. If you came after Ringo Moon and his gang, you would have to pay the ultimate price because they weren't going down without a fight. For the last twenty years, he had been successful in his life of crime and violence and had no intention of giving it up now. Especially as the lawmen planned to hang them in the public square. If they went before Judge Roy Bean, they would swing for sure.

Still, he knew he had men out there who were willing to take the risk for the gold he would bestow on the men who broke them out and made them free men again. After all these years as a successful outlaw, he could easily afford it, and the fact was well known throughout West Texas, a region full of men of reckless blood who were willing to risk their lives for money.

Of course, there was his favorite, Buck. Still, he knew if it came to one or the other, they would both do what they had to escape, even if it meant giving up his men, if it meant he went free. There was little honor among thieves when the times were dire. Additionally, it was relatively easy for any successful outlaw gang leader to recruit new members. As far as loyalty, he knew that that would always be questionable. All he had to do was look at Eric—a man he never expected to have the balls to go against him, his longtime leader.

"COME ON. Get off your lazy asses and help me drag these logs to the train tracks. We need to build a big enough fire to scare the engineer, otherwise it won't work. If we stack the wood high enough, if he decides to ram it at full speed, it'll hit the cabin and should fill it with burning wood and cinders. If we do it right, it'll work out, one way or the other. But I figure he'll stop rather than take a chance."

Black Bart stared into the distance, and when he didn't see anything, he dropped to his hands and knees and put his ear to the steel rails.

"If we had the time, we could dig up a few railroad ties and pull off a link of track," Charles Boles alias, Black Bart, said. "That would be the cleanest way to derail the train.

"That'd be too much work, boss. It's enough of a pain in the ass to drag all these logs. They weigh a ton."

"Use your horse for the hard work. We can't take all day. As it is, we're runnin' late. Had we not received that telegram back in San Antonio, we'd have never even known about this opportunity. I'm gonna make sure that Ringo Moon pays us a pretty penny for busting him out. And here I was thinkin' we came all the way from California for nothing. Then again, with all the trains crisscrossing the country, nowhere is too far if it's worth enough money."

"I think I can hear it comin'," Jessy Gabbard said as he put his ear to the tracks. "We'd best hurry it up if we want to have the fire lit in time."

Ten minutes later, they set the kindling alight with the help of a can of kerosene. In minutes, flames leaped upward, sending cinders rising into the clear blue sky. As the heat increased, combined with the blazing Texan sun, they had to back away to keep their eyebrows, mustaches, and beards from getting singed.

Narrow hips, sun-darkened, thin-lined features beneath the turned-up brim of a faded Stetson. Black Bart's mouth was covered by a bushy mustache and pointed beard. He slipped his hat off, wiping his brow with his shirt sleeve, showing the receding hairline of an aging man. He wore a long duster coat and a bowler hat. Flour sacks with holes cut out for their eyes hung from their saddles.

He was much more meticulous than the notorious Ringo Moon, who Bart considered reckless to a fault. But since he was told he had buried gold from his dozens of robberies stashed halfway across West Texas, it was an unmissable opportunity.

The telegram said he was traveling with a sheriff and two deputies. One Sheriff White from El Paso and two hired sign-on deputies, so he didn't expect too much resistance. They waited close to the tracks where they hid their horses and Bart's buggy waited. He hated riding horses, so he hired a single-horse surrey to travel the hundred miles to the place he picked to stop the train.

The Englishman, Black Bart, was known for his courteous behavior during robberies. He seldom harmed the passengers of the stagecoaches, which was his preference. However, things were getting too hot to work, as renewed pressure from the law in Southern Oregon and Northern California was mounting.

So, they hopped on a train in Boise, westbound, finally taking the rails south to Texas, which was about as lawless as anywhere in the country. They had been on their way to El Paso when they got the telegram tipping them off about Ringo Moon's capture.

Of course, he didn't know the man personally and doubted he would ever become friends with such a scoundrel, but if the money was right, he and his men were up for the job, and they were ready to get their hands dirty. In Texas, few stagecoaches carried valuables anymore with the abundant presence of trains, which were much safer and harder to rob.

Charles E. Boles usually stuck with the Wells Fargo stages, but as times changed, he and many other outlaws had to adapt their ways accordingly. It was 1883, and little did he know this was the year he would lose his freedom.

As he watched the black blot in the distance grow, he wondered if he would have the opportunity to leave one of his clever poems after they set Ringo and his gang free. As soon as they received the payment, he planned for them to be on their way. Men like Moon made business riskier, and it was already dangerous enough.

The fifty-four-year-old outlaw was accompanied by mostly men his age. The majority of his crew of eight had been with him for years. He made it a point that each of them knew they worked exclusively for his gang and never took on jobs independently. As long as they followed his carefully developed plans, they knew they wouldn't be in jail, and their robbery attempts were almost always successful.

As the locomotive came closer, a mist of uncertainty clouded Bart's face. His voice got louder as his raw-boned cheeks tightened. "Is he gonna stop or not?" The glaring sun made them pull their hats lower, casting shadows over their eyes from their brims. The brakes locked as they screamed, iron against steel.

"See the sparks?" Jessy Gabbart, Bart's right-hand man, asked. "The engineers set the brakes, boss. He ain't gonna chance ramming such a big fire. Your plan worked like it always does. I bet this Ringo Moon ain't so smart."

The gang leader patiently waited for the nearing train with his thumbs hooked on his gun belt and a smile curled at the edge of his lips. "This is gonna be a piece of cake."

At first, Jessy showed concern momentarily, but then he relaxed into a grin. He had been riding with his boss for a long time, and his wit and intelligence had led them to many successful stagecoach robberies, most of which were carried out without a shot being fired. But something told him that today wouldn't be without violence. Ringo had a reputation for vengeance and needless killings.

A brittle silence hung over the gang as they waited for the train to finally pull to a complete stop. The other men stepped out of their saddles, letting their reins trail. They wanted to launch their attack close to the train so it wouldn't turn into a battle of long rifles.

Bart's pencil ceased to scratch the parchment for a moment as he stopped and thought, then began to write again. He hoped he had a chance to leave another poem, but he wasn't going to risk his life to do it. Still, he wanted to have one ready, just in case. He licked the tip and began to scribble again as the train came to a screeching halt.

———

FIRST CAME two toots from the steam whistle. They all instantly knew that something was up. When Will looked over at Ringo, he saw his eyes sparkle in anticipation. He had expected another attempt, and this one might be successful. They were in the middle of nowhere with no help to be found.

"Just like we expected, something else is up. Henry's not blowing that whistle for nothing." Will stuck his head out the window to look down the tracks as the wind ruffled his blond, graying hair. "We've got another fire out front, but there's no bridge around here. From the looks of all that smoke, I figure it's a doozy, too."

The Texas Ranger captain and his right-hand man were tight-jawed and solemn. Everybody pulled their guns.

"You fellas might think you have everybody else buffaloed, but not me—not by a long shot. You know what's waiting for us out there. How about we use Ringo here for a shield this time, Will? That should throw a wrench into the works and give us time to see what we're up against." Gid stared at Moon with a threatening look.

"Oh God," Texas Ranger Captain Harvy said while his man cursed, but it sounded more like a prayer. "I count nine of 'em, and there are five of us. We need to even out the odds a little."

As the country yawned wide, Will's spyglass inched over the expanse. "I could swear I saw that fella on a wanted poster somewhere. Yep, that's the outlaw I saw posted on the sheriff's office wall the last time we were in California. What was his name again?"

His eyes continued to crawl out into the distance, carefully pinpointing the outlaws' positions. They made themselves ready to jump off the train as soon as it stopped, unless the outlaws opened fire first, then they would use the passenger car as cover.

Gid grabbed the binoculars and huffed. "That looks like Black Bart and his bunch. Things have just gone from bad to worse. This here is a different caliber of outlaw than Ringo."

Everyone pulled their guns and held their breath as they waited for the train to jerk to a stop. When it did, the couplings clanged, one car at a time, until it all banged to a halt. For an instant, nobody moved as the steam engine panted like an old dog.

———

"I RECKON it's time to separate the chaff from the wheat."

Will raised his Colt-45 and fired point-blank at the rider just outside the window. The gang member's body jerked from the impact and toppled to the ground. Suddenly, everyone was firing bullets. Dozens of rounds from nine guns slammed into the wooden coach like a hundred woodpeckers hammering a tree. Shards of glass and wood splinters shot across the room like Indians' arrows.

Chunks of lead slammed into the wooden wagon, whined off rock and stone, as gun smoke hovered thick in the air, and the smell of cordite overwhelmed the smell of burning wood and coal.

At the same time, everybody started firing as bullets slammed into wood, steel, and flesh. The lawmen returned controlled, accurate fire from good cover. Suddenly, five outlaws lay on the ground, each one with a well-placed bullet in their hearts. That was when Bart saw it was time to cut their losses and escape before it was too late, and he ended up dead, along with his friends.

As Burt ran for his buggy and his men for their horses, they barely escaped with their lives, even though it had been two to one. In their escape, a dust cloud followed them like dogs chasing rabbits. The outlaw's horses ran through the dirt cloud in a pandemonium of teeth and white eyes. The lawmen listened as the sound of pounding hooves slowly disappeared into the distance.

The whole while Eric sat as mute as a tailor's mannequin, hoping that nobody noticed him and he didn't get shot, too, in the excitement of the moment. He was an outlaw, too, and he apparently had enemies on both sides of the law.

Gid spat, wiped his mouth, and stared at his brother, wondering what was going to happen next.

"I heard Black Bart's polite, but he's also hard-shelled and mean, that's for sure," Sheriff White said.

"His instincts are good. Had he stayed two more minutes, he would have probably ended his career as an outlaw."

Will looked across the carriage, and the floor was covered in broken glass and pieces of wood. Then he saw the piece of glass sticking out of Wayne Hazzar's right eyeball.

"Somebody get this out of my eye before it stabs my brain," Wayne cried out. "Am I gonna die, Ringo?"

"Of course you're not gonna die, fool." As Ringo reached over, the chains on his wrist rattled. He held Wayne's head and swiftly pulled the four-inch shard of window glass out of his eyeball. It turned a mushy, dull white. When he looked at the piece of glass, the pupil hung from the end on a slimy string of white.

"I wonder what the engineer is gonna do now," Will said.

No sooner than he said it, the cars' couplings began to clank as the engine came to life and began to move forward. Will stretched his head out the window and watched as the burning logs, now collapsed, were pushed aside by the massive cowcatcher.

The granite-faced outlaw, Ringo Moon, stared stonily at the traitor. Yet another attempt had been foiled.

CHAPTER SIXTEEN

THEY WATCHED AS THE TREBLING BACKDROP OF THE western horizon left the escaping black images like marionettes with the lowering sun at their backs. First the sound, then their shapes, finally dissolved into the wavering heat.

When the sun neared the horizon, a breeze stirred. It whispered through the trees. It gave relief after the glaring white light of daylight. The train and cars crossed before the sun, vanishing over the hill one by one. When they reappeared, they were black dots on the horizon.

When the yellow disk neared the rim, it sat squat, pulsating, and malevolent. Sparks from the teapot smokestack scampered down the plains. Simultaneously, on the opposite end of the world, a pumpkin moon ascended and grew until it seemed so big you felt you could reach out and touch it. The lobe-shaped moon climbed into the sky so high that it dimmed out the stars.

Under the moonlight, beclamored with yapping

coyotes, amid cries of owls, a wild boar lingered like a puppet from the heavens with his long mouth jabbering and saliva dripping from his tongue. Cinders from the train's smokestack yawned in the night winds.

They watched as a dozen teepees, visible in the middle of nowhere, appeared under the moonlight through the window. Tethered dogs howled at the edge of the Indian camp as they bared their teeth and snapped at the passing train.

A retinue of wolves trotted silently in single file behind the pack's leader. The alpha male occasionally looked over his shoulder to ensure they followed. They cast long shadows in the silvery moonlight.

Gid spat, wiped his mouth, and stared at his brother, wondering what was going to happen next. Without saying a word, Will's brother shrugged. Nobody knew what was in store for them now. They were a couple of hours from San Antonio, where they would stop to change trains and return the gold eagles and take the last stretch to Santa Clara and lock the prisoners up in Sheriff Parson's jail.

Jim Baker looked over, scratching his bushy beard, and squinted his intelligent eyes as they twinkled with mischief. "You boys made short work of them fellas. I was gonna jump in and help, but I began to feel sorry for the outlaws that attacked the train. They were clearly outclassed. I'd hate to find myself on the wrong side of your guns."

When Will glanced at Eric, he was clearly shaken up and thrown off his game. He had a puzzled look on his face, as if he was trying to figure something out but just couldn't quite put it together.

"Well, there's only one more stop for water and coal

before we hit San Antonio and the main railway station," Sheriff White said. "I figure if there's anyone still alive and willing, that's where they'll hit us next. We'll be stopping at night too, so the risks will be even higher."

"Well, let's take turns and try to get a few winks of sleep," Gid said. "We've been awake for neigh-on two days. Maybe we can bribe the first-class waiter to bring us a gallon pot of coffee. I figure we've got two more hours to go, plus the stop, and we'll be safe and sound within the city limits."

Everyone in the car dozed off and on because they were all exhausted from the endless action they had experienced since leaving El Paso. It was a miracle that they were all in one piece. The moon stood high overhead, casting silvery light across the countryside as the train continued to run clickity clack down the tracks. All the lawmen sat and dozed with their guns in their laps, ready for any challenge that arose. They felt it was only a matter of time before somebody had another go at freeing Ringo and his gang.

Even the outlaws were worn out, especially from the last encounter with Bart and his outlaw gang. They couldn't move because they were shackled to the wall, so all they could do was try to curl up into balls as small as possible and hope they didn't catch a stray bullet. The tension of the helplessness they felt was exhausting, so they were worn out, although they hadn't done anything but sit and watch as they prayed that the outlaws would win the day, and the sheriff, deputies, and the Texas Rangers were shot dead.

But so far, it just wasn't working out for Ringo, and now with every mile they passed, he felt his chances of escape were slipping away. So far, the men with badges had made short work of every attempt to win the prize for breaking Moon out. Now he wondered if there was anyone left brave enough to give it another go. Now, he felt his only chance was the refueling stop, not an hour away. If someone didn't intervene then, they might never come.

When the engine began to reduce speed, Ringo jolted awake, startling himself. He had tried as hard as he could not to fall asleep, but his body was exhausted and had given in to the wear and tear of the last couple of days.

When the locomotive came to a complete stop, clouds of smoke spewed from under the engine as the conductor released the valves and allowed the pressure to drop, as the machine continued to pant. Beams swung into position, protruding from tanks, as water was fed by gravity, and coal filled the fireman's bin. He and the conductor worked frantically so they could get underway again before something else occurred.

Will and Gid dropped down the ladder on the farthest side of the reloading station as they waited in the dark. The Texas Rangers climbed down the steps to the loading side of the operation, and Sheriff White stayed inside with his pistols pointing at the three wanted men. An evil smile crossed his face.

"You know, Ringo, you and your men are worth just as much dead as you are alive. I bet if your outlaw friends heard we had killed you and you boys, they wouldn't be chasing us all over the Texas countryside anymore, would they? Maybe I should just kill you now and end all this violence. I've never seen a man draw as much bloodshed as you have in the last day and a half.

With all the holdups, the run is gonna take two days when the train usually takes thirty hours. You've been a nuisance from the start."

"I know you're too much of a lawman to murder me in cold blood, with shackles on me no less. You ain't the same kind of man as I am. You're among the weak, and *I am* the strong. You see, were I in your boots, I wouldn't hesitate to kill you here and now, why I'd probably empty my gun in you just for fun. We *have* been a nuisance, ain't we?" He laughed like a madman at the end of his tether. "Nah, it's just like I thought. You don't have it in ya. It's a shame because if you did, you'd send tongues a-waggin."

"You know, Ringo, you're right about that. I ain't like you at all. None of us lawmen here today are anything like you, trash. And you won't be the ones to inherit the earth because men like me and the Crockets are here to keep the balance of things, so you outlaws don't take over the world."

"Why, don't he sound like a preacher, boys? Up there on your holier-than-me pedestal. Just because you wear that badge don't mean that you're any better than me."

But one of the two gang members still alive was missing an eye, and it took all he had to deal with the fact. The other was scared to death because, unlike Ringo, he believed the sheriff was going to shoot them dead. He didn't see why one of them hadn't already.

Of course, Eric was still sitting on the fence, and no matter what he did, he didn't intend to get into a gunfight with the likes of the Crocketts and the sheriff, let alone with a couple of Texas Rangers stirred into the mix.

Now, when he looked at it all, he saw that Ringo was

holding a losing hand, and he had better stay his course and stick to the lawmen. Maybe he would still get out of this alive if he kept his wits and his mouth shut. When he started talking was when he got into trouble in the first place. He knew he was too dumb to know the right thing to say.

Will and Gid walked up and down the length of the train, but found nothing out of order. For a moment, they thought they could see somebody in the shadows, but when they turned and ran, they saw it was no more than a few coyotes.

Everybody was surprised when nothing occurred, and they were ready to get underway again. They had managed to escape what they considered the most vulnerable spot of the entire journey. Now they were only a couple of hours from San Antonio.

The Crocketts and the Rangers climbed aboard just as the train jerked into motion. The mountain man continued sitting in the corner, watching everything that happened like he was memorizing all the stories he would tell in the future. It seemed that when the beaver was all trapped out and the buffalo gone, he took to storytelling more than anything else. He still took the occasional scouting job with the army to make ends meet, but he preferred to observe life rather than participate, and of course, repeat all that he saw.

"Is everything under control here?" Will asked. "I see you didn't have to shoot any of the prisoners. You're a good man, James White. I know that was your last chance to kill Ringo, and God knows he deserves it, but you're a better man than that. I thought about shooting him myself for all the trouble he's caused us, but I didn't have it in me either. I can see we're more alike every day."

As they talked, Eric saw their mouths move, but he didn't quite hear what they said. His mind had gone past fear, worry, and dread. From what he saw at this point, Ringo seemed to be hurtling into a free-fall descent into malice and self-destruction, and he didn't want to be a part of it. Maybe he was just realizing what the difference was between good and evil. He already knew he was slow.

Perhaps he was never taught the difference, but watching Will, Gid, and the sheriff, he began to understand. Especially when compared to Ringo, and he knew things about him that few men did. He was much more evil than anyone ever suspected—the things he had seen him do he even hated to think about because it gave him nightmares. Eric harrumphed and forced a grin.

Maybe I still have time to make things right. Until now, I didn't know the difference between right and wrong. Now it's as clear as water. Maybe I still have a chance to make things right and turn over a new leaf.

Will watched as Eric's face changed as though he had made some profound revelation. "Be decisive, Eric. Right or wrong, go for it and stick to your plan. The trail is full of flat squirrels."

For the briefest of moments, everything froze, like a picture, for Smith. He looked at Will and blinked like a bird. Then he grinned so broadly you could see his back teeth. He tried to calm himself down, pressing his lips into a tight smile, but his heart rate flew off the charts, and he nearly laughed.

"I'm gonna go and check the top of the carriages.

Gid, you can check the passenger cars and first class to make sure nobody's new on the train. Captain, maybe you and your Ranger can check the livestock car to make sure nobody's hiding in there."

Will pushed his way out of the door between the passenger cars and climbed the ladder to the roof. Then he made his way across the top of the cars, making no more noise than an alighting bird as the veins on his temples pulsated like fuses. He continued beneath the slow wheel of stars pulsating light years away, but he found no one hiding in the shadows to make another attempt at busting Ringo and his men out.

Moon sat there staring blankly into space like he had forgotten where he was. The bags under his eyes had grown bigger, and the whites were completely red. He knew that he had just about run out of time. He rubbed his neck, already feeling the invisible nooses biting at his skin.

The men stretched their necks out the window, angling to gulp cool morning air and tracking several spirals of smoke rising obliquely from somewhere just over the rise. It was outlined by light from the first hint of dawn on the eastern horizon.

"There she is," Sheriff White said. "San Antonio is just over that rise. In half an hour, we'll hit the city limits. Then the train slows down to a crawl, so they don't run over pedestrians, bicycles, and carriages."

The fiery disk rose with the color of steel, and the bake-oven air returned, but now they were in the city, and with all the buildings, it was stiflingly hot without a sign of a breeze. Everything wavered in the distance just above the ground from the heat.

As Eric looked out the window, he thought the city

was full of churlish-looking White men sucking their teeth and looking around with crazy eyes. He worried about being left alone in the passenger car with the Texas Rangers and Ringo Moon. Wayne was totally out of commission due to being blind in one eye, and Jessy had lost his nerve and had apparently given up all hope. He appeared to be waiting for his execution.

Inside the cattle and horse cars, animals stomped their hooves and stretched their necks as they squealed. They smelled all the strange city odors.

"When we stop, we don't wanna be walking through the city with these sacks of gold. We'd better take our horses, otherwise, if we have trouble, we won't be able to move quickly. Gid. I'll go back and get three horses saddled. If you and your Ranger would be so kind, Captain, as to watch these outlaws until we return, it would be mighty appreciated. We don't wanna ride all the way to Santa Clara with so much gold. That will keep the local bandits off our backs."

As soon as they mounted the horses, the sheriff neck-reined his stallion toward the middle of the street as Will and Gid urged theirs with rowels to their flanks. Beige sacks with *US MAIL* stamped onto the side in black letters, hung over their horses' necks. Will's right fingers drummed on the grip of his Colt. Their eyes carefully scanned the street. There in the middle of the block, they saw the sign they were looking for.

They watched a pack of wild dogs roaming the edge of a narrow alley. They shied and backed away, save one. It stood its ground and barked at the people on the streets. A woman with a broom came rushing out of the door and shooed him away. They were after table scraps from the restaurant next door.

When they pulled up in front of the National Bank of Texas, they sighed a breath of relief. They carefully looked around before they dismounted.

"Can you lug all four sacks in by yourself, Sheriff? That way, Gid and I can stand guard out here at the front doors. We don't wanna lose those gold eagles again, do we?"

"I'll take 'em in, two at a time. I sent a telegram to the bank just before we left El Paso, so they'll be waitin' on the deposit. I told them to have all the papers in order because we wouldn't have time to linger. Keep a sharp eye out, men. We're just about to cross the finish line."

CHAPTER SEVENTEEN

"HOW ABOUT ONE OF YOU SMART ASSES COME UP WITH something clever to say now that the sheriff ain't here to save your hides. I've had my differences with the Comanche and Apache, but I can still see their side of things because we've settled on their land. But when it comes to outlaws, I have no sympathy at all. I see you're not so brave now that you don't have the sheriff and his deputies to make sure nobody harms ya. But ya see, now you're mine." Captain Gus Harvy spat a brown stream of juice on the front of Ringo's shirt.

"I ain't one of them anymore," Eric huffed, as he tried to push himself deeper into the corner. "I already made a deal with the sheriff and the Crockett brothers. I'm what you call a star witness. I'm on the same side as y'all now."

"Not in my book, you ain't. For me, you're nothin' but another no-good thieving outlaw and murderer. If you were lying on the ground on fire, I wouldn't piss on you to put it out. So don't come with your sob stories, boy, 'cause they don't hold water with me. You're no better than that trash-talking boss of yours."

"Whatcha say, Ringo?" Ranger Jackson asked. "How about we have a little contest. Do you like to play games, Moon? I sure do—especially if it's with someone like you. I'm sure you're gonna love it."

Jimmy made a show while removing five of the six bullets from his heavy 1847 Colt Walker single-action revolver. It was the Rangers' choice for its firing power, and it could be used as a club at a weight of four and a half pounds. He ejected five bullets and then slipped them into his shirt pocket. Then he spun the chamber until it stopped, holding it up to his ear as it clicked. When he drew back the hammer. The metallic sound made Ringo jump. The look in the Texas Ranger's eyes told the story.

"You think I'm bluffin', do ya?" A grin spread across his face.

Ringo shook his head from side to side as he said, "No, no, no, mister. I know you ain't bluffin'."

The Ranger pulled the trigger with an expressionless face. It was as if he didn't really care if the gun went off or not. A dull click was all they heard, but when Ringo looked down, he saw that the wooden bench under him was wet with warm piss. He frowned when he saw he had wet himself. For the first time he could remember, he was terrified. He knew that he was facing his imminent death. When he looked into the Ranger's eyes with the pistol, a cold chill shiver ran up his spine, and his teeth began to chatter.

Jimmy spun the six-chamber cylinder again, making it click until it came to a rest on a mystery. Was there a bullet head under the steel hammer, or was it empty like the last one? Ringo's eyes spread wide as he looked down at the dark barrel again, maybe for the last time.

"Are you ready to die, Mr. Moon? You'd best make your peace with your maker. I've got a feeling that this is the one. You wanna make a wager on this, Captain? A gold eagle says this one's it."

Now Ringo's shoulders shuddered as he broke down and began to cry. The stress of the last two days had left him shattered, and he knew that no one else was coming to try to save him, no matter how much money he had buried across West Texas. Now the gold and silver would go to waste because only he and the simpleton knew where it was all buried, and to him, it seemed like he was staring death in the face.

Right then, he would trade it all for his freedom, but it didn't look like he was going to get his wish. He watched as the Ranger's finger slipped into the trigger guard again and began to put six pounds of pressure on the trigger.

"Please don't kill me, mister! I don't wanna die like this! I repent. Have some compassion for a poor, lost soul. I know I'm a sinner, but I promise I'll walk the straight and narrow if you don't shoot me now." He interlocked his fingers, making his chains jingle. "Please, God, don't let them do this to me."

"That's what I thought. You're a coward to boot. Do you see what your boss is made of when the time comes, fellas? He's no more than a whining wreck. I don't think that God is listenin' to ya, Ringo. Come on, boy, it's your time to go."

"That's the way of the world, fool—to bloom, wither and die," Ranger Captain Harvey snickered. "You're like a poisonous weed that needs to be killed so you don't taint our society."

Then Ranger Jackson pulled the trigger again. The click came, but the blast didn't follow. Again, Ringo gobbled air as his bloodless face stared on in horror. He was so dizzy that he was about to pass out.

"You're a no-good coward yourself, Ranger," Wayne growled as he stared out of one eye. It was clouded with clotted blood, and a pinkish liquid wept down his cheek. "Pickin' on a man in chains. Take the irons off, and I'll show ya what kind of man I am."

When the blow came, it was lightning fast. Wayne didn't know what hit him as he went out like a light. An egg-sized bump rose on the side of his head as a rivulet of blood cut a path through his dust-covered face. As soon as he was hit by the barrel, his head spun, making him nearly black out.

"That'll teach you to sass me, fool. I knew one of you would take the bait. Now, where were we? Oh, that's right." He spun the chamber again as it clicked to a stop. Ringo felt that his luck was just about to run out.

WHEN THEY PULLED up to the watering trough in front of the bank, their horses dapped their mouths as they rose and lowered their dripping heads. They drank deeply from the crystal-clear water as beads streamed off their hairy chins.

Will leaned over his paint's head and whispered something into his ear as the sheriff gave him an odd look. He knew the Crocketts had skills second to none, but now he wondered if they also spoke to their animals. Will pulled a carrot from his pocket and fed it into his horse's mouth. His nose moved softly against Crockett's palm, licking his salty perspiration. He whispered into his ear like he was family.

The iron shoes rang loudly under their horses' hooves, as they shuffled their legs and rolled their eyes as their riders pulled back on the reins. Sheriff White stepped down, taking five strides to the door as Will grabbed his horses' reins just above the bit ring. James disappeared behind the two guards. The armed men held eight-gauge shotguns in their fists, and they were cocked and ready to fire. Everyone had been warned that an important shipment was arriving on the El Paso to San Antonio train.

The snort of an animal came from less than a stone's throw away. The Crocketts pulled their pistols and swung them toward the movement. The blood drained from the preacher's face as he rode a donkey out of a darkened alley beside the bank. He quickly wheeled the animal around and disappeared back into the shadows. The brothers let out long sighs and turned back to their objective.

Gid forced his eyelids to lower slightly until he was peering through slits with bullet eyes. The bright sunlight made things waver as long shadows formed on their western side.

Will put his guns away as his hands gripped over the other, leaning on the saddle horn as he patiently waited. But his eyes didn't linger. He kept a sharp watch on his surroundings while appearing not to be paying attention.

Long strides took the sheriff to the doorway with the mail sacks over his shoulders. He was in and out in minutes for the other two satchels, then he disappeared behind the double doors as two armed guards stood beside them. They turned a key in the lock and blocked the entrance. Nobody was getting in or out without their permission.

After a few minutes, the key rattled in the lock again, followed by the sound of squeaking hinges. The sheriff appeared with a document in his hands confirming the return of the stolen money. They even had the tally books that were originally inside the sacks, so they knew how much money was due to each account owner. Of course, the money for the party in El Paso was lost, but most of the stolen money was returned. Now, all they had to do was deal with the prisoners.

"Well, then, now that that business is done, let's get going. We still have work to do, and I plan to be finished by the end of the day." Will pressed his heels into his paint's flanks as his mouth hinted at a smile.

All three cocked their ears to a sound that was still a whisper. As it became louder, they heard the familiar pitch to the clamor of a stagecoach. They saw the driver throw his boot at the brake lever as it nearly jackknifed to a stop, sliding around a corner. The dust slowly began to settle. When they looked toward the end of the street, they saw big black puffs of smoke from the massive iron locomotive.

The world was changing right before their very eyes. The creaking, churning of wheels and jingling harnesses came racing by in an explosion of wood, leather, and horseflesh. They turned their heads as it dangerously passed by in a flash of red. Dust chased the wheels down the street as the whip cracked over the six-horse team's heads.

Gid still held his revolving pistols at his sides. The sun claimed it was eight o'clock. If they got moving soon, they would be in Santa Clara in time to tend to the horses and catch a noon lunch.

"Well, now that that's taken care of, we only have one last chore to do." The sheriff smiled. "Then all this mess will officially be out of our hands. Your boy's help has meant the world to me. I know now that I would never have made it had you two not been along. Things got a mite more complicated than I expected. But we're nearly there now. I figure I'll stay in Santa Clara for a few days and see if the judge shows. I would like to see how that trial pans out. If you two wanna join me, you're welcome. We can charge the state for the expenses. You're both still deputies until I formally sign you off. No sense letting a nice room and a bath with all the food we want pass us by. Mind you now, I never take advantage of such expenses, but I believe that the three of us have earned it."

"I doubt the folks in Santa Clara will complain after we saved their hard-earned savings." Will smiled. "I think that we'll take you up on that offer, James. But we'd better wait until we get there first. There's still thirty miles to go before we're home free."

"Why, I like the idea of all the food I can eat." Gid laughed. "Maybe by the time we leave, they won't think it's such a bargain. Not after I eat them out of house and home."

As the rush hour began, they slowed their horses, picking their way through the masses of people, wagons, carts, and wheelbarrows. They had their direction. All they had to do was follow the black puffs of smoke at the end of the street. But now they were in a city of over twenty thousand inhabitants.

———

"WHAT'S the meaning of this, Captain Harvey—Ranger Jackson?" Sheriff White asked as soon as he stepped into the passenger car.

Both Texas Rangers stood above Ringo with their guns in their hands. Blood ran down Wayne's face from the gash on the side of his head. Now he was blind in one eye and too dizzy to use the one he could still see through.

"They were gonna kill me, Sheriff," Ringo cried. "They were playin' Russian roulette with my head. Go ahead. Just ask my boys. They'll tell ya the truth."

To everyone's shock and without a word, Ranger Jackson raised his revolver, snuggled the barrel up against Moon's head, and pulled the trigger six times. Each time, Ringo's eyes squeezed shut. When he came to the sixth and last chamber, he began to cry openly. When the hammer fell on another empty chamber, he blinked his eyes in surprise that he was still alive.

"There was never a bullet in the chamber in the first place, dumbass. I'm not daft, nor am I a killer. But when I have the chance to teach an outlaw a lesson, I rarely pass, if the opportunity arises." He smiled despite the stern face of the sheriff.

Gid surprised everyone and began to laugh. "That's a good one, Ranger Jackson. I'll have to remember that one. I bet that's a good way to get an outlaw to talk."

"It sure is a good way to make 'em cry like babies." Jackson chuckled. "Just look at all the tear streaks down his face. Why, he cried a river while praying to God, but I doubt the Lord Almighty was listening. Not to trash like him."

Ringo looked questioningly from the sheriff and back to the Rangers again. He had been made a fool of, and it happened in the blink of an eye. He suddenly realized he wasn't in the same league as these lawmen. He had apparently mistaken them for someone else.

"So, you weren't gonna kill me after all?" Ringo asked, shocked. "You're a mean bastard, is what you are."

"At least I don't murder innocent souls like you," Jackson said as he slowly reloaded his large pistol. The powder load in each round was huge.

It was so real to him that Ringo could hardly believe it was all fake. He looked at Wayne and Jessy, but they turned away, embarrassed. They had seen him so scared that he had peed his pants. Moon knew he would never live this one down. He suddenly felt utterly defeated. He plopped down on the wooden bench seat, resigned from everything. He was so stunned that he acted like he didn't know that anybody else was even there. He began to mumble to himself like he was all alone.

"I'll put the horses back in the livestock car," Gid said. "You can tend to these dangerous Texas Rangers, big brother." He laughed again.

CHAPTER EIGHTEEN

As the train gained speed again, they rushed toward their destination, believing the danger had passed. In a couple of hours, they would be safe, and their prisoners would be behind bars where they belonged.

As they rode down the tracks, gaining speed, they watched as the black specks in the distance gradually grew as they came nearer. Finally, the specks turned into horses and riders. When they looked at them through their spyglasses, they saw it was the young Lotsee and his war party of Comanche boys. The silhouette of the first Indian crept across the distance like an animal, slow and with his back arched. He was the advance scout. He flashed a small piece of mirror against the sun and gave the braves the signal.

It looked like Comanche Indians running into sight, beating their ponies into a whirlwind as they screamed across the countryside with blood in their eyes, baring their teeth. Their long black hair fluttered in the wind as they rode at a sprint, all in a beeline for the train.

There was something in their eyes that made you know they weren't going to stop, no matter what. It was their final charge in a hopeless battle for freedom and a way of life on the verge of extinction.

"There are your friends again," Gid said to the Rangers. "I wonder what those boys want now." He had another look through his binoculars and frowned. "From here, it looks like they're serious."

"They're just some kids having fun. They sure do put on a show, though, don't they?" The sheriff chuckled, still thinking it was all a show, just like they did before.

Hinges creaked as the door at the end of the carriage began to open, and the men in the passenger carriage held their breaths. But it was just Will returning with another pot of hot coffee.

"The coast is clear here on the train. It looks like your luck has run out, Ringo."

When Will looked through his spyglass again, he saw the contrast of war paint against the Indian boys' dusty bodies. When he heard the arrow whine past his ear through the broken window, he knew the young Comanche warriors weren't playing. Apparently, this time, they were as serious as death.

"What the hell?" Sheriff White asked. "Are they really shootin' at us? But I thought we were all friends."

"I doubt any Indians out West think any White man is their friend after takin' all their land and running them onto reservations. Remember, lots of those who didn't bend a knee died where they rebelled. Somehow, these boys slipped through the cracks." Will removed the glasses from his eyes and wiped his brow with his sleeve.

Soon, bullets were pinging off the side of the passenger carriage. It was hard to tell how much damage they were doing because the car was already shot all to hell, and the windows were all broken. When they walked, bits of glass and broken wood crunched under their feet.

They felt their patience quickly wear away. "I never thought these young men would make a bad turn like this. I reckon all we can do is fight back," Sheriff White said.

They had been trying to keep these youngsters out of trouble, but it appeared that now they had gone too far, and it was too late. Now that they had attacked a train full of White people, and some were important from back east. They had passed the point of no return.

"I wonder what they want this time," Will said. "What's clear is they ain't friendly anymore. I wonder what happened. Those bullets and arrows say they're playing for keeps. Something has them all riled up."

Projectiles lofted across a blue sky void of clouds. They whistled like ducks flying at unbelievable speeds. An Indian ran into sight, beating his pony into a whirlwind as he launched a lance that sailed through the passenger car window, stabbing the outlaw Jones in the leg. It split his tibia into two, making him cry out in pain. Now, two of the remaining outlaws were wounded.

Hostile warriors screamed across the countryside with blood in their eyes as they bared their teeth. Their Indian ponies heaved for air as they pushed them to their limits. The young warriors attacked with wild eyes. They all knew they were on a mission, and if they failed, they would surely die. Still, they continued because they had nowhere else to turn. It was fight or starve.

They all focused on the slight possibility of newfound freedom, although they all knew deep down it was an illusion.

When the lawmen opened fire, the young warrior braves went down like ducks at a shooting contest at a carnival. Not one of the men with badges missed leaving a dozen warriors lying on the ground dead or bleeding out in less than five minutes. If they were accurate with their pistols, they were even more deadly with their rifles. Especially Will's Sharps with a range of up to a thousand yards and Gid's skills with his 1873, 44-caliber Winchester rifle. With their thirty-inch barrel, they were accurate to a fault.

Will shook his head wearily, clearing his throat of disappointment before speaking. "If only they had listened and come back to me when they wanted something to eat, they'd all still be alive. I hate to see youngins lose their lives for nothing. I wonder what got into 'em."

"Sometimes a quirk of fate makes you a housecat instead of a tiger. For some reason, these boys made all the wrong choices." Sheriff James White shook his head in disappointment.

Will heard another arrow whine past his ear and fired the last shot. It wasn't until the gun smoke cleared that he saw who it was he had hit. He hit his bullseye, knowing the young man wouldn't survive. It made his heart sink.

———

WHEN LOTSEE FELT THE BLOW, the wind rushed through his ears, and a red flash seared across his brain, and he blacked out. He found himself staring up at the sky as vultures circled overhead. Everything was spinning, and he saw stars. He shook his head to remove the cobwebs, then pushed himself up and onto his elbows as he looked across the distance, struggling for air. He saw his friends lying in pools of blood. He had unwittingly betrayed them and sent them to their deaths along with himself.

War paint contrasted with their dusty bodies. Thickening blood stained Lotsee's chest as his heart struggled to continue to beat. Three white lines of war paint ran across his brow, and white hands were painted on his horse's flanks. But the hate and blood and violence had vanished as he felt his life seeping away. He could feel the warm, damp puddle form under his body and knew that he only had seconds to live. He felt his heart struggle to continue beating.

With the wad in his cheek, the sheriff's lips hardly moved when he talked. He slowly shifted his chew to the opposite jaw. "I reckon those Indians the Texas Rangers were looking after made a bad decision when they decided to attack us. Then again, they should have known better. The captain won't have to worry about 'em anymore."

"Can you hear me, Lotsee?" Will asked as he kneeled beside the dying boy.

The Indian kid nodded as tears of defeat welled in his eyes. He tried to smile through blood-stained teeth.

"Why in the world did you try to do something so stupid?" Will asked. "Didn't you know you could come to Gid and me if you needed something to eat?"

"We are poor, and some White man paid us a gold eagle to attack the train before it hit Santa Clara. Ten dollars is a lot of money for a poor Indian." He fished in his pocket and pulled out a yellow, shiny coin with a figure stamped on the side. "He promised us another one when we completed our job. But I led my warriors to their deaths." Lotsee was struggling to breathe, using his last breaths to talk.

"So, you're their war chief, eh," Will said as he took Lotsee's head in his hands and carefully brushed his hair out of his face. He knew the boy didn't want to die alone, so he softly helped usher him on his way.

"No, I am the oldest. None of us were really warriors, so there was no real leader. Now we are no more than dead boys. I'm sixteen, so I should have known better."

"Growing up too fast is as dangerous as a bullet out here in Texas. It's not your fault, son. Had you been born in different times, you'd have made a fine warrior. Maybe even a chief."

Will saw Lotsee's eyes shift suddenly. He felt his little brother solemnly looking over his shoulder.

"Thank you," he mouthed, but no words came. He was too tired to speak.

Then Lotsee's eyes rolled back into his head. Will used his fingers to gently close his eyelids, letting the young boy rest in peace. He cooed at his bravery as he passed. One moment he was there, and the next he was gone to the Indian spirit world with his friends.

"It's a damned shame to see boys die needlessly," Gid said. "If only he had someone to guide him, he would have made a fine man one day."

"Would've, could've. It don't matter anymore anyway. They came at us, boys," James whispered, not wanting to break the spell. "There was nothing different we could have done. Life's hard like that out here in the Texan Badlands. Not every box is full of chocolates."

"At least we can bury Lotsee, can't we?" Gid asked. He was so shocked that the blood drained from his face. They were used to shooting outlaws, but this was something totally different. "They were just innocent boys caught in a grown-up's world."

"Burying them is not the Comanche way," James replied. "It's best we leave them where they lie. If they have people around here, someone will come and give them a proper Indian burial. If we mess with them, they might take offense, and then we'd have another mess. I heard that for a warrior to be taken off by the birds is an honorable burial. They make a six-foot-tall platform so they can stare at the sun with dead eyes and feed the vultures. There's nothing more here that we can do. Tell Robert, the engineer, that we'll be heading out again as soon as he's ready. I've lost count of the number of times we've stopped since El Paso."

They saw the smoke billowing out of the stack as the engine began to gain steam. Then the big fifty-four-inch wheels spun, lacking traction. Finally, they bit and took hold, and the locomotive jerked into motion yet again. The couplings clanged, and the entire train, with all its cars and caboose, jolted and immediately began to pick up speed. In no time, it was roaring down the tracks yet again.

———

EARLY THAT MORNING, the Comanche youngsters were camping in a cluster of trees. Cinders climbed skyward as they rose on thermal currents created by the flames of their campfire. Their shadows danced on the young warriors' faces as they waited, staring hungrily. The smell of the last of the horse's flank steaks sizzled as their mouths watered and stomachs grumbled.

The young Comanche warriors sat in a circle. They couldn't take their eyes off the grilling meat. Of course, they were accustomed to being hungry, but up until then, they had managed to get by. Still, foraging for food was becoming more difficult by the day. They hadn't seen any worthy game animals for over a week.

The last time they saw a buffalo was when they were still little children. Back then, the countryside was abundant with elk and white-tailed deer, as well. Little by little, the White people were making it impossible for the American Indians to survive off the land like they had in recent years. Eventually, they would all be forced onto reservations or would starve like many had already done in the past.

Sometimes, they received handouts from the Texas Rangers, and a deputy sheriff gave them a longhorn to eat. But after today, they would be scrounging for food yet again. The days of easy hunting with plentiful buffalo had long passed, and even elk and deer were scarcer every day with the constant advancement of White people from back East. Everywhere they looked, they saw hunters with sophisticated guns. They knew that soon there would be no wild game for the Indians.

Of course, they were aware they should already be on reservations, but they wanted to live their last years, weeks, or days as free men, even if they were only boys. Still, they knew they had no future, so they recklessly rode across the state, making do the best they could. At this point, everyone was a potential enemy or threat.

Lotsee was the first one of them to see the single rider near their camp. The man looked like he was part Indian and part White man. Since there were a dozen and he was only one, they let him advance as they carefully followed his movements with a few rifles. Nobody was to be trusted at this point. When he came close enough, they could see his long-hooked nose on his face.

"I come in peace with gifts," the man said in a strange accent. Lotsee nodded, raising an eyebrow. "I have two gold coins for you if you do me a favor."

The stranger pulled a gold eagle out of a vest pocket. He flicked it in the air as it tumbled through space until Lotsee snatched it with lightning speed. It disappeared into his closed fist.

Then, just to confirm, he put it between his teeth and bit down to see if it was real. He smiled, asking, "What do you want in return? Gold coins don't come free. Even an Indian like me knows that."

"There you have your gold eagle. Attack the train from San Antonio to Santa Clara, and there will be another one just like that waiting for you when you're done. Friends of mine are being held captive by White men with badges. If you free these four men, you will have twenty dollars. But you'll have to be quick because the train is nearing its destination."

"How do we know you will pay us if and when we are successful?" Lotsee asked.

"How do I know you won't take my ten dollars and not do as I asked? I have put my trust in you, so now you must put your trust in me." The stranger forced a smile, but Lotsee saw it didn't reach his eyes.

The war party leader nodded as though deep in

thought, but inside, he was so excited he was having a hard time hiding it. Twenty dollars for food would last them for many months. If they were careful, maybe a year. Two gold eagles weren't much to most White people, but to these poor Comanche, it was a fortune.

"All right. We will do as you request, and I find the payment fair. How will we locate you when we return? If we return?"

"Don't mind that. I will find you just like I did now. Do we have a deal or not?"

Lotsee nodded, and they spat on their palms and shook hands, sealing the pact. The Indian leader looked at the man bearing gifts with weary eyes. He knew that nothing in this life came for free, but at this point, they were desperate and had little choice.

Without another word, the stranger stood, climbed back into his saddle, wheeling the horse around and leaving the way he came at a slow, confident walk.

"I forgot to ask his name," Lotsee said.

"He didn't ask for our names either. Something smells bad here, and it's not rotten meat."

"Still, what have we got to lose but our lives? We've been risking them ever since we refused to go to the reservation. We are worthless without money or even food anyway. We must take a chance and hope the Indian spirits protect us. Perhaps they have sent us a gift."

He rubbed the shiny coin on his tattered buckskin shirt, then studied the imprint. He observed it featured the iconic *Liberty Head* surrounded by thirteen stars. Little did he know they represented the thirteen original states that had been the British colonies. It was one of the prettiest things he had ever seen.

"Look how shiny it is." Lotsee held it up to the sunlight as it sparkled. "It is the first gold I have ever held in my hands. I hope it won't be the last." All twelve took turns, feeling its weight and marveling at how it sparkled in the sunlight.

"Break up the camp and clean everything up. We don't want to leave any traces of our presence in case we encounter trouble. I would imagine if they were the lawmen we saw before, they will shoot back this time. Their kindness will only go so far. Now we will be the aggressors. Prepare yourselves, my brothers. For some of us, it will be our time to die."

———

IN AN HOUR, there wasn't a trace of their camp, and they were all mounted, ready to ride for the shiny steel tracks that run between San Antonio and Santa Clara. Of course, none of them had any idea of how to stop a train. Even most American outlaws found it too much of a challenge and opted for easier targets.

But if they had to try to free a White man from the law to make twenty dollars, then they would have to figure it out while they commenced the fight. They knew such opportunities didn't repeat themselves, and as it was, they were at the end of their tether.

For such poor Indians, twenty American dollars represented more money than they could even imagine, and they were all ready to risk their lives to get it, no matter how risky it was. This would determine their future as warriors, or there would be no future at all.

CHAPTER NINETEEN

As soon as they got Santa Clara back in sight, Ringo's hopes fell through the floor. Eric was so nervous that he could hardly sit still, even though he had been repeatedly promised he would be rewarded for his help. Now that he had discovered the difference between right and wrong, he was willing to do everything he could to make amends. If necessary, even doing time in prison.

All he wanted was to have a clean sheet when all of this was over and be able to turn a page in his life. Whether Ringo, Wayne, and Jessy hung, he no longer cared one way or another. He was happy just to have a chance to start over again. He left himself to the mercy of the lawmen who captured him, whom he now trusted, and eventually the judge.

Anything was better than continuing as he had been for the last few years. Suddenly, he knew what honesty and freedom meant. They weren't a given and had to be earned. This was another lesson these men had taught him. Until they met, he had never had honorable friends. Everyone he knew was an outlaw of one caliber or another, so he had nothing to compare to.

Before Will, Gid, and the sheriff, he had never been in contact with decent men. Now he saw and knew them for what they were, and he was doing everything in his power to make amends. He felt embarrassed that he had had second thoughts. Now he was thankful that he had never revealed his confused feelings to his newfound friends. In that he had been lucky for a change. Until then, the only luck he knew had been *bad*.

They felt it when the engine began to slow, and the rocking of the cars wasn't as turbulent. Less smoke rose from the teapot smokestack, and more steam clouded the sides of the massive boiler. What surprised everyone in the prisoner carriage, the outlaws included, was the dense crowd of people waiting for the train to arrive. It was much larger than the population of the small town of a thousand six hundred men, women, and children, although the latter were fewer in numbers. At this point, Santa Clara still mainly consisted of males.

They heard angry shouts through the broken windows. People hastily waved their fists in the air to show their anger. These were all the people from the county who had deposited their hard-earned money in the bank in San Antonio, only to have it stolen on its way to the renovated savings and loan in town. Will and Gid exchanged knowing looks. They both knew a dangerous crowd when they saw one. A glance at the sheriff said that he recognized it, too.

The original area around Santa Clara was attractive to the German settler population. The town's growth was primarily driven by the agricultural opportunities available. In the immediate area, construction had begun on industries such as steam and grist mills, cotton gins, and stores and warehouses, indicating a burgeoning economy.

The land around the growing town was renowned for its rich soil and expansive open spaces, which supported a thriving farming and ranching community. Crops and cattle were significant draws in the economy, attracting hundreds of settlers. Mexican immigrants were also welcome, as they came from the nearby border, only 175 miles away in Piedras Negras.

The up-and-coming boomtown already had a school and church, indicating the development of community infrastructure and social institutions. The population was set to grow by forty percent by the end of the decade. Guadalupe County was officially put on the map.

"What the hell is all this ruckus?" Gid asked, perplexed by the number of people on the streets of the usually quiet town. "There must be everybody in the whole county here, and they look like they're dammed-well riled up."

"Somebody must have sent wires on the telegraph from the places we've been through advising that we were coming with the prisoners who stole these folks' money. If you look closely, it seems more like an angry mob than a carnival or circus arriving in town."

"That means the circus is us, don't it?" Gib asked. "I don't think I like where this is going."

"Do you smell that odor, boys? It smells like boiling tar and feathers to me," the sheriff said. Then he spat the bad taste in his mouth out the window, but it didn't help. "Right now, we've gotta focus on getting these four to Sheriff Parson's office and in the jail cells to protect them from this crowd."

Will levered a round into his Winchester rifle, and Gid followed suit. "As soon as the train comes to a stop, we'll go out first and stand guard on either side of the stairs. Then you push them out at gunpoint. Let Eric lead the way. That should help keep them in line. Did you hear that, Ringo? If you escape now, I won't be able to save you. You'll be at the mercy of this crowd out there waitin' on us."

Will swung down from the steps to the carriage, pushed his fists into the small of his back, arching away the stiffness brought on by sitting on the hard wooden benches for two days straight and with little sleep. Then he reached up for his rifle, leaning on the railing. All the while, Gid had things covered from the platform.

"Come on down, little brother. I've got ya covered."

Will pulled at his shirt. It was stuck to his body with sweat. The overhead sun pushed more heat into the streets of the small town.

Ringo struggled to mask his frustration and contempt. But no matter what he did, his hatred for the Crocketts and that El Paso sheriff was something that he couldn't hide. Somehow, he still had some hope of getting out of his predicament alive. He couldn't see the writing on the wall due to his lack of insight. It must have been because he had gone for so many years and never been caught, but now he was going to pay for his crimes.

"Come on, fools. On your feet. That means now."

Sheriff White waved his pistol toward the exit. "If you don't act up, we might make it to jail. That's about the only place you'll be safe right now."

The outlaws reluctantly followed Eric out the door and down the steps. The sheriff was right behind them with pistols in both his fists. He did a balancing act as he carefully climbed down the ladder. He could see the angry look in the crowd's eyes.

When Will and Gid heard the shot ring out, they swung their rifles in the direction of the sound. The hot lead seared across Sheriff White's hip, creating a line of hot fire. It felt like a bullwhip's popper slicing through his skin.

"I'm hit! It must have been a stray bullet from the mob."

The sheriff's breath came in ragged gasps as he fought to remain standing. His body obeyed his mind's demands as he struggled with being shot. Then he looked down, and all he saw was blood. Still, he knew the wound wasn't mortal. Luckily for him, it was a *through-and-through*.

"I'm hit but I ain't dead," James said through gritted teeth. "It'll take more than a stray shot to kill me." A long cheroot was clamped in his sneer as he gritted his teeth against the pain.

"Watch yourselves now," Gid said as he eyed the angry citizens. "These folks ain't thinkin' straight, so all our lives are at risk. Easy does it, amigos."

"Everybody, stand back. I'm El Paso Sheriff James White, and we've gotta escort the train robbers to Sheriff Parson's jail. Now settle down, folks, and nobody will get hurt. I'd hate to shoot one of my own kind. As you can see, one of y'all already shot me in the thigh, so I ain't in the mood for mischief. Move aside! We've not only recovered the train robbers we deposited your money safely back in the San Antonio bank. Now let us do our job. There's nothing more to see here."

Once the crowd saw that somebody's reckless behavior had shot a sheriff, they were stunned. This gave the lawmen a few minutes to execute their plan. Everyone was in shock, so they let them pass without a word.

"Keep moving, gentlemen," Will said as he rushed the string of lawmen and prisoners along. "It's right there in the middle of the block."

––––––––

THEY QUICKLY HEADED for the building with a large white star painted on the window. Boot heels hammered the plank porch as they walked through the open door.

"Sheriff Parson. It's been a while. I assume you know why we're here, right?"

He looked tired and untidy as he sat there, his boots perched on an open drawer beside a messy desk. His hands were folded across his chest. A watch chain ran from his vest pocket, draping across his belly to a buttonhole. He was a different person than the man they saw on their last visit.

"Whaddaya say, Sheriff Parson?" Sheriff White asked. "Or aren't you gonna answer me today? I've got plenty of time. I can wait here until tomorrow if you'd like. Are ya gonna help us guard these dangerous dogs until the trial? You have the only jail in town. Don't take offense, I'm just funnin' with ya."

The Santa Clara sheriff began rearranging papers over the polished surface of his desk. When he looked up, the Crocketts were looking at him strangely. He had already met them and knew that they were way out of his league.

"You might want to tell me the which of why of things before you start usin' my facilities," Parson said as he pushed his hat back. Hair hung from the shadow of the sheriff's wide-brimmed hat, thick and glistening from the heat.

"These here fellas are who's gonna swing," Sheriff White said. "These are the ones that robbed the train."

Ringo's voice was full of gruff challenges. "Nobody in this town has the balls to hang me. You just watch. One way or another, I'm gonna get out of here."

"Well, well, I see we have a live one here." Sheriff Parson swung his legs onto the floor and laid his hands flat on his desk to make sure the four outlaws paid attention as he stared them down. "For your information, I don't give men like you a second chance, so if you try anything funny, I'll shoot ya on the spot. I don't play games. That's why I'm still alive. I guess I'm slowly learning how to sheriff the town."

Sheriff Parson grabbed a large ring of keys from the open drawer and walked back to the four cells, unlocking two. "Here you go, boys. You can share a cell. A couple of us will stay in the last bunks until the trial."

The locks groaned when the keys turned, and the hinges squeaked loudly when he pushed the doors open.

"Marshal Weston hasn't been replaced yet, but he

usually used my jail, though. The US Marshal's office is still empty. For these dangerous-looking fools, we should be enough."

"Eric here has turned state's evidence. He'll be getting a pardon with my recommendation," Sheriff White said. "I know it's unusual, but if it weren't for his help, we might not have gotten here. He deserves a second chance. I have information that indicates that he's never shot anyone, and in the robberies, he was the fella watching the horse."

Ringo dropped onto the first bunk without a word. He lay there examining the ceiling. A water stain was spreading as he watched. In the end, he was locked in a separate cell to keep them from talking and devising a new plan. But it was clear that Wayne and Jessy had had their fill of their gang leader. They didn't respect him any longer.

Sheriff Parson cocked a brow and looked at Ringo like he was garbage, and nothing would ever change his mind.

When his gang members saw him crying like a baby while the Texas Rangers were playing their game of Russian roulette, they had given up hope in their leader and now wanted nothing to do with him. He had let them down on all fronts.

The prisoners jumped when Sheriff Parson slammed the jail cell doors shut simultaneously. It was the sound of doom. Then the tumblers in the locks clanked, and the sheriff smiled.

Will leaned back into one of the chairs in the sheriff's office and sat cross-legged, tenting his fingers before his mouth as though he was deep in thought. His eyes said he was tired, but he was hungry too.

"Why don't you boys go and have something to eat and drink. You must be worn out. I'll keep an eye on these three. I reckon you'll take Eric with you. If he's not locked up, I'm not responsible for him. You understand that, right?"

"Are you hungry for a sit-down meal, Eric?" Gid asked, grinning. "I'm starving. I could eat a cow, whole."

"Come on, I'm pretty hungry, too." Will led the way out the door and turned right on Main Street. Halfway down, they saw the sign in white letters, and beside them was a painting of a cowboy riding a bucking bronco. The name said, *The Rowdy Cowboy Saloon*.

They pushed their way through the batwing doors as they whooshed closed behind them. The bartender looked up, and recognition flashed in his eyes.

"It's about time you boys made it back. I reckon you took longer than you thought. What'll it be, Will? The same as usual?"

"How are ya doin', Joe? Eric, this is our friend and favorite bartender," Gid grinned.

"Four beers and a bottle of whiskey with four clean glasses comin' up." The bartender fussed behind the counter, reaching deep into the icebox for the coldest mini keg of beer.

"It don't get no colder than this, Gid. Watch when I pour it. See the condensation form on the mug. The glass is cold too. That, my friend, is the secret."

After several whiskeys, James snapped out of the daze and grinned. His eyes were slightly crossed, but he looked happy and relaxed. He had worked all that tension out of himself with a half bottle of whiskey.

After a while, Sheriff White just stared at them all, baggy-eyed and confused. Now he was beyond drunk, and Will had a sneaking suspicion why. After all the hard talk, he felt the lawman was exhausted from being afraid twenty-four seven for the last week. He put on a good cover, but Will could see the signs. At times, in the past, he had felt the same. He pulled off his hat and shook his head, making his graying blond hair hang around his face. It had been hard on all of them. James's eyes were blurry with whiskey. He smiled when he remembered the drinks were free.

———

IT WAS after midnight and Sheriff White had already called it a night and had headed for the government-paid hotel to sleep off all the whiskey he had put away to relieve the stress from the prisoner transport. By then, Gid had eaten so much that his belly hurt. In the end, he had a circle of saloon customers around him, cheering him on to eat more and set the Rowdy Cowboy record. Finally, his little brother retired to the hotel room too.

When Gid found himself alone, he took a deep sigh of relief. Of course, the job wasn't done until the trial and the undeniable hanging, but at least the traveling and danger had passed. He turned his head when he heard the soft, sexy voice.

"Hi there, handsome."

Gid looked up, smiled, and asked, "Do you want to join me in a refreshment?"

"A refreshment?" Darlene giggled. "Why aren't we refined tonight. Where did your friends run off to, Mr. Crockett? Don't tell me you're all on your own?"

After Darlene took a seat, Gid leaned in close and

whispered into her ear, making the pretty lady laugh out loud and hard.

"You seem to know who I am, but I didn't catch your name?"

"That tickles. My name is Darlene Sadler."

He watched as goose bumps sprouted on her arms and her face turned red, but they both knew it was all in fun.

"Don't tell me you don't like it," Crockett whispered in her ear. He could hear her breathing quicken.

For a moment, she stared at him, glistening with emotion.

"Are you married?" Darlene asked. When she saw the look on Gid's face, she said, "Why, I'm just pullin' your chain." In fun, she cuffed him in the chest.

The first opportunity he got, Gid leaned in and brushed his lips against hers. She involuntarily flinched. Her initial blush disappeared, and her lips grew into a smile.

"Why, Gid, you're as sparky as a racehorse and slick as a mink."

"I don't see you puttin' up much resistance. Nobody's pushing you, Darlene."

Still, her eyes swelled at the extravagant notion, even though she knew she wasn't the type of woman to make Gid Crockett a wife.

Finally, she smiled, grabbed his hand in hers, and said with a mischievous look, "Wait a few minutes and follow me."

He smiled with a twinkle in his eyes and said, "All right, Darlene."

———

THAT EVENING, the last thing Joe saw of his friend was when he was climbing the stairs.

Gid knocked on the door.

"Who is it?" a woman asked in a husky voice.

"It's me." He heard the key in the lock, and then it opened. It clicked lightly when it closed.

CHAPTER TWENTY

OVERHEAD, THE STARS SWUNG COUNTERCLOCKWISE IN their nightly course as the Big Bear turned and Earendel winked in the farthest distance. A dozen falling stars left vapor trails streaking toward Earth and then burned out in midair.

After a few hours, the sky burst into a pink, rose, and crimson prism as it stretched from the eastern to the western horizon. Birds chirped as they awoke with the smell of flowers in the air. Somewhere in the distance, a mule brayed.

Stores began to open, and buckboard wagons rolled quickly up and down Main Street. Women came out of their homes and dumped dirty water from washing pans into the street. The smell of breakfast drifted through the air as roosters crowed behind the buildings.

In an hour, Santa Clara was bustling. These weren't just your normal citizens. People from all around the county were present. The population was even larger than when the train arrived. As the word got around, the mob began to swell. There was nobody within fifty miles who didn't know that the hearing was imminent, and nobody wanted to miss out. Even the ranchers and farmers far from town kept their money in the San Antonio National Bank, and they were all as angry as hell. The only thing they were waiting for was his honor's arrival.

All those present had already made up their minds, and if the verdict wasn't to their liking, they intended to take the law into their own hands. Ringo Moon and his outlaw gang had stolen their life's savings, and even though the Crocketts and the El Paso sheriff had recovered most of the gold double eagles, they still wanted revenge. If for nothing more, to ensure it didn't happen again.

———

PEOPLE on the street all stopped and stared when the broad figure wheeled onto the main drag. The small bell on the mule's harness served as a warning that Judge Roy Bean was present and accounted for. At fifty-eight years old, he still proved an ominous figure. Curtains of white hair and beard hung from under his tall, white hat. Another straw sombrero hung from his saddle horn. He wore a leather vest, a light-colored shirt, a bandana, and denim jeans, and Mexican sandals covered his feet. His appearance wasn't as distinguished as most judges, but everyone knew and respected him for who he was.

The Kentuckian nodded his head in greeting as he passed the pedestrians on the street. Everyone smiled and bid him good morning. In one hand, he held his reins, and in the other, he clutched his law book.

Tattered edges peeked from its sides. The news that he had arrived in town raced through the population like wildfire. They all knew that with his appearance, the show was just about to begin.

Bean was famous for his unusual verdicts, which often included exorbitant fines that he promptly pocketed, never to be seen again. Once in his saloon in Langtry, Texas, at The Jersey Lilly, a man paid his bill with a twenty-dollar double eagle gold piece. When Bean failed to return his change, the customer complained, and the judge promptly fined him $19.95 for contempt of court.

The few children in town ran down the street after the judge, rolling metal rim wheels with sticks while begging for sweets. Bean reached into his vest pockets and evenly distributed a mint each. Despite his lack of honesty regarding his financial affairs, he was still considered a fair and understanding leader of the courts. Everyone knew that no one was totally honest living this far west, especially in Texas.

Although the newspapers called him the hanging judge, he seldom condemned the accused to death. He preferred long, complicated punishments. But for the Ringo Moon gang, he had little choice. If he didn't hang them, a vigilante mob would. He had heard that they had already survived an attempt to tar and feather them and knew better than to disappoint such an angry crowd. Still, the formalities had to be respected, and despite there being no room for a verdict other than guilt, he insisted they follow the rules.

Bean made a beeline for the sheriff's office. The first thing he always did was have a look at the accused, and if possible, speak a word unless they were too unruly.

These brief meetings played a significant role in the judge's final decision. It often depended on their demeanor and whether they were repentant or not. From what he heard about Ringo, he didn't expect much. How his gang reacted may determine their future. It all depended on who committed the murders. Killing men for no reason other than just being ornery was something that even Bean didn't tolerate.

WILL WAS RUNNING through a stack of wanted posters when he heard the knock on the door. He locked eyes with a man he had never met but knew from pictures in the newspapers of him standing in front of his saloon.

"Mornin', Judge. My name is Will Crockett. I'm workin' as a deputy for Sheriff White out of El Paso. All in cooperation with the local Sheriff Parson. It looks like we're all on the same page here. The only problem is with the citizens of this fair city. It appears they want to jump the gun and hang these fellas before you sentence them. They came at 'em once, but we got lucky, and their attention was diverted."

"We can't have something like that happening, now, can we. I suggest I visit the prisoners, and then I'll set a date for the hearing. Excuse me, Deputy, but I have my way of doing things, and I'm not ready to change at my age. Be patient with me, and you'll be surprised how quickly things will roll along."

"Whatever you say, Your Honor. Come along and I'll introduce you to Ringo Moon and his gang."

When the first prisoner didn't look up, Judge Bean patiently cleared his throat. Ringo turned and stared at the person who was interrupting his nap. A snarl settled over his face, and he spat on the floor. He had no idea who it was but was disrespectful just the same.

"Whatcha want, fat man? Why are ya standin' there starin' at us like we're a bunch of monkeys? I know my rights. I'm entitled to be left alone until my trial. Where's that lawyer of ours, anyway? I need to have a word with that fool."

As soon as the words came out, Ringo knew he had said the wrong thing. Still, he was too stupid to admit he was wrong. He continued to stare down his nose at the stranger, almost daring him to say something else.

"Your Honor, this is the leader of the outlaw gang, Ringo Moon, and these are his sidekicks, Wayne Hazzard and Jessy Jones. They committed the local train heist and two murders."

"Whatcha talkin' about, Crockett? What did you call this fat man?"

"Let's keep this a secret for now," Bean whispered, turning his head. "I wanna see the surprised look on his face when I walk into the courtroom."

"It's just a fella that wanted to see what a killer looks like," Will covered. "Not everybody can say they met a real-life murderer."

"Whatcha doin'? Collecting money so they can look at us like baboons in a zoo? Bullshit. I know my rights. Until I'm proven guilty, I'm innocent by law."

Ringo growled like a dog ready to bite. The judge had a last glance from head to toe, shaking his head, and dismissed the gang leader without a word.

They moved to the next cell, and both Wayne and Jessy were wide awake and looked like they hadn't slept for days. They were sitting on the edge of their bunks.

Neither dared to look when Crockett led the robust older man to the second cell.

If nothing else, Roy Bean enjoyed a little humor, even though it was *dark*. Not telling Moon he was talking to the judge made him smile. They left the outlaw with a puzzled expression on his face despite his bravado.

"This is Jessy Jones, and the fella with a damaged eye is Wayne Hazzard."

"Did you and the sheriff do this to them?" Bean asked with a raised eyebrow. "I see one of them is using a crutch and the other has obviously lost an eye."

"No—sir. Some of Ringo's buddies were looking for a reward for breaking him out. They shot up our passenger car. Luckily, they were the only ones inside who were hurt. I can't say the same for his so-called friends who came to save 'em. I'm afraid they're all dead. We don't start fights, but if one presents itself, we don't stop until the job is done. They started shooting at us, and we returned fire. It's as simple as that."

"You don't say," Bean said, as he scribbled something on a paper in his lawbook. His mask of a face didn't belie his true feelings. Everyone wondered what he was thinking.

"That wasn't the only time some of his friends tried to bust him out, either. We've been engaged in a running battle since we left El Paso to retrieve the gold and deliver the culprits to the town authorities. In this case, Sheriff Parson. We even had a bunch of Comanche boys try to stop the train. One of Ringo's friends paid them ten dollars and promised ten more when the job was done. Unfortunately, it cost them their lives, too. I must admit, it's been a devilish trip. It's a miracle we all got here safe and sound."

———

WHEN THEY RETURNED to the front office, Sheriff Parson and Gid were just arriving with a very hungover Sheriff James White. His eyes were webbed with red lines, and the sour taste of whiskey filled his mouth and nose. His clothing was disheveled, and his face was beet-red.

"Howdy, Judge Bean," Sheriff Parson said. "Have you already seen the prisoners, sir?"

"Yah-huh, I think I've seen quite enough. Get Sheriff White sobered up. I want him to be prepared to testify at the hearing. Is that clear?"

"So, when do you want us to organize the trial, sir?" Sheriff Parson shifted his weight from one foot to the other, afraid he would anger Bean. He was one of the few men who could cost him his job. Now it was important to him, when a few weeks prior he was ready to quit.

"Tomorrow morning at nine sharp, Sheriff. I think we'd better send these scoundrels on their way forthwith. The faster we get our jobs done, the less chance the crowd in town turns into a mob. Do we have any witnesses other than appointed officers of the law?"

"We've got something better. Come in here, Eric," Will called out. "This is Eric Smith, Judge Bean. He's a witness to the robbery and much more. He's willin' to testify to it all. He used to be part of the gang, but he has turned over a new leaf in life. He has proven himself to us time and again, and we all agree that he should be set free. According to him, he can solve a half dozen murders and at least ten robberies."

"It looks like an open-and-shut case, then. All the better. When it comes time to hang a man, I hate to linger. It's an ugly business when you can't settle things with a jail term and a fine. I'm heading for the hotel. Once you have the documents in order, please ensure they are delivered to my room for my review. Good day, gentlemen." The judge's voice implied he was unhurried.

Bean's aging face was marred by crow's feet that stretched around the corners of his eyes, with deep lines across his brow. His skin was like worn leather. His mouth was tight in thought, but his voice said he was serious.

The wooden floor groaned under his weight. He walked out the door, grabbed the mule's harness, and waddled down the street.

"Do you know who you just met, Ringo?" Gid called out.

Will put his finger to his lips and whispered, "Hush now. It's gonna be a surprise. Do you wanna know what he called the judge? He called him a fat man. Just think what he's gonna feel like when he sees Bean walk into court with Ringo sitting with the accused."

"Yah-huh, some fool that wanted to see somebody famous, I reckon. Why can't I get a break? Where's that damned lawyer of mine?"

"You're too stupid to keep your mouth shut," Will said. "One of these days, you're gonna regret it. Your attorney is supposed to be here at three. You can have as long as you want with him."

GID WALKED BACK to the cell block, opening and closing his fists. Ringo looked up when he heard a key rattle in the lock. He blinked like he didn't know what was happening. Then it came to him.

Jessy clambered white-eyed, "W-w-w-watch cha want?"

"You ain't my concern, for the moment. I wanna have a talk with your boss here. You can insult this fella you call, *fat man*, all you want, but I won't have you talkin' back to my brother. It's time for you and me to have some alone time. Look the other way, you two, or you'll be next."

Wayne and Jessy instantly turned their faces toward the corner. They had seen Gid in action and wanted nothing to do with whatever was about to happen.

An iron fist came driving toward Ringo's solar plexus. It turned his nasty smile into a lopsided surprise, sending him careening backward, face-first into the wall at the end of the cell. Before he could react, Gid jabbed him three times in the lower back just above his kidneys. It took the outlaw's breath away as he fruitlessly tried to struggle for air. Crockett wanted to ensure he understood that they didn't tolerate poor manners. Moon tried to get up one more time, but Crockett hit him with his fist in the stomach like a sledgehammer.

Ringo's body was red and bruised from Gid's beating, but he was careful not to hit him somewhere it showed, although he deserved every lick he got. By the time he reached the trial, he would be black and blue, but it would all be hidden under his clothing. The only thing that showed was a busted lip and a crooked jaw.

"If you make me come back here again, you're gonna be sittin' down when you have a leak, for the rest of your life, which don't look like it'll last long anyway unless you can conjure up a miracle. The clocks a-tickin', Mr. Moon."

When Gid returned, silence crept over the sheriff's office like gray gloom. Only Will had a knowing look on his face when his brother walked out the door without another word. He stormed across the street to the saloon. He knew he was going to have a stiff drink to get the bitter taste out of his mouth. He obviously had felt it was time for someone to teach the gang leader a lesson.

Jessy's heart was pumping when he watched what happened to Ringo, and he wondered if he and Wayne were next. Beads of sweat popped onto his brow. He swallowed hard, trying to catch his breath. Suddenly, he couldn't wait any longer and began to cry.

Everybody but Moon laughed. Even his men no longer had any respect for him. In their eyes, he was the fool who got them into all this mess, and they would do anything to get out. Maybe even turn on their leader. Unfortunately, they were too late. Eric would provide all the evidence they needed.

All morning long, they had heard the saws and hammers as the town carpenters built the scaffolding for the coming event. The racket was driving Wayne crazy. He was still groping, trying to cope with his ruined eye, and Jessy had to hobble around the cell with a splint on his leg. The prisoners remained silent from then on, and no one asked any more questions. They already knew the answers.

"THINGS HAVE GONE to blazes in a handbasket," Wayne huffed. "I don't see us gettin' out of this one." A gooey secretion seeped from his eye that looked like egg white. The control of the moment was wrenched from the outlaws' grasp.

"I didn't kill anyone. It was Ringo who shot the conductor. I don't know why he did it. There was no call or reason. It's he who should hang, not us."

But nobody but his partner in crime was there to hear what he said. Ringo cursed and spat at his men, but they turned their heads away in shame.

CHAPTER TWENTY-ONE

A LINE TO GET INTO THE COURTHOUSE WRAPPED AROUND the building and went down the sidewalk, crossing the first alley and down the street. It was clear that everyone wouldn't fit. Still, they held their ground and waited for the chance to see the spectacle firsthand. The environment in Santa Clara was circus-like. The folks from all around came to see the main attraction. That would be the hanging after Roy Bean was done in court, and the jury had passed the guilty verdict. It was doubtful that their punishment would be anything less than the gallows.

Hinges creaked as the judge's chamber door began to open, and everyone in the courtroom held their breath. The voluminous figure almost gracefully walked over to the bench and took a seat. Murmurs rippled through the crowd. Will, Gid, Sheriff White, and Eric Smith sat in the witness box. Moon, Hazzard, and Smith sat at the council's table on the opposite side. Not an empty seat remained in the courtroom, and another fifty angry citizens stood crowded in the back.

"All rise. The Honorable Judge Roy Bean presiding."

Two burly men with court badges stood guard at the doors, ensuring that no one entered or exited. Each one had a sawed-off shotgun in their hands. The Ringo Moon outlaw gang had already stirred up enough trouble, and they wanted to be ready in case there was another attempt to free the outlaw. It was a stretch with all the angry people and lawmen, but so far that hadn't stopped everyone from cowboys to Black Bart and even a band of young Comanche. Nobody knew what to expect next, but they were all ready for the worst.

The Crocketts had urged the judge to expedite the process, but Bean had his protocol and would not be hurried. This meant that they had two fronts to worry about. One was Ringo's outlaw friends, and the other were the people watching the trial. They had gathered once to tar and feather, and eventually, hanged all four. Nobody doubted that they would do it again if they didn't get what they wanted.

Ringo's fear kicked up a notch when he saw who walked into the room, and his heart sank. It was obvious that the judge got his full attention. Suddenly, the truth settled in, and blood drained from his face. Right before him, sitting on the judge's bench, was the man he had called *fat man*. Despite his delusional mind, he was going to hang, and nobody was going to come and save him. It was the end of the road for this outlaw.

Roy Bean sat before him, staring him down. He insulted the one man who held the weight of his future in the balance. Still, the fact that Crockett had lied to him and covered up the truth, made him angrier and more belligerent. There was one trait about Ringo that never wavered. He lashed out without thinking, and he couldn't keep his mouth shut.

The judge placed his hands on the desk and leaned forward, ensuring he had everyone's full attention and who he was and what he intended to do. His eyes bore holes as he glared at the accused. Then he leaned back into the chair, showing a gold chain that disappeared into his britches pocket. He lay one hand on his tattered law book, and with the other, he banged the gavel on the sound block.

"Hear ye, hear ye. In reference to the city of Santa Clara, Texas, against the Ringo Moon gang, including Ringo Moon, Jessy Smith, and Wayne Hazzard. Eric Smith, an ex-member of the gang, has turned state's evidence and will be tried separately. This court is now in session."

When the crowd continued to shout and argue with one another, the judge angrily sat on his bench, a disgusted look on his face. A gunshot rang out through the courtroom. Plaster from the ceiling showered the attendees. The citizens looked dumbfounded as Sheriff Parson pushed his hat back from his forehead. He raised the pistol barrel to his lips and blew away the gun smoke as he stared threateningly at the spectators.

"Those of you who disrespect the judge will be spending the next week in my jail on bread and water," Sheriff Parson shouted with his pistol hanging at his side, but he didn't put it away, just in case. The crowd was instantly silenced. "That's more like it."

"Well, then," the judge said. "The prosecution has the floor."

A man with a black frock stood before the courtroom and said, "I call Mr. Ringo Moon."

Another employee in a government uniform and a county court badge escorted the belligerent outlaw from the dock to the witness stand and swore him in.

The court clerk asked, "Do you swear that the evidence you shall give the Court within the trial shall be the truth, the whole truth, and nothing but the truth? Please state and spell your name for the record."

Ringo snarled. "I do," the gang leader replied. "R-I-N-G-O M-O-O-N."

"Do you feel anything when you shoot people?" the prosecutor asked out of the blue, dramatically as he pointed his finger at Ringo.

The outlaw glanced toward Bean, and the judge said, "Just answer the questions, Mr. Moon."

"Of course, I feel somethin'. I feel the recoil." The outlaw snickered through a swollen lip when he laughed, and a pain shot across his side where he had two busted ribs.

"And did you and your gang participate in the theft of the gold coins from the mail car on the Southern Pacific Railroad?"

"You know damned well we did. Nobody's denying we robbed the train and stole the gold."

"And did *YOU*, Mr. Moon, shoot and kill the railroad engineer in cold blood from the back of your horse, as witnessed?" the prosecution shouted. "Was it *YOU* that murdered United States Marshal Bill Weston, too?"

"Whatcha think, fool? Of course, I didn't shoot anyone. I may be a thief, but I ain't a killer." Moon lied. "I don't know nothin' about no dead US marshal. Do I look stupid to you?"

"You're about as sincere as a two-dollar funeral," the city prosecutor replied. "If there is anyone here in the courtroom who believes a word Mr. Moon says, please raise your hand? I didn't think so. We have professional witnesses putting you at the scene of the crime and will testify that you and you alone killed the man in question."

The judge bunched his lips as he weighed his story, what little there was. To him and the jury, it appeared to be a cut-and-dried case.

The prosecutor arched his brow, almost bored, and asked, "How did it happen? I'm referring to the murder of the engineer on the Southern Pacific Railroad? Mind what you say, now. Witnesses to that murder are in this courtroom."

Ringo swallowed grudgingly as blood rose with a jolt of panic. He shook his negation, tight-lipped. "I don't know what you're talkin' about. I didn't kill anybody, mister. If you want someone to blame, I ain't it. Sure, I helped steal the gold, but I didn't shoot anybody. You have the wrong man," he said, sitting back in his wooden chair with a smug look on his face.

All the time, Moon shot hopeful glances out the pained glass windows on the sides of the room. Squares of yellow light spilled onto the floor.

"Virgin Mary and Mother," the attorney for the defendants said and gasped. "Who would shoot an innocent man like that?"

"You're out of order, sir," Bean roared. "Watch your step in my courtroom."

"Did you two participate, Wayne, or you, Jessy?" the prosecutor continued.

"I object, Mr. Hazzard and Mr. Jones have not been sworn," the defense called out, panicked.

"Sustained," Bean replied, bored. "Swear them in and let's keep this hearing moving."

The court officer swore in the other two outlaws, and the questioning continued.

"No-sir, all we did was help Ringo steal the gold," they said in unison.

"So, do you work for Mr. Moon?"

"Yes, we're his assistants, I reckon."

"Exactly. You are no more than assistants. And who did kill these people in question?"

"Our boss, sitting right there on the stand," Jessy said as his eyes filled with tears.

"Why, you no-good rotten liar." Ringo jumped to his feet and lunged for Jessy, but the court officer anticipated his action and grabbed him by the collar and sat him back down.

"Do you work for Mr. Moon, too, Mr. Hazzard?"

"I reckon I do, at least while we're doin' a job. When we ain't workin', I'm usually at home with my wife and kids."

"And what job is that—exactly?"

"Why, robbin' banks, stagecoaches, and trains. I reckon that the trains are the hardest, but Ringo is really good at makin' plans."

"If you saw all the violence that happened from Pecos to here, why didn't you quit and leave? Surely you had a choice in the matter. Couldn't you separate yourself from all of this whenever you wanted?"

"Not if you ride with Ringo Moon, you don't. He always swore if anyone went against him, he'd hunt us down and kill us and our families. Wife, children, and in-laws too."

"And why is it that you are willing to leave him now?"

"Why, anyone would do the same to save their hides, sir. We're thieves, Your Honor. There ain't no doubt about that. But wouldn't anyone here try to avoid the noose if they were sittin' where I am? Like I say, I admit that I robbed banks and stagecoaches and even robbed a train or two, but I ain't no killer and neither is Wayne."

"It doesn't look like you and your friends did a very good job if you were caught."

"We usually do better. It was just bad luck that caught up with us this time. That and the Crockett brothers, along with El Paso's Sheriff White. They all three be hard men. Harder than us, I reckon."

"Have you or Mr. Jessy Jones killed anyone on your other endeavors?"

"No-sir, never. Ringo is the only one that does the shootin'," Jessy replied as tears cut a clean streak down his dust-covered face. "He has a thing for killin' things."

"By things, what do you mean, please? I'm afraid the jury may not understand."

"Why, I've seen Ringo kill just about every kind of animal that ever walked the earth. Horses, dogs, cats, mules. Oh, and Indians. He hates Indians. Especially the Comanche and Apache. Then again, I don't think there's a law against killin' the natives, is there?"

"Would you like to elaborate, please, Mr. Jones?"

"Elabor-what?"

"Kindly explain to the jury exactly what you mean."

"You know, the things that outlaw gangs do. Stealin' and scarin' the daylights out of folks. At least that's what Ringo said to do. I think it makes him feel good, frighten' folks, but he likes shootin' 'em more."

"Who the hell are you workin' for, fool?" Ringo shouted. "You're supposed to be working for all of us. How dare you try to turn my partners against me? I have my rights."

"I am afraid, Mr. Moon, that you don't have a chance in a million years of being acquitted. But if your men are honest, I can throw them to the mercy of the court, and they might get away with a forty-year sentence. At least it's better than what awaits you, Ringo. I'm sorry that things worked out this way. But still, it's better to try to save two of you than let you all hang without an argument. I'm afraid that for you, I have no argument at all."

The prosecutor tried to stare Ringo down, but it didn't work. For some reason, he didn't seem as scared as a man who was facing the noose should. He glanced out the window again like he was expecting someone.

"No more questions for Mr. Hazzard, Your Honor. Now I would like to call Deputy Sheriff Will Crockett, if it pleases the court."

"You may step down, and Mr. Crockett, you may take the stand," Judge Bean ordered.

———

"MR. WILL CROCKETT, do you have anything to share with the court?"

"Men wear boots, and horses have shoes."

"And is that supposed to mean something?"

"Ringo left his boot prints beside the mail car where they blew the door and stole the gold. My little brother and I are trackers, so we saw it straight away."

"How can you tell? Excuse me, but a boot print sounds rather absurd."

"One boot heel is cracked. Go ahead and check his footwear. The left one will be busted." He pointed a finger at Ringo.

The court orderly walked over and grabbed Moon's boot and had a look at the heel. "It's busted all right."

"So, you see it now? Same boot, same man. My little brother and me saw him shoot the conductor, too. We saw it with our own eyes. How much more proof do you want, and why haven't you put Eric Smith on the stand?"

"All in due time," the defense, Norm Foreman said, like he had all the time in the world. "All in due time."

Ringo was so shocked that everyone had suddenly turned on him that he didn't know what to do. He was blind with fury, but at the same time, he felt more helpless than he had ever felt in his life. Not only was the whole town against him, but now his own attorney and gang members had turned on him, too. At this point, all he could do was hope another one of his outlaw buddies was interested in the reward he would pay to the man who broke him out.

"I object!" Ringo roared.

"Sit that man down or put a sock in his mouth and shut him up! I will not tolerate such behavior in my court." Bean shouted.

His voice boomed through the room, making everyone sit up straight, and a deep silence fell across the crowd. Nobody wanted to be removed, or they would miss what was turning out to be the event of the year.

Deputy Gid strode over and grabbed Ringo by the arm while digging his knuckles into his fractured ribs. "If I hear another peep out of you, I'll beat you here in front of all these people. Is that what you want?" Ringo twisted in his seat as Crockett applied more pressure. Moon's face went white, and he nearly passed out from the pain. "Now are ya gonna behave, or do we have another dance?"

Ringo nodded like a doll with a broken spring for a neck. Everyone in the courtroom was staring at him with eyes full of hate and vengeance. Now it was Moon's turn to be on the receiving end of things.

"I don't think we're gonna need that sock," Grid smiled. He glanced at Ringo and winked, making the outlaw even more furious.

"There ain't a man alive that's above the law, but this one doesn't even have the common decency to stop once he's caught," Sheriff White whispered to Will. "What did your brother do to him to make him so afraid?"

Will raised an eyebrow and grinned. "That you'll have to ask him yourself." He glanced at the prosecutor and nodded toward Eric, who sat beside him.

"My-oh-my," Mr. Foreman said, slapping his hand to his forehead. "I almost forgot my prime witness, Eric Smith. Thank you for reminding me, Mr. Crockett. I am sure, once we've heard his testimony, there will no longer be any doubts in the minds of the jury."

Twelve town citizens sat in the jury box. All of them were men. Each one looked as mad as a hornet's nest. There was no doubt in anyone's mind about what their decision would be. The only thing not clear yet was what awaited Wayne and Jessy. Would they get a lengthy sentence in the Texas State Penitentiary in Huntsville, or would they, too, hang by the neck until dead?

"So, you used to rob trains and stagecoaches, is that

not correct, Mr. Eric Smith?" Prosecutor Foreman continued.

"Yes-sir. Robbing trains and stagecoaches is a lot riskier than growing corn in Ohio, but it pays better unless you get caught. Me, I've learned my lesson. I was never much of a gang member with me bein' slow and all. I was more of a gofer for Mr. Moon. You know, go for this and go for that. I was his errand boy. I didn't even get a split of the stolen items. I get a fixed salary at the end of the month. But at the time, it seemed fair enough since nobody else would give me a job. I ain't much with numbers either and can't read or write."

When the defense finally finished, he sat down next to Ringo, oblivious to the danger. He didn't know he was sitting next to a rattlesnake.

"You don't scare easily, do you, Mr. Moon?" Foreman whispered.

"I never saw much sense in it before, and I can assure you I ain't scared now either. You just wait. My time will come, you sonofabitch. How dare you turn on me! I know my rights."

CHAPTER TWENTY-TWO

By the time the prosecutor got his turn again to resume his case, the defense had done his job for him. Now, everybody in the courtroom knew Ringo Moon was guilty of murder. They even felt a little apathy for Wayne and Jessy. How much their testimony did for their failing cause remained to be seen. He concluded his case with a few words, as everything had already been said and done.

"I have no further questions, and I rest my case, Your Honor," the Santa Clara prosecutor, Bill Willis, said. "May God have mercy on these men's souls."

"Foreman of the jury, will you please stand?" Bean asked politely. "Do you or any of the members of the jury have any questions?"

"No, sir. I believe it's clear enough for us to deliberate."

Bean instructed them on the law relevant to the case, emphasizing the role of the outlaw gang as fact finders. He explained the truth as he understood it, ensuring everyone had a clear understanding of what had transpired in detail. He didn't want any doubts when it came time for them to vote on their innocence or lack thereof.

"Now that you have all the facts, you may retire to the deliberation room until you have voted your verdict, during which time I am afraid that you will not be allowed to leave the room. There is an outhouse located just outside the door, should you need it. However, you will have to wait to be escorted by a court officer, who will wait outside the door. There have been several attempts to disrupt the process, and I want to ensure it doesn't happen again."

"I believe we've heard all we need to hear, Your Honor." The jury foreman stood along with the other eleven jurors, and they all disappeared through a door behind the jury box. The lock clicked when someone from inside turned the key. Everyone in the room would give their back teeth to know what was said behind closed doors.

Nobody expected them to take much time to deliberate and come to a final decision. Nor did the courtroom attendees believe they would even *consider* sending the other two to prison. Everybody wanted to see all three hang. That was why they were there. There wasn't a person in town who didn't enjoy a good hanging, especially when half of them saw how these outlaws rode in and robbed the train of their life savings.

Everyone's eyes went to the jury as they filed out and then to Judge Roy Bean when he, too, disappeared through a hidden door behind his bench. It was disguised with varnished pine paneling. It closed with a bang that sounded final and conclusive—almost like a tomb's door. When it was closed, a silence momentarily crept over the crowd, then they all began talking at once, and the volume grew greater by the minute.

The outlaws looked at each other with dismal faces. They were so nervous, their eyes twitched, and they bit their lips. They knew that when the judge returned, their lives would change forever, and there was nothing they could do to stop it. Seconds felt like minutes and minutes like hours, as they glued their eyes to the jury foreman's door. He would be the first one to emerge and present the judge with their decision, along with suggestions for punishments.

Still, only the judge would make the final sentence unless they were pardoned, and everyone knew that was impossible, including the outlaws. Judge Bean was often lenient, but this time, he had to consider the public's interests more than his own personal agenda. If he didn't condemn them to death, he could have his authority challenged, and this was something he had to avoid at all costs. An officer of the courts who didn't keep his people in line may well soon find himself out of a job.

———

THE COURTROOM WAS chaotic as the jurors continued to deliberate. They had been at it for over four hours, and the crowd was becoming more belligerent by the minute. Several small fistfights broke out among citizens arguing over whether Wayne and Jessy should receive life sentences rather than be hanged like Ringo. Everyone was worked up into a frenzy as they continued to wait.

At some point, everyone began to chant, "HANG 'EM NOW, HANG 'EM NOW, HANG 'EM NOW!" until the officer of the courts, the Crocketts, and both sheriffs had to forcibly quiet them down at the threat of removing them from the courtroom. Nobody who had heard the trial in its entirety wanted to be expelled and miss the fireworks that would inevitably come.

The tension had the town in a frenzy, making them capable of doing anything, even committing murder, which would be what it was if they went ahead and lynched them in a mob. Disregarding the law to such a degree wasn't something the judge or the lawmen could permit. For Bean, it would mean an unwanted blemish on his already dubious reputation. For the Crocketts and Sheriff White, they knew if they had to, they would turn their guns on the very people they had recuperated the gold for. That would be a disaster on all sides, and they had to avoid it at all costs.

Once they quietened them down, they heard a click as a key slipped into the lock. The brass knob handle turned, and the jurors filed out. The last to emerge and sit was the foreman. He had a yellow piece of paper in his white-knuckled fist.

They all took their seats as they silently waited. Everyone in the courtroom was on the edge of their pews as the tension grew. They returned their eyes to the door behind the bench, waiting for Bean to emerge. They didn't have to wait long.

When the judge retook his seat, he eyed the foreman and asked, "So, were you able to come to a verdict?"

The foreman said, "Yes, Your Honor. We *have* come to a unanimous verdict as required by law."

"And what say yee, sir?" Bean asked.

The foreman unfolded his piece of paper even though he knew exactly what it said. He seemed to like having everyone's eyes on him. The room was so quiet you could hear a pin drop. This was the highlight of his life. To be the man to voice the sentence of those guilty of the worst crime in the history of Santa Clara, Texas.

"In the case of Mr. Wayne Hazzard, we find the defendant guilty. In the case of Mr. Jessy Jones, we find the defendant guilty. In the case of Ringo Moon..." He lifted his eyes from the yellow paper and stared across the crowd. He had their undivided attention and intended to draw it out as long as he could. After taking a deep breath, he said in hardly a whisper, "In the case of Mr. Ringo Moon, we find the defendant guilty as charged. Our suggestion is for a sentence of life in the Texas Federal Prison for Mr. Jones and Mr. Hazzard. In the case of one Mr. Ringo Moon, we suggest he be hanged by the neck until dead as soon as possible, considering the situation."

"Very well, then. We can execute the accused at the hangman's earliest convenience. What do you say, Mr. Gravely? When can we expect this execution to be carried out? Please keep in mind that I have more courts to attend to and the need for urgency given the repeated attempts to break Ringo Moon out of jail."

"Is tomorrow at noon quick enough for you, Judge? The scaffolding's complete. All I've to do is fill out the pertinent paperwork and the receipt to forward to city hall for the expenses. I can assure you that there will be no holdups on my end."

"Very well, then. This court is adjourned. I'll see you at twelve sharp tomorrow, Earl."

Without another word, the large man turned and

sped to the door and out of the public's eye. A sly smile curled at the edges of his lips. Sometimes it felt good to give an earned sentence and let two men live. Despite his reputation, Judge Bean didn't enjoy hanging outlaws and eventually only hanged a few throughout his career.

———

WHEN THE COURT WAS ADJOURNED, Sheriff Parson said, "Can you boys help us see these three get back to the jailhouse in one piece. I'm still not convinced the citizens of our fair city won't change their minds and hang all three. I heard some grumbling when Wayne and Jessy were given lengthy jail sentences rather than the noose. Mind ya now, I'd have preferred they'd hang myself after all the trouble they put you men through. I would hate to see those two get out for good behavior in ten years only to go back and do the same thing again. At least we know Ringo is on a one-way train to hell."

"Come on, then," Will said as he pulled his pistols. "Let me check to see that the coast is clear. Luckily, we only have a block to go. Once we have 'em locked up again, we should be all right."

As they headed for the door, grinning, Will winked at the town law with his approval. Sheriff Parson swallowed appreciatively. When he peeked out the front courthouse doors, bright sunlight flashed in his eyes, blinding him momentarily. He pulled his hat down, shading his eyes as he gazed across the distance, looking for trouble.

"Nincompoop," Gid spat, as he grabbed Ringo's chains and gave them a sharp tug. "You're crazier than a dog humpin' a pig. You give me any trouble and I'm gonna beat you so bad they'll have to *carry* you up the thirteen steps to the gallows."

"Watch your temper, little brother," Will huffed.

"I don't need to control my temper. I need this fool to stop pissin' me off. If he doesn't shut up, Ringo and I here are going to have another round, and this time I won't be so gentle. The hangman won't mind stringing up an outlaw like this with a couple of broken arms and legs. I figure I deserve satisfaction after chasin' this moron halfway across Texas and back."

Ringo snarled, cleared his throat, and spat on the floor, splattering it on Gid's boots. "Go to hell, Law. Your brother too. Don't worry. Your time will come when I get even with y'all. Especially you, Will Crockett, for lyin' to be about who the judge was."

"You better be careful, or you might wake something that had better stay left sleeping," Will said knowingly.

The strength seemed to rise from somewhere deep inside the Gid, like liquid heat from the earth's core as a fiery anger flashed in his eyes. His voice came like daggers, and his heart started to pound. Will already knew what would come next if he didn't stop his brother but didn't care anymore. He had heard enough about Ringo's crimes that he believed he deserved all the punishment he got and then some.

That was when they heard the guns go off, BOOM, BOOM, BOOM. They instantly knew that something else was up, and it had to be men looking for the reward for freeing Moon.

Gid suddenly lurched forward, grabbing Ringo and Wayne by the scruff of their necks as Sheriff White stuck the barrel of a revolver in Jessy's back. "You'll be the first one to die if this goes south." His eyes blazed at the outlaws. "Shootin' you three will be a pleasure."

With his heart racing, Will hit the ground at a full run as he raced for the nearest horse. It was tied to the hitching rail in front of the Rowdy Cowboy Saloon—his blood sped into overdrive.

Without any warning, Gid slammed his fist into Ringo's face, making it appear to deform. When his nose snapped, it sounded like a broken twig. He laid into him so hard that from the first punch, he was unable to speak. After being hit twice more, he tried to crawl away.

"Where ya think you're goin'?" Gid growled. "I just knew we were gonna have another dance. Come back here, you coward."

Ringo's breath was trapped somewhere in his body, and he couldn't breathe from the pain. He was drenched with sweat, and his hair was matted with blood.

Ringo's heart was in a sprint, and his mind was jumbled and confused, but he knew he had to keep his head if he wanted to survive. He let his mind go there and imagined his escape. His anger flared, and again his mind spun despite his struggle for control. Moon knew his last chance was just about to present itself, so it was now or never.

The pallor of terror crawled into his eyes. Ringo Moon stood staring blankly because he was beginning to believe that he would never see his home again. As he looked at his short future, he couldn't see past the negativity. He drew in a deep breath, sniffled, shook his head, and frowned. He had never been a religious man, but now he prayed to God, but once he started, he felt stupid. How could he believe in something he couldn't see?

"Take the prisoners to the jail, boys," Gid said to Sheriffs White and Parson. "We'll take care of whatever it is that's comin' at us now."

CHAPTER TWENTY-THREE

At first, there were only a few gunshots. Most people believed it was some cowboys just off a cattle drive, blowing off a little steam. Then a woman screamed. That got everyone's attention. When she continued to yell and call for help, men went running to her rescue. There were already too few women in town. They couldn't let anything happen to those they had.

By the time the Crockett brothers laid eyes on the situation, they could see the end of the street was a powerful mass of horns, fur, and hooves. Initially, the cattle moved at a walk, or at most, a trot. But when three more gunshots rang out, they broke into a run, and that was when they began roaring down Main Street like a hairy brown train. Women screamed some more as men cried out, telling children and those unaware of the gravity of the situation to seek cover.

A few people pinwheeled through the air when hit by the power of the shoulder-to-shoulder herd of long-horns. They had just arrive by cattle drive from Southern Texas and had been lingering in holding pens to be sold and shipped back East to the many slaughter-houses. Suddenly, the street was filled with livestock from the corrals next to the train yard, and they were out of control. The ground shook as they stormed down the street, tearing support posts from porch roofs and parts of the sidewalk. Hitching rails disappeared as watering troughs were damaged and emptied.

As the town's citizens left the courtroom, they found themselves standing in the way of sixty charging cattle as the stampede began. At first, most of them didn't know what started it, because the cowboys knew better than to drive a small herd down the main street of town. None of them would be so drunk and foolish. All they knew was that gunfire ratatated through the air, and the next thing they knew, spooked cattle were running across the small city at full speed and straight for the people leaving the courthouse and those trapped on the wooden plank sidewalk.

Horses tied to hitching posts reared, trying to free themselves from their harnesses. They kicked their hind legs as their eyes spread wide in fear. Unfortunately, a few of the helpless animals were trampled where they stood, while others managed to break away and flee for their lives.

It was said it started when a rider sent a shrill whistle from across the clearing. Right after that, someone emptied one of the cattle pens into the street. A rider urged them into a stampede as he shot more rounds off into the air. Before they could see who it was, the pair of outlaws wheeled their horses and disappeared around the side of the buildings at the end of the street. It was apparently more of Ringo's outlaw friends.

The massive bovines bowled over men and women

who were trampled underfoot before they could make their way to safety. As the cattle ran wild with fear, they bawled, terrified, making them race even faster in their desperate attempt to escape a real and present danger. The pounding of hooves hammered the ground as screams drowned out all other sounds, making the earth tremble. Dust and the smell of dirty cattle filled their mouths and noses.

Gid Crockett grabbed the nearest horse, quickly climbed astride, and raced in the direction of the gunshots. When he got one of the guilty parties in sight, he set his spurs and charged the mounted outlaw, finally colliding hard into the instigator's horse, knocking them both to the ground, dazed. Crockett kicked his leg over his horse's neck and slid to the ground in one graceful motion. Then he grabbed the downed man by the hair and hammered his face with his fist. Three blows and he was unconscious.

Several of the long-horned cattle had been shot dead by the townsfolk or cowboys. Carcasses blocked the way for others, leaving them nowhere to run. Some were severely wounded, so the Crocketts went around putting them out of their misery as the livery owner, Billy Bob Thorns, used a two-horse team to drag them off the street. Pink froth showed on their colorless lips as they struggled for one last breath.

The rest of the stampeded herd ran down alleys and side streets, and others vanished into the brush on the edge of town. Two dozen cowhands raced their horses up and down Santa Clara, lassoing the last of the strays, rounding them up to return them to their holding pens. Within minutes, the situation was back under control, and one of the perpetrators was captured. Gid grabbed him by his ear and dragged him toward the jail. He yelped as his massive paw yanked harder.

Will wove his horse through the thinning cattle to see if he could help the injured, but he found little more than cuts and bruises and a couple of broken arms. All in all, things worked out, and they successfully warded off another attempted jailbreak. This time, they had even captured one of the assailants. This appeared to be the least professional attempt to date.

They listened until the last hoof-clop died in the distance. When the tension ended and their bodies relaxed, they exhaled deep breaths. The nervousness from the trial added to the stampede, leaving them all frazzled. All they could think about was hanging Ringo, so all this chaos would be over, once and for all.

Gid continued to drag the man who had set off the stampede by the ear. His horse lay panting on the ground, injured from the clash. The outlaw wailed as his ear got redder when Crockett twisted it to get his attention. His eyes blinked as he fought back tears.

"Where's the other fella that was with ya?" Gid asked, twisting harder. The man's eyes spread wide with pain as he whimpered, trying to speak, hoping to appease his captor and get some relief.

"He was just ahead of me. I swear, I don't know where he went. We hadn't really planned that far ahead. All we were focused on was creating a diversion to break Ringo out of prison. Beyond that, we figured that your prisoner would know what to do. We would have to stay with him until he paid us anyway."

"Why did you start the stampede in the first place? How much money did Moon offer you two?"

That was when Gid almost tore his ear off. "Answer

me, or I'm gonna rip it right off your head and make ya eat it!"

"We did it for the reward. Two thousand dollars, each, if we break him out of jail. I swear, I don't even know the man, but every bandit or outlaw from here to El Paso knows about the offer. Maybe even over the border in New Mexico. Desperate men will travel a good distance for that kind of money. I was just after the gold eagles and thought the cattle would make a good ruse. I didn't mean for 'em to stampede or hurt anybody. We're no more than a couple of worn-out cowboys that have fallen on hard times." He scratched his face with scarred and calloused fingers.

"Well, mister, I hate to inform you, but your luck is just about to get a lot worse. If you think that you've fallen on hard times in the past, I promise you what's comin' will make your head spin."

The captured outlaw looked at the deputy with vacant eyes. He had just stepped into a situation he never imagined. The possibility of capture had never even crossed his mind.

"Here's another one for the jail. If we keep this up, they'll have to build another cell or two," Gid said as he looked across the street at the mess.

The man they caught, who was responsible for the stampede, would pay in the same way as Ringo. By swinging from the end of a rope. Sheriff Parson promptly accused him of attempted murder of the town's citizens and assault on those who were injured. Judge Roy Bean would have more work to do in Santa Clara in a week or so, when he returned. In the end, somebody might still get lynched by an angry mob after all was said and done.

WHEN THEY RETURNED to the jail with their new prisoner, all three members of Moon's gang were locked up tightly in their cells. Both sheriffs sat on the porch with their guns on the table, readily in reach, and their Winchester rifles lying across their laps with rounds already levered into the chambers. Now they weren't taking any chances and were ready for whatever else might be thrown at them.

"Is it just that one outlaw, Gid?" Sheriff White asked. "How's that life of an outlaw workin' out for ya, boy? We can stick him in Ringo's bunk. I figure they're friends anyway."

"He claims he don't even know him. He said that the word's out that Ringo will pay a reward for anyone who breaks him out. The fella claimed it's known all the way to New Mexico. No wonder there were so many of 'em." Gid shoved the new guest into the first cell block where Sheriff Parson locked him up. Everybody was stained with blood, hair, and mud.

On the world's rim, the sun sat perched like a bird, as a carpet of stars began to roll out across the vast sky, reaching the western horizon. A prism of colors arched across the heavens like giant arrows while coyotes howled somewhere in the not-too-far distance. Their shadows grew long as the sun sank over the horizon, finally disappearing altogether.

Gid stood at the washpan in the corner, washing blood off his knuckles. He scooped water and rubbed his face, then he ran his fingers through his hair. Wet beads ran down his neck, tracing over the lines of his muscles.

"I'm so hungry that I could eat a buffalo, whole," Gid grumbled. "I must have used up all my energy on Ringo and his new friend. I wonder what was goin' through their minds when they thought they could pull something like this off. It's amazing what greed will do to a man. From my observation, it makes most folks dead stupid, I reckon. It has certainly been a long trip from here to El Paso and back. Tomorrow this time, Ringo Moon will be no more, and it'll all be over."

"I could eat something, too, but most of all, I could use a stiff drink and a cold beer chaser. It's been a hell of a dry, dusty day." Will wiped his sleeve across his brow.

Outside, the wide clearing was illuminated by the orange glow of windows. They could see people eating around tables inside. The yellow glare of kerosene lanterns reflected in the slightly steamed glass. They climbed up and onto the damaged porch, ducked under the drooping roof, and stepped into a large room full of sweaty bodies.

Of course, with the hanging in town the following day, the population had swelled to half again its original size. Everybody with transport made the trek across the county to the city to see the event. Even those not affected came, unwilling to miss out.

"Tossin' your rope before buildin' the loop don't catch the calf," Will said.

"Those boys didn't know what they were getting themselves into. The one I caught claimed he was no more than a down-and-out cowboy. What a way to waste your life. I think Ringo's mother mated with a scorpion. I don't think I've ever disliked a man this much."

"I don't believe anyone is unaware of that, little

brother. There's hardly a white patch on his black and blue body. He troubles me like women sometimes do."

Vultures made lazy circles high in the sky, waiting for their next meal. Dozens of crows lined tree branches with an eye on food as they cawed nonstop. A coyote snuck through the bushes, getting ever closer to the smell of blood. Every scavenger within five miles would be there waiting for whatever scraps they could snatch away before the humans butchered the steers to make steaks.

CHAPTER TWENTY-FOUR

When Ringo awoke long before the sun was up, he sniffed the air. He could still smell the pine sawdust from the previous day. Now, all he could hear was a hammer driving the last of the sixteen penny nails into two-by-fours by lamplight. He knew that at twelve o'clock the trapdoor would be released, and he would be standing on it. He briefly wondered how it would feel to fly through the air, as free as a bird, until the length of the rope went taut and his neck snapped.

The hangman was a narrow-hipped fellow with large hands and broad shoulders. He wore a tattered black stovepipe hat and a long, black coat too heavy for Texas weather. His face was as pale as the moon, his hands spindly, and his fingers long. Earlier that day, he had tested the trapdoor to ensure everything would work as smoothly as silk. It was vital for him to execute his job to the best of his ability. A proper hanging ensured that the victim was killed instantly with the snap of his neck.

Inexperienced individuals left their victims

swinging as they struggled to breathe, taking endless minutes to strangle. Gravely didn't believe in needless suffering. It was gruesome enough when well done. A black velvet hood hung from his left hand as he watched the noose swing in the stiff Texas breeze. When he looked down, he saw the hate in the outlaw's eyes, but he returned a compassionate smile. He always liked to send his victims along their way as gently as possible.

He knew this one was going to be difficult, which was usually worse for the victim. If he resisted and moved around when it was time to slip the noose over his head, he might displace the knot, and then he too would suffer a prolonged and painful death. When Gravely smiled, it appeared gruesome, but if you looked into his eyes, all you saw was resignation and pity.

Ringo was so angry his eyes glowed orange like branding irons fresh from the fire. Despite having the gallows standing before him, he still didn't believe he was going to die for what he had done. For some reason, this reality escaped him. Or perhaps he thought that there would be another attempt to free him as he stood in front of the thirteen steps to the top of the platform.

The first step creaked, making the crowd fall silent. Everyone's eyes were on the gang leader that the judge had condemned to death the previous day. When Sheriff Pason offered his hand to steady him, so his ankle irons didn't tangle, he spat and jerked his arm away. They all saw that Ringo's eyes were full of hate. He appeared to be consumed with it to the point of loss of all reason. He didn't seem to understand the situation he was in.

———

INSIDE THE CELL, Wayne eyed the distant clouds. He could see through the small barred window high up on the wall. From where he lay, he saw freedom, something he would never feel again.

"Do you think it was worth it?"

"Whatcha mean was it worth it?" Jessy replied.

Now they were locked in separate cells to enhance security. Still, they knew that once Ringo hung, nobody else would be coming to save them. Despite all their attempts, it was beyond their understanding how they hadn't managed to sneak off in all the chaos.

"You know. Spendin' the rest of our lives in jail. I figure maybe I'd rather hang here and now. I don't know if prison will suit me well. Especially now that I'm a cripple. The doctor said that I'll never be able to walk without crutches again. To be honest, I find it a nuisance. So, whatcha think? Especially with you being blind in one eye. If the truth be known, I wish I'd never laid eyes on Ringo Moon. In the end, he brought nothing but bad in his wake."

"There were some good times, too. I liked having all the money I could spend and do anything I wanted and when I wanted." Jessy moved his chew to his other jaw. It made him mumble when he talked.

"Now, you're never gonna do what and where you wanna for the rest of your life. That's one hell of a long time. Do you think they'll make us work?" Wayne asked.

"Of course, we're gonna do hard labor for what we've done. Maybe if Ringo were with us, he might have been able to buy contacts inside the prison walls. Just think, all that money and nobody but us and Ringo know where it's buried. Whatcha think is gonna happen to it? He always claimed to have a half dozen hiding spots."

"If I read the angle of the sun right, Ringo is just about to swing any minute now. Then it'll be just you and me. Just think about what we could do with all that money. There're thousands in each location. Why would a man with so much silver and gold keep on riskin' his life like he did?"

"I reckon he liked the lifestyle more than he did the dollars in paper and coin. I know for a fact that he liked to kill people too much for his own good. That's what got him hanged." Jessy scratched his head like he was stuck on a thought.

"I figure that Ringo would be as useless as a two-legged donkey without us. He's so crazy he needs men like you and me to keep him balanced and on even keel."

"Those are some mighty big words. You've got to admit nobody planned a robbery like Ringo did. His only problem was his mean streak. If we had just stolen the money and not killed anybody, I reckon they might not have even formed a posse and followed us. But with the marshal and the engineer dead, we went over the line. I wonder how the lawman was killed. Moon had ordered him tied and locked in his cell. I reckon Joey went too far."

"Right now, Ringo's only problem is the noose around his neck. I figure it'll be gettin' tight about right now."

As soon as they heard the loud bang and the crowd cheered, they knew that Ringo was swinging from a beam. When the fireworks went off, it sounded like the

Fourth of July. Orange, green, yellow, and blue explosions burst high in the sky in the shape of palm trees.

"Ringo couldn't lead a fat man to a pie-eating contest and ain't worth the time of day. All he did for us was get us life in prison," Jessy grumbled.

Like before, tears began to stream down his face, but this time, he wasn't embarrassed and didn't hold them back. They flowed like a fountain.

"Some of that trash we stole from weren't people. They were no more than prairie maggots," Wayne snarled. "Money doesn't have owners anyway. It only has spenders."

―――――

SHERIFF PARSON LIFTED the gun belt from the wall peg and strapped it around his waist. He picked up his star, huffed on it, and polished the tin on his shirt. It shone like new. From outside, they heard a solid knock. They moved their hands toward their guns, ready for anything.

"Who is it?" Parson asked with a ring of suspicion in his words. He was no longer sure of anything.

"It's me, Gid Crockett." The door opened two feet, and he slipped his way in.

"If I were you two, I wouldn't be makin' a fuss over your sentences," Will said. "Feel lucky you ain't beside Ringo right about now, swinging from a beam. I bet he ain't lookin' too healthy with a purple face and a swollen tongue."

Everyone went silent for a moment, then Will chuckled to fill the void and ease the tension. Despite the situation, they began to laugh, even though there was nothing funny. It was nervousness that provoked the reflex, but the laughter didn't reach their eyes.

Sheriff White spat out the stub of a cigar and turned his boot on it.

———

WHEN THE TRAPDOOR disappeared beneath Ringo's feet, he felt his hair go limp as he dropped into the void. First, he had heard the mechanism click when the hangman pulled the lever, and the X under his feet disappeared. He peered from under the hood and looked at his feet like they were foreign bodies unattached to his torso.

Right after the bang of the trapdoor, he felt the noose around his neck tighten when it jerked out the slack, making his body dance at the end. The last thing Ringo heard was a loud crack. It sounded like dry wood breaking, and then his lights went out. Somewhere in his self-consciousness, he heard the rope squeak on the wood above. The hanging was executed perfectly, as always, by the professional, Mr. Earl Gravely.

CHAPTER TWENTY-FIVE

As soon as Ringo Moon was cut down from the gallows and placed in a wooden pine box, the townsfolk turned their attention to the new prisoner. He was one of the two men responsible for the stampede, which endangered every citizen on the street and severely damaged the town's storefronts, not to mention the lost cattle. All these things cost the citizens of Santa Clara money, and they were tired of the thefts and outlaws running amok and had finally decided to put a stop to it themselves.

Will, Gid, and Sheriffs Parson and White were in the local law office when the streets began to fill with an angry mob. They must have been two hundred strong by the time they reached the jail. As nightfall neared, they carried torches, sending dancing shadows on the storefront walls. Cinders flew downwind as a stiff breeze sawed at the fires. The mob members carried sticks, hammers, and guns as they taunted the remaining prisoner.

"TARRED AND FEATHERED, TARRED AND

FEATHERED, TARRED AND FEATHERED!" the mob chanted to the dismay of Willy Burns, the outlaw who helped start the stampede. Never in a million years had he expected this to be the outcome of their reckless act of violence. At first, it seemed simple enough. But as soon as it started, they realized that they really didn't know what they were doing.

"You ain't gonna let 'em tar and feather me and lynch me, are ya, Sheriff?" Willy Burns pleaded as his eyes stretched until all you could see were the whites. They saw his chin begin to tremble and knew he was about to break down and cry. He suddenly realized he wasn't as brave as he had believed, either. Right then, he was more scared than he had ever been in his life.

"All these outlaws act like they're plenty brave when robbing unarmed innocent folks, but when their time comes, they're nothin' but cowards," Gid growled. "Ain't you even ashamed of yourself, crying like a baby in front of grown men. You ain't made of much, are ya?"

It was clear that he and his brother weren't happy about the decision, but they were only deputies and not the town sheriff. When they looked into the eyes of the El Paso sheriff, they saw that he would rather shoot Burns himself than turn him over to the angry mob. But it was Sheriff Parson who would have to deal with his people. After all was said and done, this would be no more than a memory, and in the end, the wrong decision could cost him his job, if not his life.

"This time, I don't know that they can be stopped," Sheriff White said. "Especially as Judge Roy Bean rode off on his mule as soon as the noose was slipped around his neck. I don't know if it's good politics to take on the whole town after all that's happened."

"Maybe it's time to let them work things out for themselves," Sheriff Parson suggested. "We've done just about all we can do and shootin' locals ain't my idea of keeping the law. I've gotta stay here and y'all don't."

"It rubs wrong lettin' something like that happen before my very eyes, but this time I don't see how we can stop them short of gunplay, and as far as I'm concerned, that's out of the question. I don't wanna be on the front page of every newspaper in the state of Texas." Sheriff White rubbed his three-day growth of beard. "Whatcha think, Pete? You have the last word. You're the town law, so I reckon it's your call."

"You're right, James," Will said. "Whatcha wanna do, Pete? It's your decision. If we leave 'em too long, they'll tear your jailhouse down. If you had a back door, we could try to sneak them out and whisk him away to San Antonio to stand trial. He'll never get a fair shake here in Santa Clara after what he's done."

As the darkness deepened, so did the anger of the mob. Finally, they were hammering their fists on the sheriff's door, and it was just about to give and break down. Things couldn't be put off anymore.

"Stand back!" Sheriff Parson shouted as he opened the door with his pistols in his hands.

"Whatcha gonna do, Sheriff? Shoot us all? You know we're due this revenge for all that these men have done. It was bad enough that Judge Bean let Wayne and Jessy get off with a lengthy prison sentence. If you don't want us to come after him, too, let the last prisoner out. If not prepared to suffer the consequences."

Sheriff Parson reluctantly slipped his Colt-45 revolvers back into his holsters, so he posed no threat. He could feel the sweat rolling down his back as fear made the hair on his neck stand on end. He knew he was the only thing between the angry mob and the man they wanted to tar and feather. Was the outlaw worth risking his life for, and possibly one or more lives of the mob? All this raced through his mind at the speed of light because he knew that he didn't have time to ponder.

"Let him out, boys! There's nothing more we can do for this outlaw. I ain't gonna get shot for scum like him. Stand back! I'll warn ya now, we ain't gonna let y'all in. Just hold your horses and you'll have what ya want."

"Damn," Will swore under his breath. Turning the prisoner over to a lynching mob was against everything he believed in, but he, too, saw that now they had no choice in the matter. They could all four end up dead at the hands of a furious mob over two hundred strong. "Come on, little brother. I reckon we have little to no choice."

"Are you sure, Will? Won't this make us as bad as them? I don't like how this is workin' out."

"Sometimes you've gotta do what you've gotta do to save yourself. A town jury would sentence him to hang anyway, and then we'd have to risk our lives to rescue a man who is guilty of attempted murder and jailbreak. I reckon it's time to turn the law over to the town. As far as I can see, it's not our call. It ain't our town. It's Sheriff Parson's now."

An uncomfortable silence fell over the four lawmen. Eric sat in the corner, terrified that the Santa Clara citizens would remember him and decide to hang him, too. He pushed himself back into the shadows of the corner of the cell block where he felt safer. He watched Willy's face as he realized what was about to happen. He gave him a pleading look, but they both knew there was nothing they could do. If the law was ready to give him up, he was toast.

"Come on, Mr. Burns. I don't like this any more than you do, but the mob has left us no choice." Sheriff Parson backed away from the mob and toward the front door to his office, never turning his back on the crowd. He kept his guns holstered to avoid any misunderstandings. A moment later, Burns was pushed out the front door, and it slammed shut behind him. They heard the heavy key turn the large lock. The lawmen carefully peeked out the window to see what happened next.

"No!" Burns shouted as he clawed at the door, but it stayed shut. "You can't do this to me! You're the law, for Pete's sake. I have my rights."

Outside, on the porch, the crowd pressed in, and the outlaw disappeared from sight.

"You lost your rights when you committed the crime, so you can beg all you want," Billy Bob Thorns said to their prisoner. "Your pleading will fall on deaf ears."

The liveryman tossed a ready-made loop around his neck, and the mob cheered. More participants joined in as they all moved as one toward their next stop. By the time they reached the fire where the tar was making black bubbles pop on the dark surface, the crowd was nearly out of control. The lawmen watched from the safety of a locked door as he shook his head.

Somebody had brought a long pole. After they tied him up, they slipped it through their hands and feet and carried him, two in the front and two in the back. Many of the town's folk poked him with sticks and pelted him with stones. Sweat mixed with blood matted Willy's hair. Trussed up, he looked like a hog ready for the spit.

Black smoke rolled from the metal drum as the oil boiled inside. As they approached, they sliced off his clothing with knives. Then they painted him with wood tar. Finally, they rolled him around in a pile of chicken feathers, until they stuck. In minutes, Willy Burns looked like a giant chicken. He continued to resist until someone hit him on the head with a bat, and he momentarily passed out. By the time he came too, he was covered in fluffy white feathers which tickled his throat and nose.

————

THE MOB CARRIED him to the gallows. The trapdoor remained open from Ringo's execution. Before he knew it, Willy was struggling not to fall as he climbed the thirteen steps to the top. This time, there were no masks or formalities. The mob was angry and handled their prisoner brutally.

There was no black hood to cover the victim's face. Nor was there anyone professional enough to ensure the knot was placed in the correct position to prevent the accused from suffering needlessly. They even preferred it that way. The more pain and agony he sustained, the better it would entertain the angry mob. Finally, they would get their moment of revenge just like they did when they watched Ringo Moon hang. This was even better because they were doing it themselves.

When the trapdoor on the floor of the gallows was set back in place, it clanked almost as loudly as it did when it opened. Billy Bob moved over toward the lever as Willy stood on the X painted on the floor. The noose was thrown over the beam above them and tied off.

"PULL THE LEVER, PULL THE LEVER, PULL THE LEVER," was repeated louder and louder by the now-belligerent crowd, and unknowingly, they were committing mob-murder.

Lynchings were widespread across the United States in 1883. In many places, there was little to no law, so it was only natural for the town's citizens to take the law into their own hands. Although the majority were ethnic minorities, often outlaws just like the Ringo Moon gang or the man captured, Willy Burns, were common too, especially in out-of-the-way places. Most of these lynchings occurred in the Southern United States, yet racially motivated lynchings also happened in the Midwest. The largest single mass lynching was of eleven Italian immigrants in New Orleans.

The term *lynching* came from the Justice of the Peace, Charles Lynch, who administered rough justice in Virginia. Everyone from horse thieves to murderers and highway robbers to murderers were victims of lynching mobs, along with countless innocent victims because of the lack of due process.

Everybody startled and jumped when the trap door went *BANG*, and Willy found himself struggling while using his bound hands and fingers to pull the noose from his neck.

"Watch 'em dance." Billy Bob grinned.

When the crowd realized what they had done, they momentarily fell silent. Then they broke the spell, and they all returned to their vengeance and hate for those who had tried to take what was theirs.

The crowd watching went nuts as their victim

kicked his legs fruitlessly. It took a full ten minutes for Willy to finally fall still. The only sound was the creaking of the rope against the overhead beam. Some of the spectators began tearing the gallows down so they could take away pieces as souvenirs.

By the time the two hundred people were done, there was nothing left of the platform and steps. Of course, the first thing to vanish was the noose. It was later found hanging from one of the rafters in the livery barn and stables. Billy Bob Thorn had pocketed it when he cut him down.

"Frontier justice was served," Billy Bob said later that night. "Drinks are on me." The Rowdy Cowboy Saloon was bustling with people from all around Guadalupe County.

CHAPTER TWENTY-SIX

"WHEN'S THE NEXT STAGECOACH TO EL PASO?" GID asked. "It's time for us to be on our way. I've had enough chaos to last for the rest of the year. How about you, brother? Don't you think it's time to go?"

"Whatcha mean, stagecoach?" Will asked. "Why pay for a trip that takes twenty days when we can get there in two by train? I know we're not in a hurry, but I wanna get to Arizona someday. Hopefully, nothing will happen, making us turn back."

"After what we've been through in the last weeks, all I wanna do is go slow and sleep in a bed at night. One that's not rocking back and forth twenty-four hours a day, either. If you'd like, we can ride our horses, but for now, I'm done with trains. All I want is a quiet trip back to El Paso and then onward to New Mexico and eventually Arizona. Do you have a problem with that, big brother? That *was* our original plan."

"Not really. To be honest, I'm tired of riding trains, too. You're right. We ain't in no hurry and we have money, so why not take our time? We can ride some of the prettier stretches by horseback and the hard and empty desert by stage. I agree, little brother. It's time for a change. To be honest, I can't wait to get out of Santa Clara. Mind you, I like the town and its folks well enough, but too much has happened in the last few days for me to hang around. I must say, all this has left a sour taste in my mouth, especially the lynching."

"I thought you had a fancy for that daughter of the other banker. Linda, you said her name was. Don't ya wanna stay in contact with her? It might do you good for a change. All I know are percentage girls, and in my opinion, they don't make good wives."

"Oh, I like Linda all right, but she ain't the one. I'm not even sure if there's a woman out there waiting for me. We've been bachelors for a long time. Maybe we aren't even capable of such a change."

"The stage won't get here until six or so, the day after tomorrow, but it'll make the return trip first thing in the following morning." Sheriff White looked at his new friends as if they were crazy. "Why would you want to break your backs on such a rough and tumble ride? It just don't make no sense to me. Why, fewer people ride the stagecoach lines every day. The train is ten times faster."

In 1883, stages were a vital, albeit uncomfortable means of travel. Various lines connected small communities across Texas. The stagecoach routes also facilitated the movement of mail, passengers, and light freight. While the railroads were beginning to make inroads, stages continued to play a significant role, especially in areas still far from the shiny steel rails.

Until they reached all destinations, they would be a valuable means of transport. But they were laying track as fast as the grass grew, and it was evident that in the following months and years, the entire country would be crisscrossed with the scars of steel tracks.

Stages were established along lines with regular stops for changing horses and providing meals and lodging for passengers. It was a more interesting way to travel because six people were hurled through space in a small carriage, which was a more personal experience, and communication was unavoidable. San Antonio to El Paso was a notable route, along with the Houston and Austin Mail Stage Line.

Traveling by this means was always uncomfortable, and sometimes the passengers even had to step down to help push their stagecoach out of mud holes and marshes. Despite the inevitable, the expansion of railroad lines marked the beginning of the end of the stage as the primary mode of long-distance transportation for both Texas and beyond. The San Antonio to El Paso route was originally a hunting path that was used as the state expanded westward. It left a lasting impact on its development and infrastructure.

"Because, soon, the stagecoaches won't be around anymore. Don'tcha see how fast things are changin'? Soon, there won't be enough passengers to amount to a hill of beans, and the Butterfield Stage Company will be out of business. I don't disagree that trains beat stagecoaches, hands down. But don't you wanna have that last stage ride before they, too, disappear like the beaver and the buffalo? It may well be our last chance to ride a stage in Texas. Who knows how long it'll be before we get back to these parts?"

When he staggered in, it was clear that the sheriff had been drinking. It was as if he were looking through filmy eyes. He stood, planting his feet so he wouldn't sway. Still, the Crocketts couldn't blame him. That first night, they had a drink or two too much, as well. They knew the sheriff drank to take the bad taste out of his mouth about all the things that had gone wrong in these past days. Notably, the imprisonment of Wayne and Jessy. It was still stuck in his craw because he believed they should have hanged. Then there was the lynching which was something that he couldn't get off his mind.

Will nodded...then he sat silent for a spell. "It's funny how that worked out. We rode all the way across Texas without as much as a scratch—something that I can't say about the outlaws that we chased, killed, and captured.

"From now on, that's one thing that I can promise fellas like this bunch we caught. If you commit a crime on my watch and don't surrender, you die. I'm tired of draggin' outlaws, zigzagging across the countryside. This prisoner transfer was the worst one yet. I can't remember having so much trouble."

"That Ringo Moon wasn't any more than a scalawag," Gid spat. "Nobody's gonna cry over his death. Do you hear that, Mr. Hazzard and Mr. Jones? Tomorrow you'll be heading for your new home. The Texas Federal Prison, and I don't think that with Ringo gone, anybody's going to try to break you out of the prisoner transport wagon. You two are gonna rot in a cell for the rest of your lives with no chance of parole."

"I've got one thing to tell you that you had better remember, Eric," Will said as they locked eyes. "If you don't make your life purposeful, you risk declining into vice and violence just like your three old friends. It'll be unavoidable. Now, you have a second chance in life. You had better make the best of it. Not many people get an extra go at things. Don't make me track you down and bring you in for breaking the law because if I hear such a thing, you can bet your britches I'll be following you."

"You're not a stupid man, Eric," Gid said. "Bad people have been telling you that when it ain't true. You are misinformed, but you are fortunate, my friend. I, for one, won't hold whatcha done against ya. But like my brother said, if you mess up again, we'll feel obliged to track you down since it was us that are responsible for you going free. Make the best out of it, even if you find it hard at first. Remember how important such a gift as a second chance is."

"Now I know they were never my friends. They just used me to do all the things they didn't wanna do. They never even gave me my share of the money they stole while I was riding with them, so I was never really part of the gang in that sense. I reckon I was too stupid to understand that what I was doing was wrong back then."

"Well, don't just stand there like half-struck noon, get a move on. As far as we're concerned, you're a free man. Ain't that right, Sheriff White? Your name has been cleared, and you won't be on any more wanted posters. As far as the law is concerned, the reign of terror of the Ringo Moon gang is over."

———

TWO DAYS LATER, when they were ready to go, to the Crocketts' surprise, all the towns' members stepped forward, offering their hands. Everybody liked the brothers, even those who had just met them. Now, the sheriffs felt like old friends.

Grass was tucked up to the watering trough as their horses pulled at tufts and slid their jaws while whisking their tails at flies. Gid's horse had a shotgun blast of brown and white with a long strip down its face. His mane was white and wild. The mare lifted its head, staring at its master, bright-eyed and intelligent. The horse neighed and shook its head. When he rode him, it was as if he were an extension of his body.

Tears flushed Darlene's eyes, but there was defiance there, too. She knew it wasn't meant to be, but she wanted it just the same. Her heart suddenly began to thump in her throat. Still, her heartbeat was full of dread, fearing she would never see Gid again. She waved at him from a distance, so she didn't embarrass him with her unannounced presence, but he didn't see her.

Linda walked right up to Will and pushed a wisp of hair out of her eyes and gave him a hopeful smile. He drew in a sudden, deep breath as his eyes widened.

"Maybe, one day," Will said, shrugging. "Don't worry, I'll be back along his way soon enough. With the railroad now everywhere. It's just a few days away."

For Will, it wasn't her pretty face, flowing hair, and well-formed figure that made her so beautiful. There was something in her voice. Still, he knew that if he were to court a banker's daughter, he would have to spend a lot of time in Santa Clara, and right then, all he could think about was getting away.

Linda wondered if he could hear the bass drum hammering in his chest. *Sometimes women are just jealous of how simple a man's brain is,* she thought.

She looked back and tossed him a wistful smile, then blew him a kiss. Then suddenly she was gone, lost in the growing crowd. Linda Chapman met Will at the first hangings. She was the daughter of the only other banker in town.

Suddenly, Darlene appeared, much to Gid Crockett's surprise. When her eyes grew wide, Gid couldn't stifle a smile. She had a crush on him, but she knew that since she worked in a pleasure palace, she had no future with a man like him. If only they had met in a different situation, maybe, just maybe, things would have worked out.

The sun hung over the horizon like a big red rubber ball as it brought on a new day. The air was fresh after a cool night.

Will slouched in the saddle, one leg hooked over the saddle horn. When his little brother caught up, he swung his boot back into the stirrup.

"Come on, let's ride on the top for the first few miles and give the shotgun guard some company."

"All right," Gid replied, stepping out of his saddle.

Will grabbed the reins close to the bit rings as he tied the leads to the back of the stage. Once the team was hooked up, he glanced at his tarnished tin-plated watch. It was surprisingly on time. That was more than he could say about their last train ride.

As Will and Gid took their seats on top of the stagecoach next to the shotgun guard, they stared into the distance like sharp-eyed vultures, ready to swoop down for their next meal. They both wondered what their next adventure would be.

CHAPTER TWENTY-SEVEN

Eric really hadn't thought about what he would do after he was set free. All he knew was he wanted to get out of Santa Clara before the townsfolk changed their minds and decided to tar and feather and lynch him, too. The image burned into his mind forever as a warning of what could have happened.

The following day, after a good night's rest, he walked eastbound and out of town. The truth was, he felt as free as a bird. Eric briefly thought about Wayne and Jessy sitting in their dismal bunks, as they waited to die of natural causes in the Texas Federal Prison in Huntsville. It was built in 1849 and was more like dungeons than the cells found in Santa Clara or El Paso.

Will and Gid Crockett had returned the money he was carrying in his small leather coin pouch when they arrested him, so he wasn't broke. Since it wasn't stolen but hard-earned, they considered it his. It was from his last wages.

The simpleton whistled as he walked because he felt so good. He was no longer under the thumb of Ringo

Moon and was free to do whatever he wanted. All he had to do was keep his promises to the Crockett brothers and walk a straight line. As a matter of fact, to his recollection, he had never felt so good. Musical notes of "The Farmer in the Dell" floated through the air.

At night, he walked off the trail and made camps in places surrounded by stands of trees or in gulleys or small canyons where he wouldn't be seen. He would spend hours staring up at the stars until he fell asleep with a smile on his face. Life was good for a change, and he was happy that evil people didn't surround him. He was enjoying his time alone. Usually, he was at the beck and call of Ringo and the other gang members to do all their dirty work and chores they were too lazy to do.

Now, he was only responsible for himself and was his own boss. He almost felt as though he had been freed from slavery or something similar. There was nobody around to insult him for being a dim wit. He couldn't help that he was born with an intellectual disability.

One night, a white-tailed deer stepped into his camp just before dusk. They locked eyes, and to Eric's surprise, it didn't run away. He smiled when he realized the animal didn't feel threatened in his presence. Then again, animals had always been friendly with him until Ringo and his gang hired him. He hadn't realized the change until right then. Again, he smiled.

That night, he had an old dream that he hadn't had for weeks, if not months. He and Ringo were stashing the first significant gold heist. Back then, Eric had no idea of where it came from, but he remembered vividly where it was buried. He remembered how Ringo had that crazy look in his eyes and how it frightened him. He had been scared of Moon from the day they met.

———

THE NEXT MORNING, when he awoke, he blinked the sleep away and stared at the clear blue sky. He had overslept, and the sun was already wavering in the distance. That was when he remembered the dream. He suddenly realized he was the last person alive, or at least free, who knew where Ringo's gold and silver were buried. It dawned on him that with this find, he was wealthy beyond his wildest dreams.

It suddenly occurred to Eric that he had been given an important mission in life. Since he didn't know who the actual owners of the valuables were, he decided to spend his days helping the poor and the needy. He had been in the same position and knew how hard it was to be destitute and feel inadequate. Now he thought that he might be able to make a difference, at least for some.

Now, he had a chance to return his good fortune. He suddenly thought about Gid and Will Crockett. Right then, he knew they would be proud of him for what he planned to do. Hopefully, he would run into them again one day, and he could tell them all about it.

That thing called greed didn't affect Eric in the slightest. Living like a rich man never even crossed his mind. But he did see the opportunity to help the needy, just like Will and Gid had enabled him to start a new life.

A LOOK AT: PATHFINDER: A WESTERN DOUBLE (LEVI JOHNSON MOUNTAIN MAN SCOUT BOOK 1)

BY ASH LINGAM

He left Indiana with a rifle and a dream—now the mountains will decide his fate.

Pathfinder

Levi Beaver Johnson was born to the woods of southeastern Indiana, where he earned the nickname "Trapper Boy" long before he came of age. With a sharp eye and a steady hand, he became known as the best shot in the state—and the traps he built were second to none.

But Levi wanted more than a reputation. He wanted the wild. So he left home and headed west, determined to become the mountain man he had always dreamed of being. His journey takes him to the frontier forts of Kansas, where he signs on as an army scout to earn his way into the Rockies and beyond. The road ahead is unknown, and danger waits at every turn.

Rusty Steel

At a frontier rendezvous, Levi and Captain Bill Forrester meet Rusty Steel, a rough-edged mountain man with a past as wild as the mountains he now calls home. Alongside Rusty and his crew, Levi and the captain ride deep into the Western Rockies, where they find a compound of three cabins—home to seasoned trappers who've survived in the wilderness for decades.

As Levi and Bill learn the brutal lessons of mountain life, they face a question every greenhorn must answer: can they rise to the challenge, or will they fall like so many who came before?

AVAILABLE NOW

ABOUT THE AUTHORS

Robert Vaughan sold his first book when he was nineteen. That was several years and nearly five-hundred books ago. Since then, he has written the novelization for the mini-series Andersonville, as well as wrote, produced, and appeared in the History Channel documentary Vietnam Homecoming.

Vaughan's books have hit the *NYT* bestseller list seven times. He has won the Spur Award, the Porgie Award in Best Paperback Original, the Western Fiction-eers Lifetime Achievement Award, the Readwest President's Award for Excellence in Western Fiction, and is a member of the American Writers Hall of Fame and a Pulitzer Prize nominee.

He is also a retired army officer, helicopter pilot with three tours in Vietnam, who has received the Distinguished Flying Cross, the Purple Heart, The Bronze Star with three oak leaf clusters, the Air Medal for valor with 35 oak leaf clusters, the Army Commendation Medal, the Meritorious Service Medal, and the Vietnamese Cross of Gallantry.

———

Ash Lingam was born and raised in Southern Ohio, not far from the mighty Ohio River. His family was among the early settlers in pre-Revolutionary America. He has traced his lineage back to around 1746 when his ancestors immigrated from Europe to the aspiring American Colonies.

A retired marketing executive, Ash devotes his spare time to training police dogs and writing novels. He has found his niche in the Western, historical fiction, and adventure genres.

https://www.ashlingam.com/

www.ingramcontent.com/pod-product-compliance
Lightning Source LLC
Chambersburg PA
CBHW012000050726
47499CB00011BA/3277